I0671863

Pressing Past the Past

*It's hard to move forward when
your unresolved past presses against you.*

JULEE JONEZ

Pressing Past the Past
Purpose Publishing
1503 Main Street #168 ♀ Grandview, Missouri
www.purposepublishing.com

ISBN: 978-0-6927081-7-0

Editing by Felicia   Murrell
Book Cover Design by PP Team of Designers

For permission and requests, write to the publisher:
1503 Main Street, #168,
Grandview, MO 64030.

Author Inquiries may be sent to juleejonezspeaks@gmail.com

This book is available at special quantity discounts, contact publisher for more information on bulk order discounts

Pressing Past the Past

Chapter One

Where am I? Yolanda panicked. Drenched in sweat, she sat up. After realizing she was in her own bed, her heart beat slowed down. Yolanda peered at the clock and saw it was three a.m. She had four more hours to rest. She stretched and thought about the recurring dream that always arrived before she had a message to preach.

In the dream, Yolanda was in the pulpit teaching a lesson. At the end of her sermon, a big black cloud would appear all around her. As she tried to run away from the cloud, it became heavier, engulfing her in its presence. The people in the congregation stood and ran out of the sanctuary. As she felt the black cloud swallow her into a deep abyss, a hand appeared to pull her out. A voice faintly cried, "What is done in the dark comes to light. Take my hand and follow me." Then, she would abruptly wake up.

Yolanda knew the dream had a spiritual interpretation but she couldn't imagine what it might mean. After all, she had been saved for quite some time now. Yolanda didn't do much of anything in the dark anymore except pray. When Yolanda told her husband the dream, Michael said it just meant she was still paranoid and guilty about her previous lifestyle. "You need to stop tripping. Everybody has a past. But you can't keep living in it." He scowled as he often did when he felt she was being too hard on herself. "Nobody's perfect, Yo. Not even them holy rollers you preach with."

Yolanda looked at Michael, as he lay on his side with his mouth slightly open. She kissed him softly on the back of his neck and rubbed his wavy black hair. He was the one aspect of her life that was constant. They'd always shared their life together. But things had definitely taken a different route than what she expected. They partied together, drank together, and now, they were saved together.

When Yolanda answered her call into the ministry, many of her friends and family members turned their back on her except Michael and her other lifelong friend, Kennedy.

Kennedy encouraged her to keep pressing past the past, giving a biblical illustration. "Honey, you got to press toward the mark of the high calling. Take hold of that for which God took hold of you." When Yolanda looked at her blankly, she calmly responded, "Baby...that's in the Bible. Paul said it." Yolanda was quiet. Kennedy said, "You are going to study and know the Bible, aren't you? You can't be no preacher without no word to preach."

Yolanda began to study the Word in-depth. She felt even stronger than when she first gave her life to Christ. She had peace. Her language changed. Relationships of ruin became restored. She and her mother were closer than ever, though there were still some hiccups in their dealings. She and Michael fought less and prayed more. Well...at least at first. But still, all was well - except one issue.

Her daughter, Noel.

Once Yolanda became a stable figure in Noel's life, she figured all would be fine. She didn't realize kid's memories were like Polaroids - quick to develop a permanent picture.

Yolanda gave in to every desire Noel had. If she wanted new clothes, she got them. A weekly hair appointment and manicures at the age of fifteen? No problem. Noel used her mother's guilt to her advantage. Deep down, Yolanda knew she was doing the wrong thing. Noel had become spoiled. She was selfish and easily angered when Yolanda told her no, but she felt bad for not being there for Noel all those years when she needed her. It felt like the least she could do. However,

Michael didn't agree.

"Yo, it is one thing to feel bad, but get over it." he exclaimed. "She is playing you like lotto. She doesn't pull that mess with me because she knows I'm not the one to put up with it. We both could have been better examples and parents. But buying her a sixteen-hundred-dollar Louis Vuitton purse instead of first getting her braces that she *desperately* needed is not good parenting. It's straight up stupid." She knew he was right.

Yolanda lay in bed pondering her relationship with her daughter. She heard a door close. She bolted out of bed, wondering if she should wake Michael. He snorted and rolled onto his back, snoring loudly. Yolanda grabbed her terry cloth robe and wrapped it around her waist.

She walked into the hallway and looked around. She noticed a light on at the end of the stairs. *I didn't leave any lights on.* She realized Noel was coming in the house. Yolanda didn't even know she'd left.

She braced herself for what was about to take place. She knew confronting Noel would be mentally exhausting, but she couldn't let this blatant disobedience take place in her house. Yolanda tightened the belt around her waist, sighed inwardly and asked God to intervene.

As Yolanda descended down the circular stairwell, Noel tiptoed up the stairs. The two collided into each other. Noel tumbled backwards down the stairs. Yolanda, in turn, fell on top of Noel. Both landed in a crumbled heap at the bottom of the steps.

"Dang, Mama. Get your big, crusty toe out my nose."

Yolanda forced herself up, wobbling as she stood. She reached and pulled Noel to her feet. "Excuse me, sister girl. Why are you coming in my house at almost four a.m.? You're lucky my foot ain't up another orifice of your body. Where have you been?"

Noel looked at her mother. "I was where I was. A friend needed me and I came to her rescue. Isn't that something Jesus would do?"

Yolanda seriously considered hitting her daughter in the mouth. She was used to Noel sarcastically making references to her mother's ministry. She could handle her little digs. What she didn't like was her daughter's blatant disrespect of the God she was taught to reverence. *Jesus, if I pop her in the mouth you'd understand right?*

Yolanda straightened her posture and took a deep breath. "Jesus would have told his parents there was an emergency, not snuck out of the house. What kind of emergency could a barely seventeen-year-old *girl* have?" Noel rolled her eyes and put her hands on her hips. Yolanda stepped closer to Noel. So close she could smell a familiar scent on her breath. "And for the record, sneaking out of the house to get drunk is not an emergency. It's something that could land you locked in your room for many years. What is your problem, Noel?"

Noel took a deep breath. "Look, Mama, forgive me. Yeah, I snuck out. Yeah, we were drinking. It is something I just...decided to do. I haven't done it before." Noel took off her silver hoop earrings and looked at them in her hand.

Yolanda knew where this could lead. She'd started her old lifestyle this way. "I appreciate your honesty, Noel. But, why would you do this? We did not raise you to do anything that could lead you into trouble. Not only have you disrespected the boundaries your father and I have established in this house, you should know from *my* story how this could end." Noel sighed, exasperated her mother once again made it about her bad decisions.

8

"Mama, just because you went AWOL as a teen doesn't mean I will." She folded her arms defiantly across her chest. "Every time I mess up you go into your testimony. That's your story – not mine!"

"Okay, my story isn't yours but this is *my* house. You don't pay for anything and as long as you are here, you will do what we say." Heat ran up the back of Yolanda's neck. She knew if Noel said one more thing, she might physically hurt her.

"I did it because I wanted to. Besides, you didn't raise me to do anything. Mama Sable raised me. Or did you forget in your white robe behind your pulpit you were once off drunk all the time doing what you wanted?" Hot tears fell down Noel's cheeks. "Now you know how it feels to wait up for someone...at least I came home. You never did." Noel screamed frantically, which Yolanda usually didn't tolerate. This time something within her told her to not react –yet.

Noel continued, "You can step to me with all this preachy mess about how I don't pay for anything, I'm disrespectful and all that. Okay, you're right. To keep it one hundred, I'm not doing anything that wasn't dished out from you." She wiped her eyes with the back of her hand. Eyeliner stained her eyes. "I am sorry, Minister Howard. Let me just go to bed." Noel brushed past her mother, lightly pushing her shoulder out of the way.

Yolanda grabbed Noel by the neck and slammed her back into the wall. Noel's eyes widened. Her mother had never touched her. Noel considered hitting her but she did know one Bible truth - honor your parents so your days may be long. Noel had the fear of God in her heart, at least enough to fear Him striking her if she struck back. Plus, she knew her mother could fight *for real.*

Sensing her fright, Yolanda's grip on her neck eased up. Her face was less than an inch away from Noel's. "Do not ever touch me

9

disrespectfully again." Though her voice was soft, it was firm and veiled with rage. "I have let you get away with a lot, Noel. I have tried to make up to you for all the years I was not there. I will not allow you to hold it over my head year after year. Do you understand me?" When Noel did not respond, Yolanda re-tightened her grip on her neck. Noel, scared of not breathing, nodded.

Yolanda backed away. "Go to bed," she barked. "You have a few more hours before I have to get you up for church. And put on something decent today. I am preaching and I need you to represent me." Yolanda tightened her robe around her waist. "You are not going to a fashion show but to the house of the Lord. Show some respect." She looked at her with disdain. "Though I wonder how much you know about that."

Noel watched her mother storm off. She thought about going to hug her and apologize. *No, I'm not.* All her life she had felt sorry. Sorry for being born to a mother who didn't seem to want her until a few years ago. Sorry her grandmother knew her better than her own mother did. Sorry for never having any stability in her life when she needed it most. She was tired of being sorry. It was her mother's turn for that.

Noel tipped quietly up the stairs of the immaculate mini-mansion they lived in. In Noel's opinion, her mother cared more about designer paintings, soft leather furniture, and statues than making the house a home. Noel opened the door to the one place she felt solace –her room.

She turned on the light. She knew she needed to rest but decided to write in her journal. Noel opened the thick black book and wrote in a frenzy. She recalled the events of the evening: going to a college party, having several Jell-O shots and meeting a freshman named Bryan, who thought she was twenty. As she wrote about the fight between her and her mother, her eyes became heavy with sleep.

Her last thoughts did not have to be written in her journal. They constantly plagued her all the time. She was glad her mother got her life right, but she knew all too well what it was like to love someone yet hate them at the same time.

Michael honked the horn of the cream-colored Escalade truck three times before leaning on it. The irritating sound lingered for more than a minute. "What is wrong with this child? Noel moves like she is older than your mama."

"Michael, stop it! My spirit is agitated and you are not helping, baby."

"Your spirit? Are you sure it's not just your monthly causing that?"

Yolanda looked at her husband and rolled her eyes. Suddenly, she burst out laughing. Michael often joked about exorcizing the hormonal changes that plagued her every month. He called them the "period demons". Yolanda leaned over and kissed him on the cheek. "Boy, you are so silly. I love you, though."

"Are you nervous about your sermon today, Rev?" Michael stroked his wife's hand. "I saw you all weekend in your books and writing your little notes. Let God do His thing. Stop trying to live up to an image you think is so minister-like."

Yolanda remained quiet. She did not want to have this argument before they hit the church parking lot. Ever since she accepted her role as a minister at New Life Worship Center, Michael always made similar comments. People watched her as a member of the pulpit and she wanted to be the type of minister people could admire. Michael argued that she wanted to look a part that was unrealistic. From her style of dress, to the appearance of her family, outsiders believed they were the most perfect, godly family. Nobody knew the struggles in her household. While Noel was the main source of trouble, Michael had his days. *Many, many days.* With their business growing and flourishing, Yolanda stopped her consulting job to go into full-time ministry. She had always been a co-partner in their construction firm, which they opened primarily with a hefty life insurance policy her biological father left her. Although her ministerial salary was very generous, choosing to work at the church became a source of contention. Michael was okay with her being involved in ministry, but made it clear he wasn't thrilled to become a ministers' husband. When Yolanda gave him the reigns of their construction business, she had hoped to win him over. It worked to a degree. Yolanda loved her life; she wished her husband did, too. He couldn't seem to walk with her in her calling.

For starters, he wouldn't let go of his old buddies. After he started to run the construction company, he hired his boys from the block to work under him. True, they were great workers. But all of them were lousy husbands or mates. Part time gigolos. Drunkards. Liars. And if rumors were right, they often frequented strip clubs. Even though Michael didn't partake in the same activities with them, or so she hoped, it bothered Yolanda he refused to become involved with some of the men at the church. It was as if he wanted to make it plain that his wife's ministry work was hers and he wanted nothing to do with it. Yolanda silently prayed that her husband would at least be friendly at the end of service when the ministers and spouses lined up to speak with church members.

Yolanda was about to go into the house and snatch Noel when she stepped out the front door. Her long, black hair was pulled into a chignon, which emphasized her lovely facial features. Almond shaped eyes framed her long, curling lashes. Her high cheekbones were doused with bronzer. Her deep copper skin looked kissed by the sun. Noel knew how to apply cosmetics like a professional makeup artist. Her lips were carefully lined with a coral pencil, while her pouty mouth had a deep peach gloss painted on. To top it all off, she had a small mole above her lip. A beauty mark that added exotic flair to her looks. Yolanda marveled at her daughter's beautiful face. She sighed with appreciation until she noticed something silver flashing in Noel's mouth. Somehow, she had failed to notice it during their heated exchange the night before.

"Hey y'all!" Noel forced herself to sound happy in the face of a pounding headache. "Natural beauty is one thing but fineness takes time." She kissed her dad on the cheek and looked at her mother, wondering why she was staring at her so intently. "What's up, Reverend Mama? Your figure is banging in that suit. You better hope Deacon Moss ain't sitting behind you. That's a whole lot of booty for him to peep."

Michael rolled his eyes, backing out the driveway. Yolanda was still trying to figure out what was in her daughter's mouth. "Thank you...I think. I'll have my robe on. What do you have in your mouth? I keep seeing something silver or metallic or something."

"What? You mean this?" Noel opened her mouth to reveal a recent tongue piercing. Yolanda screamed.

The screech of her voice startled Michael. He jumped and lost temporary control of the car, almost sideswiping an angry Mercedes driver. The driver yelled an obscenity at Michael. Michael in turn waved his fist at him and then sped around him. "Michael, was it necessary to act like a heathen at this moment? Have some dignity." Yolanda turned back to Noel. "Open your mouth again so I can see that thing."

When Noel did, her mother grabbed the silver ball and tried to yank it out. Noel screamed and clamped down on her mothers' finger. Yolanda yelped and snatched her fingers out of her daughter's mouth. Both looked at each other with an intense glare. Then, Noel turned away to look out the window.

13

"Dang, Rev, isn't that child abuse? Trying to snatch your daughter's tongue ring out? I don't like it myself but what would Jesus want you to do?"

Knowing he was trying to be humorous, Yolanda retorted, "How would you know? On Sunday you read the Word looking for revival and on Monday you can't find your Bible. How can you tell me what Jesus would do?"

Michael simply shook his head. He got tired of Yolanda trying to beat him with the Bible all the time. After all, didn't she read First Peter chapter three? Peter said to win the husband over through an attitude of submission, not of sista-tude.

He got out the car and walked to the passenger side to help his wife out. When he opened the door, Yolanda was pleasantly surprised. "Thank you, honey," she said, holding his hand as she stepped down from the SUV. Noel had already gotten out of the car and was switching her behind into the building to find her grandmother.

Though Sable was her grandmother, Noel felt she was a better mother than her own could be. Noel was glad when her mother got saved. They spent time together, getting to know each other. But as soon as the call into ministry came, her mother shoved her aside again. She wondered how God felt about that. When Noel entered the sanctuary, she spotted her grandmother on the back row and strutted off to meet her.

"Noel! Noel! I know you hear me. Where do you think you are going?" Yolanda managed to catch her daughter before she could get out of her reach. Yolanda smoothed down the front of her skirt and waited for her daughter's response.

14

Noel sighed and rolled her eyes. "Mama, I want to sit with Mama Sable. I don't feel like sitting all up in the front so you can either put me in your sermon or make us stand up like some kind of freaks so you can show us off."

"Amen," Michael said under his breath. "Yolanda, you need to be in the back for the consecration period. If you don't consecrate, you will keep acting like you are on your period." Noel laughed at Michael's joke. Yolanda pursed her lips tightly together and crossed her arms over her chest.

"Do what you want. This is just the enemy trying to steal my peace. Have the decency to at least stand with me at the end. Can you do that?" Yolanda did not wait for a reply. She hurried off searching for her girl Kennedy.

Yolanda's hands started to sweat while she made her way to the podium. Every eye in the sanctuary was focused on Yolanda. This was only her third sermon and the last left people wondering if she'd ever speak again. Yolanda got so off focus, she stuttered, stammered and mistaked her way through the half hour teaching. She got choked up in a coughing spell that ended when Pastor Griffin hit her on the back. Upon his firm thump, Yolanda reeled forward over the podium. As if that were not embarrassing enough, her left breast plunged over the top of her bra and peeped out the side of her blazer.

Needless to say, at the next minister's meeting, a vote was taken to make wearing robes mandatory when preaching.

Yolanda silently asked the Lord to help her speak without error and only do what He wanted. She felt at ease and godly confident.

"Can we please stand and receive the word of the Lord together?" Her strong voice bellowed in the microphone. "We will be reading from the book of Jeremiah, chapter 29, beginning at verse 11." Yolanda continued. She felt the Spirit give her more boldness to speak. As the anointing rested on her, Yolanda spoke with a power she didn't know existed within her.

The congregation erupted in cheers. Choruses of "amen" bounced off every wall in the sanctuary. Mama Sable waved her pink hanky in the air. Michael stood up clapping and grinning from ear to ear, proud of the power that exuded from his wife's barely five-foot body. Noel sat between the two looking amazed at her mother. After their episode the night before and earlier this morning, she thought her mother would be shaken up. Noel realized God Himself must have intervened today, for she had never heard such authority from her mother's voice.

As Yolanda watched the responsive crowd, her eyes fell on a young woman in a hot pink suit. Not wanting to break the flow, Yolanda tried to stay focused on the move of the Spirit. However, she noticed the woman was scowling at her. After locking eyes with her, Yolanda sensed it was time to offer an altar call.

"I am going to close. Right now, I plead with you, whatever you are holding onto," she peered closely at Ms. Hot Pink Pantsuit, and spoke as if they were the only two in the room. "Anger, bitterness, unforgiveness, addiction...no matter what it is, Jesus will forgive you for it. That which binds you now, will have to go."

People came to the altar for prayer and to receive the Lord. Yolanda felt physically drained but she knew that ministering to God's people was her call. No matter what she had to give of herself, she was determined to see lives changed.

Her life was His. Even if she had not fully faced some old parts of it.

16

✝✝✝

The ministers stood in line to greet all the members and shake hands. Yolanda was grateful Michael had decided to join her. After church, he pulled her to him and hugged her hard. When she pulled away, she noticed tears in his eyes. Before she could ask him what was wrong, he grabbed her hand and led her to the front of the church.

Yolanda was pleased with his actions but knew Michael was struggling with something. She made a silent vow to pray for discernment about it later. For now, she had to smile and play church politics.

Mother Stone, Kennedy's mother-in-law was next to shake Yolanda's hand. Mother Stone was one of the church folk who thought everyone was in sin but her. Never mind that her husband had left her for a woman twenty years his junior. She ignored the fact her brother was no longer on the building fund committee due to stealing funds for his own house. Her son may have been the lead deacon, but there was no doubt the Stone's had skeletons in their closets.

"Girl, you sho' nuff preached today." Mother Stone exclaimed, grabbing her hand. "I didn't know you had it in ya, baby. And keeping your breasts in really helped."

Yolanda smiled through gritted teeth. "I give all thanks to God that things went well today. We all have fiascos. How is your brother doing? You know God says let stealing hands steal no more."

Mother Stone stopped smiling. "Yes, He does. Well, he is fine, thank you." She rushed past Yolanda on to the next minister, muttering, "No, that heifer didn't."

"Baby, did you have to go there?" Michael whispered in her ear. "It was

17

funny. Dang, baby...you just got out the pulpit. You didn't have to take it there." He laughed. "At least you're not lying."

"The truth shall set you free," Yolanda calmly responded. She was too tired to let some gossiping, want to-be-holy, nosy old woman insult her. Not today.

Suddenly, the lady in the pink suit interrupted Yolanda's thoughts. She stepped in front of Yolanda and stared. Taken aback by the woman's intense gaze, Yolanda managed to utter, "God bless you, my sister."

She rolled her blue contact eyes and laughed. "Girl, please. Stop. If you really wanted God to bless me, you would have communicated with me before today."

Yolanda was confused. She had no idea who this woman could be. The lady tapped her foot impatiently at Yolanda. Yolanda stared at her blankly. "Do I know you?"

"Yes! You used to hang with us back in the day. I know I got fat, but shoot after being pregnant four years in a row, you'd be living large, too. It's me...Rochelle. You all used to call me Rocky."

Yolanda knew exactly who Rocky was. She got nervous and didn't know how to respond. She cleared her throat and stammered, "Rocky, so good to see you after all these years." Rocky looked at Michael smugly.

"Hi, Michael. You too good to speak to me? You used to kick it with me back in the day in your B.C. or before church days. I see y'all some heavy holy rollers, huh? Who would have guessed it?"

Michael rolled his eyes. "From what baby daddy's house did you come from today? Or have you still not found out which baby belongs to

18

whom?"

"Michael! Sorry, Rocky. It's good to see you in the house of the Lord. Excuse my husband. He's just a little cranky."

"It's all right. I'd be cranky too in his situation. I guess it don't matter none now, does it? You all have moved on like you don't have any connection with me and my family. I know we are family like the song says. Family needs to come together." Rocky looked expectantly at Yolanda.

"What do you mean?" Yolanda's heart beat rapidly. She knew very well what Rocky was talking about. This was a part of her life she chose to close the door on. She knew one day it would be opened. She always believed the past would catch up with her but right now, she was not prepared to handle it.

"Look, I know the real deal," Rocky whispered. "It wasn't a great situation at the time but don't you think you should open your arms to your...extended family?"

"Hold it, Rocky!" Michael barked loudly causing other people to look at him. He cleared his throat and quieted his voice. "I made it very clear from that point on that we were moving on with our lives. It was agreed that neither you nor any of your people would ever have involvement with us again. After what went down, we all could have gone to jail. Be grateful that didn't happen. Don't you dare come interfere with us now or I promise you will live to regret it." The look of rage in Michael's eyes was so intense, Rocky slowly backed away.

"Okay, fine. How can you live with yourselves knowing there's a lie in your household? You all aren't the only ones who've changed. We, too, are new people and deserve to have our family together. You ain't right. But it will catch up with you. Real soon." Rocky turned around and

19

walked toward the doors of the sanctuary. Before she exited, she glanced back at Yolanda one last time.

Yolanda thought she might faint. Michael placed his arm around Yolanda's waist. "Baby, don't even let her bother you. We got everything taken care of. Trust me."

"Michael, what if she is right? Should we just resolve this?" On the verge of tears, Yolanda's voice shook. "I always assumed no one knew – except my mama, obviously. I guess this was bound to come out sooner or later. Maybe we should talk to Sable and Noel. The truth can set us free."

Michael pulled his wife to him and hugged her close. "Not now," he whispered. "We'll discuss it in our own way, in our own time. We need to do it when we are ready. I don't think you're able to face that part of your past."

Yolanda buried her face in her husband's shoulder. She always knew one night a little over seventeen years ago would come back to haunt her. It was a piece of her past that would never go away.

This piece was ordained to exist for however long God had planned.

Chapter Two

After Kennedy pulled in front of Olivia's Soulfood Shack, she pulled out her compact to check her make-up. She was meeting Yolanda for their weekly lunch, nicknamed "the sista's gab-fest". They spent hours eating their favorite dishes and discussing the various issues going on in each of their lives. Sometimes the conversation got so intense tears fell, causing extra attention from people around them. They were so used to each other's emotional outbursts, neither were concerned about embarrassing themselves.

As Kennedy got out of her green BMW, she saw Yolanda had already arrived. Her Escalade was parked right in front of the restaurant. Knowing Yolanda, she probably got there right when they opened. When Kennedy entered the place, she saw Yolanda sitting in one of the plush booths in the back. The hostess nodded in acknowledgment at Kennedy. Kennedy smiled at the young lady who stood at the front of the place. She was accustomed to seeing Kennedy and Yolanda every week in the same spot.

"Hello, Mrs. Stone," the hostess said, smiling broadly. "Mrs. Howard beat you here by a landslide. As soon as we unlocked the doors, she was already pulling on the handle. There must be a lot to gab about today."

Kennedy laughed, heading to their usual spot. "Look at you, hot mama. Does the deacon know you got your bosoms out like that?"

Kennedy looked down. She had on a cashmere V-neck sweater that left little to the imagination. It was extremely low-cut and tight, definitely something the deacon *would* rant about.

"Don't hate me because I am bountiful and beautiful, my sister. Let's not forget, a few weeks ago, your left one fell out. In the pulpit." Kennedy laughed at the memory. "Because you had all the elders sweating, now you all have to wear them hot robes."

Yolanda blushed from embarrassment. "Don't remind me. The women in the church rolled their eyes while their men salivated as if they'd never seen a breast. You would have thought I did it on purpose." Yolanda buttered a roll and bit into it. The sweet rolls Olivia made were one of her favorite items on the menu.

"You know how folk are there. They look for stuff to talk about. I got the number one gossip in my house."

Yolanda shook her head. Kennedy often complained about her husband. She could go on for hours about his irritating habits, arrogance and obsession with maintaining a holy image. As a minister, Yolanda believed it was her duty to remind Kennedy God expected her to respect her husband. Then Kennedy would argue though God may have said it, He understood her dilemma saying, "Respecting someone who doesn't respect you is tough."

"What's the problem?" Yolanda asked, not really in the mood to have another conversation about Deacon Stone.

"Yolanda, I need you to be my friend not my pastor, okay? You can be biblical another day, not now. I know the Word as good as you and I don't want a lecture. I need you to really listen to me. Really listen, okay?"
Yolanda was annoyed by Kennedy's reaction. True enough they were best friends but she didn't see how Kennedy could expect Yolanda to

leave God out of anything. Many years ago, Yolanda listened to Kennedy beat her over the head with the Bible but now that the roles were reversed, she didn't seem to like it. Yolanda bit her tongue and nodded. "Let's order first. I can tell this is going to get real deep." Yolanda waved over their favorite waitress.

Holly beamed at them and came to the table. "How are my favorite gals doing today? Is it going to be the usual?" She looked at the ladies expectantly.

"For me it is. Kennedy?"

"Me, too. Except this time bake my catfish and instead of lemonade could you bring me a vodka and tonic with a touch of grenadine?"

Yolanda was shocked. She had never witnessed Kennedy drinking any type of alcohol. The closest she'd ever seen Kennedy to liquor was having some Nyquil for a cold. Yolanda and Holly both looked at Kennedy with surprise. Kennedy noticed.

"What?" she sighed, exasperated. "A sister can't have a drink to calm her nerves? I'm not going to hell for vodka. Stop looking at me, Holly, and get our orders."

"Okay, sorry," Holly said, quietly. Her smiled faded. "And you're right. It's none of my business. I guess...you being who...you know..." Holly didn't know what to say. She knew Yolanda was a minister and Kennedy a prominent deacon's wife. To see her drinking at eleven in the morning surprised her. Still, she didn't want to be judgmental or upset Kennedy. Holly turned to take their orders to the kitchen.

"You know Holly didn't mean any harm. You're an example and it probably just caught her off guard that you ordered a drink. Don't say you can't blame her." Yolanda looked at Kennedy pointedly.

23

Kennedy sighed. "You're right. I'll apologize later. But I am tired of this Deacon Stone's wife stigma." Kennedy lowered her voice. "Everywhere I go, that man's position in the church follows me. Shoot, I have to go to the lower east side of town to get away from people who know him."

Yolanda laughed. "You know Kansas City isn't that big when it comes down to it. Everybody knows somebody that knows somebody who knows you. For real, I have never seen you drink."

"I know. Shoot, you drank enough for both of us back in the day." They both laughed before Kennedy's facial expression hardened. "Seriously, I have to talk to you about something. In confidence."

Yolanda was offended. *Kennedy should know after all these years I would never tell any of her business.* She pursed her lips together tightly and nodded.

Kennedy's eyes dropped into her lap. "Lately, things have not been going so smoothly at home. Eddie is always gone. He ignores me, talks over me, talks at me. I just can't take it. To top it off, he only wants sex on his terms." Kennedy fidgeted with her hands. "Yolanda, I have never met a man who didn't...you know."

"Know what?" Yolanda was surprised to hear this. Judging by the deacon's past as a ladies' man, she would never guess there would be any problems getting him to play mattress aerobics. Yolanda waited for Kennedy to go into more detail.

Kennedy paused as Holly brought her a drink. "I made it light, Kennedy.

Kennedy nodded and smiled. "Thanks, Holly. Sorry for my little outburst. It's about that time. You know?"

Holly smiled and walked away. Kennedy waited until she was out of earshot to continue. "As I was saying. Look at me, Yolanda. You know I used to have to fight brothers off of me."

Yolanda laughed. "You look all right. You're not me with your amazon behind but you *okay*--for a man who likes 'em big." She laughed again.

"Listen, you little oompla loompa. I'm being serious, okay? Besides, you need a foot stool to reach most men so don't hate because I am big and beautiful."

Yolanda rolled her eyes. "If you like having a husband who is eye level with your breasts, who am I to hate? Continue girl, because we could crack on each other all day."

They both laughed and high-fived one another. "You right," Kennedy agreed. "I'm not use to begging someone to have sex with me."

Yolanda was quiet. In all their years of being friends, she didn't know Kennedy even had sexual relations before Eddie. Yolanda figured she wasn't a virgin but never thought Kennedy had slept around. In fact, sex was a topic that only came up when Yolanda talked about her past conquests. Even to hear Kennedy talk about marital sex took Yolanda by surprise.

"Yolanda, I have tried everything from lap dances to walking around naked for twenty-four hours. The man didn't budge. In fact, he said as the man, he would let me know when we would come together." Kennedy got angry the more she talked about it. "He has specific days and times he wants to do it. And it's always the same, no fun whatsoever. I mean, you're a minister. Didn't God create sex for our enjoyment within the confines of marriage?"

"Yes. Have you expressed your frustration to him?"

"Every day! He accuses me of tainting the act of sex because I like to be creative. Doing it on the same day, in the same place the same way every week is boring, Yolanda."

"Why does he set those standards for sex? We all know he was no virgin."

"Right. We all have a past and in his, he was a big male whore." Kennedy practically shouted. She noticed the stares of people around her and quieted her voice. She drank a swig of her drink. "He was very sexually active with all sorts of women for years. When one of his exes caught HIV, it scared him. Then, he rededicated his life to the Lord. He committed to keep sex pure—which is fine. But why do I have to suffer?" Tears sprang to Kennedy's eyes. Yolanda reached over and patted her hands.

"Maybe the kind of sex you want from him reminds him of the past. Marriage requires long-suffering, Kennedy." Yolanda softened her voice. "You may have to sacrifice your fetishes for the sake of Eddie. After all, the Bible says we are to let the husband lead and we submit to his authority."

Kennedy's anger rose. "This is why I didn't want to tell you. I'm not one of the church members you counsel with. I asked you to listen as a friend and now you're judging me. As if you have a right!" Kennedy grunted and rolled her eyes. "I hope you've submitted your whoring days to your husband's authority."

As soon as the words left her lips, she wished she could retract them. Yolanda snatched her hands away from Kennedy, a look of shock on her face.

26

Kennedy took another swig of her drink. "I'm sorry. That was totally uncalled for. Please forgive me, Yo." Her eyes pleaded with Yolanda's.

Yolanda sighed. "I forgive you. But God has cleansed me from my past and I'm pressing past it. I don't need you or anyone else to remind me of who I *was*. You asked my opinion. As your friend, who's a minister, I can only tell you the truth." Yolanda folded her arms defiantly across her chest. "If you can't take it or don't like it, don't ask me." Yolanda spoke with such force Kennedy was taken aback.

"You're right. You aren't the only one with a past. I have one too, but I don't let it affect me." Kennedy paused and dabbed at her eyes. "Let me tell you something I have never shared, Yolanda. Sex has actually been a sin I have always struggled with since I was young."

Yolanda was surprised. She always assumed Kennedy abstained from sex. It was nothing she ever talked about. Yolanda couldn't remember her dating a man seriously until Eddie. "I have to admit; I can't imagine you having sex. As sexy as you may be and even when you dress provocatively, I never heard the word sex uttered from your lips. I know you complained about fighting the brothers off, but you never said you...gave in." Yolanda quieted for a moment as she thought. "In fact, where did these sex partners come from? You didn't date anyone in high school and only once in a while during college. You never went on second dates with the few I knew you had because they were like dogs in heat."

Kennedy sighed and explained. "Of course I wasn't proud of it. Besides, no one ever saw my little conquests. They were usually people from out of town I would meet while on my debate tournaments." She took a long sip of her drink before continuing. "Sometimes, it was strangers that I'd pick up. We'd do our thing and part ways. It was a weakness. What can I say?"

27

Yolanda was still at a loss for words. "But you were so...churchy. Good-girl like. Straight and narrow. Boring. And you slept around?"

Kennedy glared at Yolanda and rolled her eyes. "I was in church and knew better. It was an area of my life I hadn't yielded to God. I wasn't ready to bring that area captive under His authority at the time."

"How long had that been going on?"

Kennedy almost lied to Yolanda, but decided to be truthful with her best friend. "I have never told a soul what I am about to tell you, Yolanda. Well, outside of my husband and my mother. When I came clean, I still felt the guilt, so please don't judge me for it."

"Never. As if I *could* judge anyone."

"My first sexual awakening happened when I was seven, by my uncle who was only...twelve or thirteen at the time." Kennedy dropped her head in shame.

Sympathy washed over Yolanda's entire being. "Kennedy," Yolanda's voice filled with emotion, "You were molested. I'm so sorry. I had no idea. Have you ever dealt with it?"

"What?" Kennedy looked confused. "Why? I mean we were both kids. I know what he did was wrong but I don't believe he was trying to hurt me. It's just that after it happened, I searched for ways to please those urges I felt." Kennedy got defensive about her revelation. "Yes, you can call it molestation. I get it. Still, it's not like some adult raped me. He was a tween himself." Kennedy tried to brush it off, but knew the truth. Despite his young age, her uncle had sexually abused her.

28

Yolanda knew Kennedy needed help. Losing her innocence so young, even at the hand of another youth, had damaged her. Sex was one action that opened the door to the enemy of one's soul.

Oddly enough after such a startling confession, Kennedy seemed very cold hearted toward the reality she was sexually abused. Her voice hardened. "Look, Yolanda, before you psychoanalyze me, understand, it was something that happened to me as a kid by another kid. Period. It's not the same as other ab..." Kennedy stopped mid-sentence. This was the first time Kennedy ever referred to her uncle's actions as abuse to anyone outside her mother and Eddie. Her heart beat rapidly as the word almost slipped from her mouth. What she always wanted to cast aside was coming out from the depths of her past. Kennedy took another drink and fidgeted with the saltshaker on the table.

Yolanda did not respond verbally. She grabbed Kennedy's hand and silently prayed. *Lord, you know the pain she has suffered through the years. You know how it has affected her, even if she doesn't want to admit it. You are acquainted with all her ways. In the end, open the door so she may be healed. In your name, Jesus, amen.*

Kennedy glanced at Yolanda to read her reaction. *She's praying for me.* Kennedy took her hand away and attempted to change the subject. "I'm okay. Really. It's nothing. It was just something we did as kids," Kennedy stated matter-of-factly.

"Who are you trying to convince - me or you? Not to be insensitive, but realize when it happened, your life changed from that moment on. And unless you deal with it, you will never be healed."

Kennedy's face warmed with anger. "Look, I'm okay. He apologized to me years later and admitted he was wrong. He cried and pleaded with me for forgiveness, so I did. God forgave him and it's all good."

29

Yolanda could not believe what she was hearing. Her best friend, who had known the Lord all her life, had hardened her heart. She was unwilling to admit the problem. Sex was a coping mechanism for her. "Kennedy, if he apologized, then apparently it must have affected him. When he came to you, what did he say?"

Kennedy regretted this conversation. At first, she thought it might be a good idea. But now, Yolanda was going to blame her, just like her own mother did when she found out. "He said for years he had nightmares. He tried to push it in the back of his mind. Finally, when he was twenty-one, he went to counseling because he still felt guilty. He deemed the whole thing as rape." Kennedy paused. "Yes, he did violate me but he was a kid, too, right?"

"Kennedy, whether you admit it or not, if that affected him like it did, surely it did something to you. I admire that he was humble enough to come to you and get the counseling he needed. Maybe you should do the same."

Kennedy threw her fork against the table, making Yolanda flinch. Although her voice was a whisper, it shook with rage. "I am *not* going to sit here and let you tell me what I need to do. I am fine! Nothing is wrong with me. Nothing. Never mention this to me again, okay?"

"Just because you are a minister, doesn't mean you have the answer for everything. Besides, you haven't been called that long, no how. Now let's drop this and you counsel your little church folk. I knew Jesus when you blew Him off." She shoved a bite of fish in her mouth and then continued her rant. "Don't come in here getting in my face like you are so much better than me. We come from two different lifestyles. You just caught up to mine. Don't dare compare me to some molestation victim." Kennedy knew she was wrong for the words she said. Right then, she wanted Yolanda to hurt like she did. She was embarrassed about her outburst, but was even angrier Yolanda suggested counseling.

Yolanda was offended Kennedy disrespected the position God had called her to. Who was she to judge her? Yolanda noticed lately when they disagreed on something, Kennedy brought up Yolanda's relationship with God. "You know, Kennedy, I may have given God my life later than you, but He doesn't count that against me. He called me not you to this particular area. Every time I say something you don't like, you want to throw my past up in my face or make it clear I am just your friend, not your minister. What's up?"

Kennedy sat quietly. She knew why she brought it up but didn't expect Yolanda to call her out. "Sometimes, I guess I can't handle the fact that you don't need me anymore." Kennedy tried to no avail to prevent the tears gathered in the corner of her eyes from falling. As her tears flowed, she confessed to Yolanda how she felt about her new life.

"I was so happy when you got saved. I had no idea God would use you like He has. You have purpose in your life. You have meaning. You have a task. I remember how you would call me back in the day; needing advice and I would minister to you. When the roles reversed, it seemed like you didn't need me anymore." She took the cloth napkin from her lap and wiped her face. "I get jealous sometimes because God chose you and not me to help others."

As Kennedy wiped her eyes, Yolanda's heart softened. She knew how Kennedy felt all along. She wanted *Kennedy* to admit it. "I *am* God's woman but I'm also *your* friend. If you wouldn't have been planting seed in me all those years, I may have died out there doing drugs and all kind of devilish stuff. *You* helped me when I needed you most. I love you for that and always will. God has used you in my life tremendously. He has a plan for you too. Don't be envious of my call; support me in it."
Kennedy nodded while Yolanda spoke. "I still need your friendship. I can't go back to the old friends who are out there. A lot of people at

church remember my past so they don't want to get to know the new me. We can't let the devil come between our friendship. I need you, Kennedy. I always have." She paused trying to carefully phrase in her mind what she wanted to say next. "Don't be prideful because now you *can* need me too. Let me be your friend and minister to your heart."

Kennedy stood and moved to Yolanda's side of the booth. She kissed Yolanda on the cheek and wrapped her arms around her. As they embraced, Kennedy was comforted in the arms of her friend. After holding each other in silence for a minute, Yolanda pulled back and looked at Kennedy. "I love you, Ken. Please remember that."

"I love you, too. Even with that cheap eyeliner you got on. Why can't you spend an extra dollar and get some good waterproof eye makeup? As much as you boo-hoo during worship, you'd think you would know how to be pretty when you do it." Kennedy laughed.

"Oh, you got jokes? Well, when we go exercise, do us all a favor and get rid of those cheap bras. You need something to hold all that in and not let them fall all over the place. That sports bra you had on the other day was so cheap your breasts were running their own race. One hit your eye; the other hit your thigh." Yolanda cracked up at her own comeback.

Kennedy had to laugh since she knew it was true. "Okay. You just check your nose really good before you preach next time. The monitor was all up in your face and you had a booger in your left nostril."

"What?" Yolanda asked incredulously. "The *whole* time?"

"No," Kennedy replied. "When you talked about God blowing an east wind on our life, He must have blown one on you because the booger flew somewhere. Hopefully on my husband's head."

32

They laughed and finished eating. After some peach cobbler, Kennedy looked at Yolanda as if she wanted to ask her something.

Yolanda looked back at Kennedy, "What now? Make it quick. I got a meeting today."

"This may freak you out, but I have been curious about something. Two things, actually. It's not unbiblical to get massages or anything...just to unwind, is it?"

"No, just keep it professional. Go to a therapist, preferably a woman, and stay out of the parlors. A licensed office and a private parlor are two different things." Yolanda was confused. "You already knew the answer. I hope the second issue is not that stupid."

Kennedy became indignant. "Look, heifer, I just wanted a second opinion. The other is...if you maybe play a little bit online or on the phone, that's not cheating is it?"

"Of course, it is. Anytime you engage in any sexual activity with anyone other than your spouse, you defile the marriage bed." Yolanda pondered why Kennedy was asking her these questions. "So don't be playing on nobody's phone or having cybersex on the laptop, you freak." Yolanda laughed. "I know you didn't think I knew of a secret scripture which would make it okay, did you?"

Kennedy laughed. "I was hoping you did. Can't get mad at a sister for trying." They left Holly a generous tip, exited the booth and headed for their cars.

When they got to Yolanda's truck, they hugged goodbye. Kennedy looked over Yolanda's shoulder and saw Michael. She held on to Yolanda tighter to prevent her from turning around.

Yolanda coughed and gagged in Kennedy's tight embrace. "Girl, I love you but let me out of all this mess. Those DD's will kill somebody. No wonder the deacon tries to take it easy."

Kennedy held on until Michael disappeared. "Sorry, my bad. I just felt the love. I had to hang on a little longer. So, you'll call me later?"

Yolanda started her truck and rolled down the window. "Yes, after dinner, about eight. Michael said he's going to work on finishing this house today so I won't see him until late. Bye, sweetie." Yolanda blew her a kiss and sped off.

As Kennedy walked to her car, she wondered who was with Michael. She'd never known Michael to be unfaithful. Sure, she heard the church gossip about some of the spots he liked to hang out at but no one had ever seen him on an official date. She assured herself it was probably a client of his. As much business as his construction company was getting, he probably had to take a client to lunch. It wasn't like he only had male customers. But he wouldn't have held their hand or kissed them. The woman by Michael's side looked more like a girlfriend than a client.

Whatever is done in the dark, Kennedy vowed to herself, *will come into the light*. She prayed in her heart Michael would do Yolanda right.

✝✝✝

Kennedy looked at the clock. It was already a quarter after five. She walked into the bathroom to freshen up before Eddie came home. Perhaps he would actually be in the mood tonight.

After brushing her teeth and pulling her hair into a chignon, Kennedy put on a black tank top with some cotton boxers to match. She walked into the kitchen and got the George Foreman grill out to prepare grilled chicken and vegetables for dinner. As she sliced her zucchini, she heard her husband come in the front door.

"Baby, come on out here. Deacon wants to celebrate!" Eddie ran into the kitchen, picked Kennedy up and set her on the counter. Kennedy was too confused to be excited.

Eddie tightened his hands on her hips and pulled her close to him. She wrapped her legs around his waist as he kissed her long and deep. "Wow! Whatever happened today, it needs to go down *every day* if I get greeted like this."

Eddie smiled slyly. His baldhead glistened with sweat. He only sweated on his head for two reasons, anger or excitement. Judging from his pearly whites, and the one gold tooth, he was definitely thrilled about something.

"Baby, Pastor done gave me a full-time job at the Lord's house. I can use my CPA for my G-O-D! No more moonlighting on the side. I am the official church accountant for New Life Worship Center. Not only that, but Pastor Griffin is my nig-, I mean, my boy. He offered a brotha fifteen *thousand* more than what I make at the firm. Shoot, I gave my notice today."

Kennedy's mood deflated. A job at the church too? An uneasiness came over Kennedy. The last CPA was shown to the door when the funds were a little off. And conveniently the money was funny just as the first lady was given a Mercedes for her birthday.

"Congratulations, honey. What about your retirement? Can you roll it over?"

Eddie jerked his head back as if she had slapped him. "What you mean?

Ain't nobody even worried about that. I'll withdraw my money and start another one."

"In other words, your boy doesn't have any type of retirement plan for you?" Kennedy asked curtly. She didn't mean to get disrespectful but considering they lived off one income, they needed one good retirement plan.

"I didn't ask all those questions yet. I believe this is perfect for us. I was working for the Lord. You know I *am* the lead deacon. Now I am working *in* the Lord's house. Come on, baby. This calls for a little somethin' somethin' like that heathen Maxwell sang."

He threw Kennedy over his shoulder and patted her behind. When they got to the bedroom, he threw her on the chaise lounge and looked deeply into her eyes. "Baby, I love you. You are so sexy. You're beautiful. A good home keeper. You are my queen." He kissed her again and Kennedy threw her arms around his neck. At this point, he could work until he died. She did not care about a 401K or anything else. She was getting some action out of her otherwise lukewarm husband. Maybe the pastor could tell him how to handle his bedroom business, she thought to herself. *After all, he checks me out enough.*

Just as Eddie got undressed, the phone rang. "No, baby," Kennedy whispered sultrily. "Let it go to voicemail. Don't break the mood."

Eddie moved away from her. "I'm expecting an important call about Sister Jean's funeral. Her daughter is distraught. This won't take long," he promised before picking the phone up.

Kennedy sighed. As he went toward the phone, she peeled off her clothing and walked up behind him. She took his hand and put it on her bare thigh. Eddie turned around and covered the mouthpiece of the phone, "Baby, I'm focused on the Lord's work. You can't be all nasty while I'm talking church business. Now, go sit down." He turned his back to her and continued his conversation. After a good fifteen minutes, Eddie returned.

"We got an emergency situation at the church." Eddie lay back on top of her. "Seems as if I gots to fire the accounting secretary. Some funds are missing and as the *manager of the ministry,* I got to exercise my authority," he boasted proudly. "But I'll exercise with you first. It shouldn't take us too long. We need to be done by six twenty. Come on, girl!"

He aimed to kiss her, but Kennedy held up her hand. His face smacked against her palm. "Forget it, Eddie. I want to make love, not haste so you can get up to the church for something that can wait. Why would the pastor call a meeting after hours? Can't this wait?" Kennedy sat up and put her top back on.

"Don't be like that, baby. I can handle this. Really quick though. The Lord's work is never done. We make ourselves available when He calls."

"Key word, when *God* calls. Not Pastor Griffin." Kennedy angered at how her husband worshipped the ground he walked on instead of the God he claimed to serve. "Aren't you a little leery of taking a job where everyone seems to get fired for money mishaps? And usually the mishaps occur when your pastor gets something new. You better hope you did the right thing by taking this job," she warned.

Eddie got up and backed away from her. "I rebuke the devil," he pointed his finger at her forehead. "This is the enemy trying to wreak havoc in my home and I bind him. The devil is a liar!"

"Fool, stop poking me in my forehead." Kennedy got off the chaise. "You got your finger a-pointing, not the anointing. Now excuse me while I get dressed and make dinner." She put on her clothes and sauntered out of the room.

"If that's how you want it," Eddie yelled after her. "And I won't give you none of this good loving when I get home."

"I'm used to it, anyway. Go on to your meeting. I can take care of myself. I've had to over the past year or so anyway."

Eddie pulled on his pants and ran after Kennedy into the kitchen. "Oh, so now you having relations with yourself? That is an abomination unto the Lord. You can't do that, thinking lustful thoughts and all. What is wrong with you?"

Kennedy sighed. "What are you talking about? I have not had any type of sexual touching since...shoot, I forgot. The last time when you maybe had ten free minutes? I want to be touched by my *husband* - not myself. But if you can't do it, don't even worry about it."

Kennedy went back to cutting vegetables. Eddie stared at her, torn about what to do. He loved his wife and wanted to meet her needs. He just had so much to do: work, church, meetings, house visits. While his body yearned to satisfy her, he had work to do for God. He promised God he would work for Him the rest of his days. He had to make up for all he had done.

At the same time, he didn't want to lose Kennedy. But if she was *really* the woman of God she said she was, she would stick by him.

At least he prayed so. Eddie sighed and shook his head. He was confused about what to do. He finished getting dressed and grabbed his briefcase. Before going to the car, he stopped in the kitchen to kiss Kennedy goodbye.

"Don't wait up. Unless you want to."

Kennedy looked him directly in the eye. "I won't. Don't want to. Bye." She turned back to the counter and marinated the chicken breasts.

As Eddie left the house, Kennedy planned in her mind how she would spend her evening. She walked over to her book bag that sat on the kitchen table. She dug deep within it and pulled out the Wild Weekly, a free weekly newspaper. Earlier Kennedy noticed an ad in it that stood out to her. It read:

BM, 40. 6'4 with muscular build. Lonely husband with busy wife. Looking for a friend to talk to. I am a good man in a bad situation. Looking for a woman to do what my wife won't...talk and maybe then some. Prefer African American descent and a woman with spiritual insight. Call my voice box, code 8493.

Kennedy assumed from the ad that they might have a lot in common. His wife wouldn't talk to him. Her husband wouldn't talk or do much of anything else with her. He was looking for someone with spiritual insight - which Kennedy had. Kennedy pondered whether or not to call him.

After her husband's promotion, she knew she'd have a lot of time on her hands. It would be nice to share it with someone else.

"Lord," she said aloud. "Forgive me. Forgive me." Kennedy picked up the phone and dialed the Wild Weekly hook-up hotline.

Pressing Past the Past

Chapter Three

Yolanda yawned as she tapped her pen against her yellow legal pad. Two hours had passed and she was still stuck in a ministers' meeting. *If we were talking about the ministry instead of these folks' misery, we could take care of business,* she thought to herself. She sat up straight trying to keep herself awake while the other members argued loudly.

Elder Whitmore was an old school, gray-haired Barry White look-alike. He argued that for their Faith Festival one of the men should conduct the service honoring Pastor Griffin. His voice went from second to first soprano. "Not all Baptist want some little woman in they face preachin'," he screeched in his high-pitch Michael Jackson voice. "It ain't my church, but if it were, I sho' would have my real soldiers for Christ winning souls. How you gon' soul win in some heels and a skirt? A woman is made to submit to the man. Now the Word say it." He took off his reading glasses and looked to his running partner, Elder Ryan.

Elder Ryan was hard of hearing, mean, senile and prejudice against women working for the kingdom of God. He was so old Yolanda joked that he and Moses went to school together. Every birthday surprised Yolanda. She just knew any day now they'd be planning his eulogy.

Elder Ryan slowly nodded his head in agreement, while Minister Caine stood up. She put her hands on her full and rounded hips. Minister Monica Caine was a former gang member. She came straight from the streets. She had a tendency to intimidate anyone who did not know her. Although her temper could flare up like a scalding inferno, she was loyal to her call. Always interceding in prayer for everyone she knew, she was truly a woman of God. A woman of God with a bite like Mike Tyson, though.

Everyone became silent when Monica jumped to her feet. She cleared her throat and tucked her hair behind her ears. "The Word may say submit but not be walked on like a doormat. I am not your first, second or third wife, Elder. And if you really knew what submission was, your marriages would last longer than the twelve-month grace period." She paused and took a swig from her bottled water. "And what you nodding your head for, Ryan? Your woman went home to be with the Lord and from the looks of it, you will too real soon. Don't lose your reward not doing what is right fooling with your homeboy over here."

The tension was so thick in the air you could slice it with a knife. Poor Elder Ryan tried to open his mouth to give a smart-aleck comeback. As he opened his mouth, his dentures fell out. Yolanda burst out laughing, and then tried to cover it with a cough. All heads turned to her as she continued her fake choking spell.

"Excuse me," she said between coughs. "Elder Ryan, do you need some help putting your teeth back in? I can grab you something to hold them in place if you'd like."

Elder Whitmore snapped his head around to give Yolanda a response. "He don't need y'all to do nothing but let us have our peace. Besides Minister, if you spent more time worrying about your own man, he might not be running around in them...them...dance hall places. As a woman of God, your own man don't respect you. How do *you* think you can preach to *anybody* under those conditions?"

Yolanda was stunned. How did they go from discussing the Faith Festival, a community event to win souls for Christ to her husband's hangouts? She silently admitted Elder Whitmore's comment had a grain of truth. Ever since Yolanda obeyed the call on her life, it was a struggle between her and Michael. He may have been a new creature but one with old habits, which included frequenting bars. She looked helplessly at Pastor Griffin, whose eyes were fixated on a piece of paper. The other five ministers in the room, Monica included, suddenly had nothing to say. No one could look her in the eye.

Yolanda gulped, praying for God to intervene. She knew God wouldn't send a whale to swallow anybody so she had to trust Him to give to her the right response.

"No disrespect, Pastor and Elders," Yolanda began in a soft voice. "We are here to meet about serving the needs of the people outside these walls. As Christians we are called to reach out to the unreachable. Ministry is our job. Not to judge or attack another person's household." She paused and looked everyone directly in the eye. "And for the record, I serve and submit to my man very well. I do it because I love God. I reverence Him. So whatever habits my husband may struggle with, God can take care of it."

Monica clapped, giving Yolanda affirmation she said the right thing. "Yes, Lord! See the body of Christ is to build one another up. And look what we have done in the Lord's house as His leaders. We need to support each other, no matter what the struggle, as Minister Howard so eloquently put it." She sat back down and turned to Yolanda, whispering, "Minister, you keep trusting the Lord and those twenties and fifties he gives to them harlots will be used to build the kingdom." She winked and spoke to the pastor.

"Pastor Griffin, when are you going to take charge over these issues presented today? We've been sitting up here for hours and have yet to hear from you."

Pastor Griffin looked up and sighed. "Well, all of you made awesome

43

points." Yolanda could tell from his composure what was next. He'd say they'd pray over everything but not accept everything unless God ordained it for His higher purpose.

"Let's pray about all the issues addressed and wait for His timing. We don't accept anything unless God ordains it for His higher purpose."

Minister Dennis Leems moaned and looked directly at Pastor Griffin. "Pastor, you've been saying the same thing for so long and nobody has seen His higher purpose for these meetings. We come in, throw around ideas and then attack people for who they are."

Pastor Griffin stood. "When will we as God's leaders stop running around chasing things that the world does and focus on His work for our lives? Elder Whitmore, you are one of our strongest leaders. However, I do think you overstep your boundaries. We have a new breed here, ministers from all backgrounds. You have a hard time accepting they are called, particularly the women. In Christ there is no man, woman, Greek or Jew. We are all one."

"Amen." Monica yelled. She rolled her eyes at Elder Whitmore, who was now ready to leave the meeting. It was a move he usually made when things were not going in the direction he hoped. "Where you going, Elder? Don't be no punk. Stay here and hear what our pastor has to say." Monica smiled broadly.

Elder Whitmore sucked his teeth. He tightened his tie and looked at Pastor Griffin. "So you want to try and check me? Boy, I was here when this church was On the Rock Tabernacle. Back when my granddaddy was still on the board. Don't come chastising me. I'll put you on my knee."

Before he could finish, Minister Dennis stood and interrupted him. "No disrespect, Elder, but you can't talk to the pastor like this. All of you are treating him with total disregard for his position here. He is our leader. Not you or anyone else." He looked pointedly at Monica.

"I know you not looking at me all cross-eyed," she sneered.

Pastor Griffin smiled and patted him on the back. "Thanks, young blood. As I was saying, all of you are valuable. However, for all of us to work together, we need to be on one accord. I don't care if you came from a gang, a crack house, or if you were a pimp or prostitute. God saved you to use you. Let's not act like the thing God called you out of."

Pastor Griffin walked to his seat. As he picked up his Bible, he addressed the group one last time. "We will have Minister Leems, Minister Boyd and Minister Caine speak at the Faith Festival. If no one can respect my decision, you may leave your position now."

Everyone looked at Elder Whitmore to see his reaction, since he was the one having a problem with who did what for the church. All of a sudden he became interested in reading his Bible. Whatever he was reading must have been good. He did not look up at anyone. Yolanda knew the threat of leaving his position was enough to shut him up, although not for long.

The meeting ended with Dennis closing out in prayer. As Yolanda got ready to leave, Pastor Griffin pulled her aside. "Minister Howard, I'd like to speak with you if I may."

"Of course, Pastor." Yolanda smiled and moved to sit beside him. When the last person left, he got up and closed the door.

"Is something wrong?" She hoped he would not bring up anything concerning her husband.

"Not with you, no," he stammered. "Minister, God has done a wonder in your life. I am so proud of you. It brings me so much joy to have you as a part of our ministry team. You may have come from the crooked way of life, but God has set you on a straight path. You represent the Proverbs 31 woman."

Yolanda was pleasantly surprised. She wasn't as confident around the other ministers because of her past. She didn't have the strength to be as transparent about her life as Monica was. Nor could she laugh about her previous lifestyle as easy as some of the others did. Deep down, Yolanda knew why. There was a part of her life she hadn't been honest about. Yet.

"But Elder Whitmore brought up a point of interest." Pastor Griffin paused.

"My husband, right?" Yolanda asked, slightly irritated that after he had esteemed her so highly, he would turn the conversation to Michael. "No offense, Pastor, but I'm the one who's called to this ministry. What does my husband have to do with it?"

Pastor Griffin raised his eyebrows in disbelief at her response. "You can't be serious, can you? Surely you didn't think you could walk into the pulpit and that *not* be an issue."

"You can't be serious about believing all the rumors around here." Yolanda's tone became rigid. "Never once has anybody *asked* me if my husband has a problem. Everyone just assumes it. He has his friends and I admit, some of them are not saved. But come on, who in this building has friends who all walk the straight and narrow?" Pastor Griffin nodded. Yolanda softened her tone. "Pastor, my husband is my mate. I'm committed to help him through whatever issues he struggles with." Yolanda stopped to take a deep breath. "Everyone wants to judge him for something they know absolutely nothing about." Yolanda knew in

46

her heart her husband's reputation challenged her credibility.

"Don't get me wrong, Minister. I know he is a man of God who struggles with the same things all men do. Because of your position in leadership here, it weakens your believability. For instance, when you spoke about being a woman of influence on Mother Daughter Day, your sermon was powerful. Awesome." He stopped and rubbed his temples. "But there were people who wondered how you can talk on being a wife when your husband can't stay at home. Now some made comments out of utter jealousy, as you are a beautiful woman. Then the others..." he trailed off. "My concern is we maintain a positive image around here, including keeping the family in check."

"I understand, Pastor. My heart is in this. My soul feeds on doing the will of God." Yolanda's eyes pleaded with his for understanding. "If by chance he doesn't get where he needs to be, that doesn't affect my position here, right?"

Pastor Griffin's silence answered the question. "I can't say it does with me. For others, it may be an issue. Just try to work on things. I want you to be a reliable source for our women, which is my main concern." Pastor Griffin stood and put back on his navy sports coat. Yolanda stood as well. A part of her was angry because she knew her husband's lifestyle did not represent the faith he claimed to have. She was also furious people would discredit her because of a man she could not control. *Everyone wants to forget about free will. I can't make him do anything. All I can do is pray for him to do something different.* Yolanda thought they put up a good front but now she knew some people didn't buy it.

She put on her coat and followed the pastor outside. As she unlocked her car door, Pastor Griffin touched her on the shoulder. "For the record, I *know* where your heart is. I have no doubt in the sincerity you have for the ministry. Understand as leaders, our whole lives are on

47

display for all to see and judge. Whether right or wrong, it's something we all have to deal with. Be strong." He patted her shoulder one last time before walking off. When Yolanda got in the car, the tears she held in flooded down her cheeks.

After a moment of releasing her emotions, she picked up her cell phone to call home. No one answered. Strange. She had told Noel to be home by five. And Michael should have been home from work.

Yolanda dialed his office. The phone rang several times before the answering machine clicked on. She hung up and called his cell phone. When he picked up, Yolanda heard music in the background. "Hello? Hello?" Yolanda yelled over the background noise. She heard muffled voices, the laughter of several men and conversation she couldn't pick up. *He must be out with the boys again.* Every time they got a new construction deal, they would go out and celebrate. Yolanda didn't have a problem with that. It's just that the celebrations happened more and more often. And Yolanda was never invited.

Not that she was one to hang out in pool halls or clubs. Yolanda found it odd she was no longer included in the success celebrations of the company she helped him build. She had convinced herself it was because he wanted to reward his construction workers.

"Yolanda. Yolanda! Can you hear me?" Michael yelled over the noise.

"Yeah, I can hear you. I was sitting here for five minutes before you noticed I was on the line. Where are you?"

"Out with the boys. We got another big deal so we had to kick it. I'll be home later. Don't wait up."

"Where are you?" she asked again.

"Baby, you're breaking up. I can't hear you. I'll have to call you back. Hello? Hello?" Suddenly, the line went dead.

Yolanda was more than a little ticked off. "Did he try to play me with the old 'my phone went out' game? I taught him that." Irritated, she started her car and headed home.

On the way, she thought about her husband. She wondered what all went on at his little celebrations. He never volunteered to tell her where they went. *Maybe it's because he knows I don't like him at the club.* Then she thought back to Monica's comment on the "twenties and fifties" being used for the kingdom instead of the harlots.

Did she try to insinuate prostitutes were servicing Michael? *Certainly not!* She knew Michael was not sexually active with anyone. Impossible. Between working all the time and then spending weekends –well, some weekends with her- she didn't see an affair happening. He had given up the strip clubs. Michael loved the strip joints for years but when they gave their lives to Christ, he gradually lost the desire to go.

Or so Yolanda thought.

Whatever was going on, Yolanda was determined to find out. She knew when she accepted her call it would challenge their lives. Michael said he wanted her to obey God and he would support her. Now it seemed like she was having to choose him or ministry. She didn't want to give up either one. If she had to choose between the God-ordained purpose for her life and her husband, she would.

Yolanda's heart said she'd choose God. Her feelings still dreaded the idea of having to do so. She spoke to God aloud. "Lord, Michael is the one man who can handle my past, the present situation caused by the mistakes of my past and he loves me. I love him. Please Lord, work

49

things out for good. Work them out for Your will."

✝ ✝ ✝

When Yolanda pulled up at the house, she noticed Youth Minister Boyd coming out of the front door. A clean-shaven young man with short dreadlocks, dressed in his velour sweat suit, he looked much different than when he was at church.

Minister Boyd saw Yolanda pull up. To her dismay, he looked startled. Instead of pulling in the garage like normal, she parked outside. She wanted to see why he was so uneasy.

"Good evening, Minister Howard. You are looking lovely as usual. Your sermon was off the hook Sunday, too." He smiled broadly at her.

"Thank you, son," she said dryly. "Why are you coming out of my house? And why are you all...jumpy? For a young man so debonair and suave, you seem a little shaken, Minister."

"Oh, me?" He laughed nervously. "I...I was just in a daze so when I saw you pull up, it caught me off guard."

"Really? What had you so in a daze, as you say?"

"I was...uh...err...uh...reflecting on how much work we did today," he seemed to get a boost of confidence suddenly. "We came up with ideas for the youth tent at the Faith Festival and we went to sing at the nursing home. It was very productive."

Yolanda smiled. "That is really good. So you had a productive day, not a *reproductive* one, right? I ask because to see you coming out of my house where my daughter is and no one else is home, unnerved me.

50

You understand?"

Minister Boyd looked at her with a stunned expression on his face. "Oh, no ma'am. It was all professional and productive. Not reproductive at all. I would not disrespect you, Minister Howard. Besides, Noel is a little young for me. A brother is twenty now, ya know?"

Yolanda still had her suspicions. *As handsome as he is, he wouldn't need to hook up with a seventeen-year-old. Besides, he dates the older sisters in the church.* Yolanda suddenly felt remorse for her assumptions. *You did the same thing to him people do to your husband, assume and accuse.* Her face softened as she smiled at Minister Boyd.

"Minister, I'm sorry for my reaction. We had a long hard meeting and I'm just a little loopy right now." He opened his arms to give her a hug. As she entered his embrace, Yolanda smelled fresh vanilla. Yolanda inhaled deeply, enjoying one of her favorite scents. *Funny, I didn't think men used vanilla products.* Then again, Minster Boyd was a pretty boy who pampered himself like one of the girls. Always smelling good, manicured and pedicured, he was the epitome of perfection.

"I trust you, Minister Boyd. I just jumped to a silly conclusion. Forgive me?" She held her arms out to hug him again.

He reached out and hugged her back. "It's cool. I understand how it must have looked. Tell your husband I said what's up. Maybe we can ball together sometime. He is working on my aunt's basement next week."

"Really?" Yolanda was surprised. Michael hadn't told her he was doing Sister Goode's house. She thought he was having one of his other contractors do it for him. A silent warning went off inside of Yolanda. Though she tried to ignore it, she could not.

"Is everything alright, Minister Howard?"

She smiled broadly. "I'm fine. I hope her...basement turns out good. Tell the family hello."

"Lord, let thy will be done. Let thy will be done." Yolanda prayed aloud.

Minister Boyd hurried to his black Ford F150. After he sped off, Yolanda pulled her car into the garage then headed into the house. She laid her purse and briefcase on the end table and went upstairs. She heard a shower running.

Noel was in the shower of her bathroom. Yolanda opened her bedroom door and walked through the clothes on the floor. She grabbed the bathroom door. It was locked.

"You know I do not go for locked doors in my house." Yolanda yelled out. "You better open up this door!" Yolanda banged on the door. After the tenth bang, Yolanda heard the water cut off. "Noel! I know you heard me. Why you got this door locked? Open it right now."

"Hold on." Noel yelled. "Can a homegirl put on her panties before you come demanding what I need to do?"

"Who you talking to? Considering this is my house, I make the rules. One of which you have directly disobeyed. What have I said about locked doors, Noel?" Noel refused to answer while she put on her underwear. "Girl, I will snatch out every hair on your head if you blatantly ignore me. What do I say about locked doors? I saw Minister Boyd as he was leaving. Mind telling me why he was so jumpy?"

Noel yanked the door open. "Why the questions? Daryl was fine when he dropped me off, so I have no idea what you're talking about.

Secondly, according to you, locked doors in an open house means someone wants to hide," Noel said, sarcastically. "Where did you get that from anyway? Locked doors mean I need a little privacy." Noel rolled her eyes and began brushing her hair.

Yolanda snatched the brush out of Noel's hand and smacked her on the head with it. Noel yelped in pain. "Don't get smart. I will beat you like there is no such thing as DFS, you hear me?" Noel nodded with a sheepish look on her face. "So he's Daryl now, huh?" Yolanda paused. "Why are you taking a shower anyway?"

Noel's eyes widened. She mocked her mother with a look of shock. "Did you ever think that I could be... how can I say this?"

Yolanda's heart beat rapidly. *Lord, don't let her have the nerve to tell me she has been fooling around with Minister Boyd. I will hang him by his dreadlocks.* Yolanda looked expectantly at Noel. "Well? Say what you got to say so I know whether or not to hug you or harm you."

Noel laughed. "I was about to tell you I was dirty from being in this summer heat. You hurt my head. You sure have been a violent little thing lately. Try this rough stuff with daddy and maybe he'd stay home."

As soon as it slipped from her lips, Noel knew she'd gone too far. Her mother didn't look angry anymore. She looked hurt, as she dropped her head. When she raised her head, Noel noticed she was tearing up. "Mom, I was out of order. I'm so sorry. Please forgive me." She reached out and embraced her mother in a tight hug.

At first, Yolanda kept her arms at her sides. She longed to be held by *somebody*, so she eventually embraced Noel back. Noel kissed her mother on the neck. "I love you. I didn't mean to hurt you. It was a stupid thing to say."

Yolanda untangled herself from Noel's arms and walked out the room. She didn't know what hurt the most. The fact that Noel had noticed her father not being home or the bottle of vanilla body gel and two washcloths in Noel's shower.

✝✝✝

Yolanda was in a deep sleep when the unlocking of the front door startled her. She jumped, sat perfectly upright in bed and glanced at the clock. It read 3:45a.m. *I know this heifer has not come in my house at a quarter to four.*

Yolanda put on her favorite robe and headed downstairs. She walked down the hall and ran smack into Michael's chest.

"Hey, baby." He chirped cheerfully. "I didn't mean to wake you, honey. I was just...I was ...uh...just...well..." Michael couldn't even finish the sentence. He knew Yolanda was steaming mad.

"You were just what? Just getting home? I am going to say this once and one time only. As long as you are married to me, you will not walk up in the house any ol' time you feel like it. Any decent man would not be out until the crack of dawn. I know them weed smoking, philandering drunks you work with have no respect for their home life but *I don't play that.*"

Michael wiped his face with the back of his hand. "Dang, baby. You didn't have to give a brother a shower. I think you spat on me on purpose. I know I came home late, but we had a situation go down."

Yolanda folded her arms across her chest and sighed. "What in the world could possibly keep my husband out until four a.m.? What, Michael? Unless you were evangelizing a lost soul or rescuing an old

54

lady from a fire, there's *nothing* you can say to excuse this."

Michael looked at the floor. He hated face-to-face confrontations. If he were on the phone, he could lie and make it sound like the truth.

"Why can't you look at me, Michael?" Yolanda asked, knowing she was taunting him. "Take your beady eyes and move them right here." She jerked his chin down, forcing him to look her straight in the eye. "Whatever lie you concocted is not good enough to get you out of this. But try me. I just like to entertain myself with your stupid stories and excuses. You must think everyone is dumb but you."

Michael started to get irritated. Yolanda often scolded him for the littlest thing like she was his mother. True, he was out doing something he had no business doing, even if he were single. Although Michael was fully aware his story might not win her over, he did not like the condescending tone she was hitting him with.

"Look, I have a mama I don't answer to, so don't try to act like her thinking you can punk me. I ain't one of your little church groupies. Don't start talking that trash about me being the husband of a minister and how what I do affects you. I have a God I am accountable to and we know that's not you." He looked her up and down and rolled his eyes. "Get out my way so I can go to bed." He shoved Yolanda to the side. Her shoulder slammed against the wall.

Yolanda yelped in pain. She balled up her fists and punched him in the back. "Where have you been? Don't walk away from me!"

Michael turned around just as she swung at his back. Unfortunately, she ended up hitting him in the chest. He doubled over in pain. She had knocked the wind out of him. He picked Yolanda up by her waist and hoisted her over his shoulder. Yolanda slapped him on the back.

55

Michael carried her into the bedroom and threw her on the bed. He pressed his body against hers and clasped his hand over her mouth. "Listen, I have never put my hands on you, *ever,* even when it was warranted. Don't ever touch me again. I restrained myself because I have never hit a woman. Do me like that again and the first time will be with you. Now are you going to let me explain where I been?"

Eyes wide with fear, Yolanda nodded. Michael had never even subtly threatened her. She looked intently at Michael as he rose from on top of her and undressed.

"Reggie got drunk and needed a ride home."

"And? Reggie is drunk all the time."

"He had an argument with Vera again over the checkbook. Do you know she went to buy a $3,000 purse on a credit card and she still has no job? Then she had the..."

"I am not trying to hear anything about their Young and the Tasteless, ghetto soap opera life. Okay? Get to the point quick."

"Oh. My bad." Michael took off his shirt and sat down on the chaise lounge. "I had to take him to one of cousin's house across the river. You know his people stay past Claycomo, baby. Anyway, there was a police standoff on the way there. Couldn't nobody get through for about an hour. When he got to his cousin's crib, they had fallen asleep and wouldn't answer the door. I had to take him up further north and there was a traffic wreck. They stopped traffic for an hour and a half to clean up. Then when we got to his other cousin's house, they said Vera called and wanted him to come home so they could talk. So I had to go all the way to Kansas City, Kansas and now I'm here."

Yolanda almost laughed. *The brother was never good at creative writing.* She decided to make him sweat it out by going into S-mode. Total silence. Sometimes silence was so loud it was more effective than a loud argument. Yolanda took off her robe and went back to bed. She pulled the covers over her head as she turned away from Michael.

"What?" Michael asked. "You don't believe me? You think I'm lyin'? See that's the kind of mess I'm talking about. You always so quick to accuse me of being at the strip club or with another woman."

Yolanda dropped the plan of being silent. *He has basically told me what has been going on. Nobody accused him of anything. Why do men tell on themselves **before** they get busted?* Yolanda sat up and looked him straight in the eye. "Sweetie, nobody said nothing about you being in the strip club or with another woman. I guess I didn't have to say it because you just did. Whatever I needed to know, you gave it to me."

Michael sat on the bed. He grabbed Yolanda's hands and held them to his chest. "Baby, I was just talking," he stammered. "I didn't do none of them things. I was just imagining some of the things you may have *thought* I did. Especially with some of my friends being so buck wild." He looked down at the comforter and back into Yolanda's eyes. "I would never hurt you. Ever. Keeping something from you is like hiding it from myself." His eyes pleaded with her for understanding.

Yolanda wasn't giving in.

"From what player handbook did you get that tired line? You up in my face acting like Forrest Gump or some remedial brother trying to play a game you can't even play well." Yolanda's voice rose in anger. "If you don't keep anything from me, why didn't you tell me you were doing trampy Sister Goode's basement? You know I can't stand the ground she walks on and here you are helping her out. What's up with that?" Yolanda jerked her hands away from Michael and flopped back down on the bed.

"Such a shame. You are allowing your anger at yourself to be thrown upon some innocent woman. A woman who is a member of the body of Christ. A client of mine who is paying a great fee to get served." Michael shook his head slowly. He knew Yolanda well enough to know that questioning her actions as a Christian would be enough to make her back off.

Yolanda took the wedding photo album that rested on the nightstand and threw it, hitting Michael in the head. "Did you hear what you just said?" Yolanda screamed. "Are you sure you stopped smoking weed? First, you basically tell me what you have been up to, telling me what I accused you of. Which I did not...yet. Now, you say Sister Goode is getting served. You sleep on the couch. Any man that stupid doesn't deserve to be in bed with his wife. And remember, you can jack up if you want to. You ain't going *nowhere.* If you even try, you'll end up back at your momma's house like your other shiftless brothers." She'd previously wondered if Michael had ever strayed. Part of her was in denial, but tonight's charade confirmed the possibility.

Michael rose from the bed and grabbed an extra blanket out of their linen closet. Before going downstairs to sleep, he turned and looked at Yolanda. "I am sorry," he whispered. "I really love you. You made me into the man I am today."

"That's not saying much right now, Forrest."

"Maybe not, but if it weren't for you getting right with God, I have no idea where I would be." His voice trembled as he continued to talk. "I haven't done anything. I promise. I've been out kicking it. I did have some drinks. I played pool. I was late getting home. I forgot to tell you about Sister Goode. But I am not guilty of anything. Anything except...except..." his voice trailed off.

"What? What are you guilty of?"

"Loving you."

Yolanda peeked at him from under the covers, where she was buried. She noticed a tear rolling down his cheek. Her heart softened. She questioned whether or not she had jumped to conclusions. She knew she was out of order in her behavior. She definitely did not operate in Proverbs 31 or 1 Peter 3 mode. She had been an accuser - angry, slanderous and filled with rage. All of which Yolanda knew were sins. Yolanda motioned for him to lie next to her.

Michael smiled broadly and practically jumped in the bed. He kissed her softly on the lips and pulled her tight. Within a few minutes, she was asleep. Michael breathed a sigh of relief. *Whew, that was close.* Michael knew right now he couldn't afford to lose Yolanda. He'd stay, even if it meant putting up with her temperamental tirades and obsession with their public image. She needed him to play the husband role. He needed her to keep his role. He loved Yolanda; he just wasn't sure if he could continue the rest of his life with her. The deeper she got into ministry, the deeper he got into trouble.

Pressing Past the Past

.

Chapter Four

Kennedy was sitting in the back of a restaurant in eastern Kansas. A little bit over an hour away from home, she was a few cities and three counties away from being Mrs. Eddie Stone. She sipped her apple martini and waited for her guy to arrive. She was nervous but excited about what could possibly happen this afternoon. She knew what she was doing was wrong. At the moment, she had no desire to be right.

She had called the ad from Wild Weekly and talked to a man named Marcus. He was an architect and from what it sounded like, had as much to lose as she did. Both were married. He told her he was a Christian, too. Although sin was lurking around them, they were desperate to fulfill their needs not being met by their spouses.

Kennedy's phone vibrated in the pocket of her blazer. It was the church. Kennedy pondered whether or not to answer it. Would it look too suspicious if she didn't? Or if she did, would she invite trouble by someone inquiring of her whereabouts? Kennedy decided to play it safe and ignored the call. *If they really want something, they will call back.* Besides, she and Marcus were just going to have lunch and then be on their separate ways.

Maybe.

Kennedy checked her watch. Eleven fifteen. Marcus would be here any minute. She remembered he said he would be in a pastel blue, long sleeve shirt and khakis. He didn't give her too much of a description except to say that he was "tall, dark and fine." Kennedy was so starved for some affection she wouldn't have cared if he looked like Gary Coleman in his mall security uniform. She was excited but nervous about this meeting.

A baritone voice came from behind her. "I think you are waiting for me. From the looks of you, I hope you are."

Kennedy turned around and gasped aloud. A six-foot-four Taye Diggs look alike smiled at her, revealing perfectly aligned, stark white teeth. *I am Stella getting my groove back.* Deep dimple in his left cheek, his muscles bulged *everywhere.* Kennedy swore she saw muscles where she'd never seen them before.

"I take it from your smile you must be Kennedy?"

"Yes, Taye, I mean Marcus." she fumbled. "It is nice to meet you. Have a seat."

"I believe I will." He slid into the booth across from her. "It sure is nice to put a face with a sexy voice. You are gorgeous. If I were your husband I'd have to keep you in the house."

Kennedy looked down as her face flushed from embarrassment. It warmed her on the inside to have a man look at her with actual...interest. Maybe even a little bit of lust. "Thank you," Kennedy stammered. "So uh...do you want to order?"

"I see you already got started." He glanced at her empty martini glass.

"I was nervous, sorry. I needed to relax." Kennedy's face blushed. "I was never a drinker until recently."

Marcus leaned in toward Kennedy with a look of concern on his face. "Really? What in your life would cause you to pick up a habit like drinking?"

Kennedy sighed. "I don't know."

Marcus sat back. "I don't like women who drink excessively. Some family members suffered with alcoholism so I've seen what it does to people. I keep myself free of things like that."

Kennedy was confused. This was the same man who put a want ad out for some booty but couldn't deal with a drinker? "Excuse me?" Kennedy said with surprise in her voice. "You mean you can see a woman, who is also married, and do whatever but you have a problem with alcohol? That makes no sense."

"I don't see what one has to do with the other," Marcus responded as he read the menu. "It's like...a preference. I prefer lobster not shrimp. I prefer yams not sweet potato pie. I prefer big hips over slim ones. I prefer non-drinkers over drinkers. It's quite simple."

"But...but..." Kennedy stuttered. "I don't see how you can even concern yourself with a social drinker and you are a social philanderer. That is what makes no sense."

"So you think you're making sense? If you find what I do so wrong, then why did you drive all the way to Topeka, Kansas to meet me? What made you, a married woman, pick up the personal ads and decide to meet a perfect stranger?" He looked pointedly at Kennedy as he waited for her response. "You call me a philanderer as if you are not guilty."

"You make a good point. I am just as guilty as you are. Maybe I should just go home."

"No, no, no. I didn't mean to make you feel bad." Marcus smiled gently and Kennedy's hard resolve softened.

"It's funny because before today, I didn't realize how empty I feel in my marriage. My husband is so involved being everything to everyone else that he can't come close to meeting my needs. I love my husband but...he puts everyone before me. I can't remember the last time he held me in his arms. It has been ages since we've laid in bed just enjoying the warmth of our bodies." Kennedy stopped to take a deep breath and gain control. She was grieved for a couple of reasons. One was the very nature of what was going on in front of her. The other was admitting for the first time her husband's neglect bothered her more than she realized. Kennedy lowered her head and silently prayed not to cry. "I'm sorry. I didn't mean to get so emotional, especially since we just met."

Marcus nodded and reached over. He stroked Kennedy's cheek softly. "You need an emotional outlet. You need a man who can understand your hurt. Someone who knows what it's like to be ignored. A person who knows a simple touch can make a difference in how you feel." He stopped and smiled. "I think we're a match, Kennedy. Except, I have one request."

"What?" Kennedy's heart beat with anticipation.

"Let's never discuss our spouses from this point on. Unless it gets to a point where we decide to walk away."

"You mean divorce our spouses?"

"No." Marcus snapped. Taken aback by his reaction, Kennedy leaned further back into her side of the booth. Marcus realized his reaction caught Kennedy off guard and softened his tone. "I meant walk away from each other. If feelings get too intense, we need to let it go. Let me make one thing clear, I am not looking to move on to another relationship. I'm looking to enhance my life while I *put up* with my at-home relationship. Understood?"

Kennedy breathed a sigh of relief. She knew she would not allow herself to get caught up in Marcus too much. *At least, I can have an outlet physically and emotionally.* She smiled at Marcus seductively. "I can live with that."

"Good. Now, let's seal it with a kiss," Marcus leaned over the table. They slowly brought their lips together in a long, soft but passionate kiss. Excitement exploded through her entire being. It had been a while since she shared that same passion with her own husband. Although Kennedy knew there could be repercussions for a sexual affair, she allowed herself to block out her convictions and go with what her body longed for.

"Goodness! People are trying to eat for heaven's sake." The waiter's high-pitched voice invaded their lustful moment. They pulled apart. The waiter stood looking at them with his hand on his hips. He shook his head. "Hmm, hmm, hmm. Why don't you all get a room? Some people don't want to see all that." He looked from Kennedy to Marcus.

Kennedy got ready to tell the waiter where to go and how to get there but before she could respond, Marcus spoke up. "If you bring us the ticket, we'll do that. Thanks, player."

The waiter was dumbfounded. "I wasn't serious. You are so tacky. Y'all are out of order." He sashayed off, mumbling, "Such a waste. I'd give anything for a man that fine."

"Did he say we were out of order?" Kennedy asked. "Please. He has a twist in his hips worse than mine." Kennedy and Marcus laughed. "You threw him off by saying we were getting a hotel. He wasn't expecting that."

"Neither was I. However, since it was suggested, why not? You didn't come all the way here just to have an appetizer, did you?"

"No. I...I...was going to eat lunch too." Even though she was enticed, she didn't want to move too fast. She feared doing something she'd regret. After all, she'd just met Marcus.

"We can do lunch. Then, I can do...you."

Kennedy's knees shook with fear and eagerness. Her knees hadn't shaken since her honeymoon. No longer thinking about the sin of what was going to occur, she stood up. Before she realized it, she had uttered two words. Two words that would change the course of her life. Two words that would take her opposite of God's will. Two words she never thought she would say after walking down the aisle.

"Let's go."

✞✞✞

As Kennedy headed back home, she tried to erase the vision of what had occurred just a little over three hours ago. Although Kennedy purposely did not revel in the memories of the amorous tryst, it became impossible to control.

The harder Kennedy fought to erase the reality of the incident, the more she envisioned Marcus kissing her from head to toe. Holding on to his perfectly chiseled chest. His heart beating on top of her bare skin. The animal-like lust taking over as they had sex. Pure ecstasy consuming any conviction for the sin they were committing. The long, hot shower they had taken together which led to another session of sexual acts Kennedy had not done in a year. Finishing with a half hour nap, as she rested in the arms of her lover.

Afterwards, when he walked her to her car, he kissed her gently on the forehead. "Thank you," he whispered. His simple touch made the hair on her arms rise and sent chills down her body. They promised to e-mail or text each other so they could meet up again. She wasn't worried about getting caught. Eddie didn't like technology- he didn't even use the data plan on his cell phone. Kennedy got excited at the thought of seeing Marcus again.

As she turned off the exit ramp, she noticed her cell phone in the seat. The display read, "Seven missed calls." Kennedy chuckled at the thought of Yolanda looking for her all day long. *She probably thinks I went to the shopping outlet in Branson without her.*

As her car slowly approached her block, Kennedy became nervous. She knew her husband wasn't really gifted in the area of discernment but there was still fear he would know something was up. When she pulled in the driveway, her mouth dropped in shock.

Mother Stone was on her front porch, hands on her hips. She tapped her foot as she pointed at Kennedy. Eddie's mother was nosy, miserable and a horrible gossip. Kennedy often referred to her as "church folk". While she was often one of those who ran around the church like she was in the spirit, as soon as she left the church parking lot she was another person: a foul-mouthed, ill-tempered, meddlesome woman who could smile in your face and spit in it within minutes.

Kennedy didn't see her husband's car in the drive so she assumed he was still at the church. What she didn't like was coming home to his mother who was more like a prison warden. *Lord, forgive me for my sin and please have mercy upon me now. Let this woman not cause me to send her home immediately...and keep my hands from reaching out and*

67

touching her. Amen. Kennedy realized her prayer was a little flesh-oriented but she thought it was worth a try.

"And where in the devil's name have you been all day?" Mother Stone belted out as Kennedy closed her car door. "I know you been somewhere serving the devil. We done been calling you all daggum day and your phone went straight to voicemail." She paused and looked at Kennedy from head to toe. She rolled her eyes and crossed her arms over her chest. "What you got to say? I am waiting for you to explain yourself to me. You got to tell me something, now. Gone all day and ain't checked in. When Eddie told me to come over here to meet you, I had to pray myself up for this kind of atrocity."

Kennedy's face became enflamed. "First of all, this is my house. Second, I have a God and a momma that I am accountable to. You are nowhere on the list. So get off my porch and take your fat..." Kennedy stopped. There were several profanities about to roll off her tongue.

Mother Stone grabbed her heart and fell back against the door. "Lord, I need my heart medicine." She pulled a crumpled tissue from her bra and wiped her forehead, which was completely dry. "When I start sweatin' like this, Lord, it's because you made my blood pressure go up about thirty numbers high."

Kennedy laughed out loud. "This is coming from a woman who ate almost a whole fried chicken in one sitting. Girl, if your blood pressure is high, stop drinking at them bridge parties you go to. You eat so much fried food Crisco is running through your bloodstream." She stepped to the front door and pushed past Mother Stone. "You can stand out here on my porch all day spouting a web of lies and dramatic scenes that are a part of your imagination. But I do not owe you any explanation on what I was doing today."

As Kennedy walked through the foyer, Mother Stone followed close behind. "Now wait a minute, missy, I'm tired of playing nice with your Rahab behind. You about to make me act like I lost my salvation."

"How can you lose something you probably never even had?"

"Oh, so now you want to say I am a heathen?" Mother Stone screeched, while taking down her bun. "Shoot, I shout more than anybody. I can even speak in tongues and everything. You the one that's been some sex-starved hussy since first grade."

Kennedy halted in her steps. She could not believe what she just heard. The one thing she had entrusted Eddie with he had told his mother. It hurt immensely to find out the issue she tried to ignore for many years was now known to the woman who was dubbed "Mega Mouth" by most of the church members. Kennedy not only prayed she would keep her mouth shut, but also that she wouldn't hurt Eddie for telling his mama the most hurtful secret she could ever have...before today.

"Yes, Eddie told me how you been having sex all your life." Mother Stone's voice was filled with disgust. "I asked him when he married you was he sure you had your issue under control. You know what they say about women like you."

"I don't. But, I'm sure you'll tell me. What do they say about women like me?"

"You can't make a whore into a housewife." Mother Stone smiled slyly at Kennedy. "You hide behind your 'Thank you Jesus' yells and helping the kids at church. You even keep a decent home. On the other hand, I still see the spirit of sex all up and down your body."

Without thinking, Kennedy pulled her arm back ready to slap Mother Stone into the next room. As she got ready to swing, Eddie had come inside. Mother Stone fell to the floor, grabbed her chest and cried out, "Lord, save me. Protect me. I rebuke you, Kenned...I mean Satan! Leave my daughter-in-law alone. You can't have her. You can't have herrrrrrrr!" She let out a squawking scream and then rolled over as if she was slain in the spirit.

Kennedy almost laughed until Eddie grabbed her. He penned her arm behind her back and had his other arm around her throat. Kennedy didn't know if he was trying to role-play like the NYPD or what. "What are you doing? Let me go, idiot." Kennedy screamed.

"I have seen enough." Enraged about what he assumed had taken place, Eddie sobbed. "I cannot believe my wife, the lead deacon and church CPA's soul mate would hit her mother-in-law." He released Kennedy and ran to his mother. Rubbing her back, he wailed as if she had died. Mother Stone opened her right eye, winked at Kennedy, and then licked her tongue out at her. Kennedy had seen enough.

"Look, you blubbering mama's boy, I didn't hit her. I wanted to and I admit it wasn't right but I am not going to listen to someone call me a whore in my own house."

"Whoa, whoa." Eddie stood up, immediately void of all the tears and dramatics. A wave of relief wash over Kennedy. *Finally, Eddie is going to be a real man and stick up for me.* She wanted to grab Eddie and hug him. She wiped out of her mind the earlier indiscretion. "Mama, you promised me you would never say anything about what I told you," Eddie's voice filled with exasperation. "I expected you to keep your promise, Mama. No matter what is said behind closed doors, you can't disrespect her to her face."

Immediately, Kennedy's heart dropped. "You've been talking about me behind my back?" Tears welled up in her eyes. "You told her the one thing I thought you would take to the grave." Eddie turned around and looked into his wife's eyes.

"Look, you know as well as I do you've had some issues. You still carry around that carnal spirit of lust. I never judge you for it. I accept it, but it doesn't mean I can't express my concerns about it to the woman I trust more than anybody." He paused. "You know that's Mama. You right behind her, though." Eddie had the audacity to smile, like his words consoled Kennedy.

"Oh, baby. Mama is so sorry. I didn't mean to hurt your *beautiful* wife." Mother Stone dragged herself up to a sitting position. She held her arms out for Eddie to hug her. He ran into her arms and then helped her to her feet. "I sure didn't mean to cause any harm. You know Mama ain't no hell raiser. When you been looking for your *wife* for an entire day, it made me act out in the flesh. Forgive me, daughter." Mother Stone smiled, but Kennedy read the rage in her eyes. She was truly an evil woman.

Kennedy decided to play along. After all, she now had an outlet. Someone who could be there to meet her needs. Fulfill her fantasy. A man who wouldn't judge her. Granted she was in sin, Kennedy figured it was better than dealing with reality. Hers was a husband who loved his mother, church members and others more than his wife. A spouse who told the secrets that plagued her early in life. A mate who sold her out. While Kennedy was enraged about him revealing her secret to his mother, she realized she couldn't say too much. She had a second life that would keep her occupied. A good distraction. To divert attention, Kennedy knew what she had to do.

"I forgive you, Mother. Besides, if I can't forgive you, God can't forgive me, right?" Kennedy smiled through gritted teeth. Eddie smiled so wide she could see his back molars. *This idiot actually believes this. I have seen ten-year-olds less gullible.* Mother Stone clenched her teeth as

71

Kennedy pulled away from her. "Baby, Mother loves you. Let's forget your old nasty...I mean this old nasty incident and break bread together." Mother Stone grabbed Eddie's hand and pulled him toward her. "Son," she murmured sweetly, "Go ahead and sit in the dining room. Your lovely wife and I will serve you dinner in a few minutes."

Startled, Kennedy snapped her head back. "What? I didn't cook before I left today. It will be longer than a few minutes before Eddie will be served." Mother Stone chuckled as she pulled a red handkerchief from her bra. She delicately wiped the sweat that was forming on her forehead. Kennedy laughed to herself at the simple pleasure of irking her mother-in-law. The doorbell interrupted her.

"That must be dinner." Mother Stone had a smile on her face, with an icy glare in her eyes. "I ordered some Red Lobster for carry-out. And wouldn't you know, Bessie May's grandbaby was working there? He agreed to deliver it to us so we could enjoy a nice meal."

Eddie squealed with delight, practically knocking Kennedy out of the way to hug his mother. "Mama, you are something else. Boy, if they could bottle you up and sell you in stores, a lot of men would be happy." He gave her a big kiss on the cheek and practically skipped off to answer the door.

"I see you stepped in and took care of things, huh?" Kennedy snapped at Mother Stone as soon as Eddie was out of earshot, "Well, at least we can enjoy some good grub despite the company." Kennedy rolled her eyes and turned to walk away.

"Uh, baby, you can roll them little slanted, squinch eyes all you want. Since you seem to be too busy to take care of my son, I had to step in." Unexpectedly, she laughed. "I don't know why you walking in there. You better make a ham salad sandwich. I didn't order nothing for you. Puh-lease. You been out all day doing Lord knows what and think I am going to feed you?" She sauntered off to join her son, who seemed more like her man.

Kennedy stood with her mouth agape. She could not believe this woman. For years she had put up with her snide comments, backhanded compliments and insinuations about her being a tramp. *But to come in **my** house and disregard me like hired help,* Kennedy silently screamed and prayed for strength not to slap her. As she toyed with the fantasy, Eddie interrupted her thoughts.

"Sit down, Mama." He whisked her by the hand and dragged her toward the dining room. "Kennedy, I take it you ate already," he called to her without even turning around. "You been gone all day, so you just go to bed. I'll deal with you later. Hope you had it good today."

If you only knew how good I did. She sighed and walked down the hall toward their bedroom. Kennedy fell out on the cream plush comforter and pondered on the day she had. She missed Marcus already. At first, she thought maybe this would be a one-time thing but after tonight's drama, which she coined 'A Man and His Mama', Kennedy knew there would be more times to come. Without undressing, she drifted into a blissful sleep.

Kennedy felt something heavy on her head. Thinking she was asleep, she rolled over only to be whacked in the back. Kennedy screamed in pain as the sting of the blow tortured her body. She sat up straight to find Eddie grimacing over her. "What is wrong with you?" Her voice filled with rage. "What are you trying to do to me, Ike Turner? I am not Anna Mae. I have no problem whooping your tail."

"I had to do something. I called your name but you didn't do nothing but snore and turn over." He paced back and forth across the marble floor. "I'm sorry I hit you. I wasn't trying to hurt you." He looked down at the floor and sighed. "I love you too much to hurt you." His voice was softer. Kennedy gulped and held back her tears. Seeing him appear vulnerable was touching.

"So what did you do today, Kennedy?"

"I had a me day."

"A 'me' day? And what does one do on a 'me' day?" Eddie frowned.

"Things that concern me and are about me and for me."

"Next time you have a 'me' day, let this 'me' know what you-me is doing. Is that clear? I don't appreciate being embarrassed at the church when they trying to call my wife and she is nowhere to be found."

Kennedy was flabbergasted. She thought he was concerned about her cheating on him, but once again, it wasn't about her. It was solely about the church members as usual.

"Had brothers cracking jokes, talking about you were probably with one of them youngins who check you out," Eddie's voice became louder as his anger heightened. "Everybody else's woman was accountable for...except mine. You know I am in a position of authority there. If anything looks out of sorts, folks will run with it. Do you hear me?" Chest and potbelly heaving, he looked her directly in the eyes.

Kennedy was furious. "Because you are too much of a punk to take a joke, you coming at me all crazy? I mean, what's *your* concern? What you assume I was doing or what assumptions *they* made?"

"Don't twist this on me," Eddie scoffed. "I get tired of all them men like

74

dogs in heat looking at you. Lusting in their hearts to get a piece of you." He sat down on the bed beside her and leaned in so close she could see a piece of garlic stuck in his gap. "You got it so good. Can't nobody take care of you like me. You haven't worked in years. Probably couldn't get a job if you had to." He looked her up and down. "What I don't like is other folk questioning me about how I run my household."

Kennedy could not believe what she heard. She fell back on her pillow in disbelief. He was so arrogant he couldn't imagine her cheating but was mad over his image? "So your concern is not where I was?"

Eddie sighed and looked up at the ceiling. He took a deep breath, and looked forcefully at Kennedy. "I'm mad because I think you purposely did not answer our calls. I think you were with one of your silly girlfriends or Yolanda. You did this to be spiteful. Mama said for all I know you could be lying around with someone, but I can't see that. After all this you got here?" He laughed loudly. "You can't afford to mess up. You'd be right back in that cramped flat with your mama and you know it. You aren't stupid."

"You know before I met you, I had what I wanted so I am not the little ghetto Cinderella you had to save from the big bad hood." Kennedy stood on her feet and snatched the comforter off the bed. She balled it up, plucked up a pillow and headed out the bedroom.

"Where you going?"

"You insulted me to the utmost for the last time." Kennedy shouted. "I am going in the guest room. Do not follow me. Don't wake me in the morning or look for me tomorrow."

As Kennedy headed down the hall, Eddie called out behind her, "You will be in the house tomorrow. For your behavior and not sleeping in the bed, I'm taking your keys."

75

Kennedy stopped in her tracks. "What? You trying to *ground* me? I am not your child. I am your wife. Wife, Eddie! I am your equal. You, your mama, your deacons, your church folk do not run me. Stop treating me like I am a second-class citizen around here. Everything and everyone comes before me."

"See, I can't even talk to you when you all riled up like this. Get you some rest and we'll discuss this in the morning. I should have listened to Mama and made you work at the church with me."

"If you like listening to your gossiping, two-faced, tongue-lashing Mama, sleep with her tonight. Maybe you should have married her." Kennedy ran to the guest room and slammed the door. She threw herself on the bed and cried softly until she fell asleep. She was convicted because she knew what was right but more willing to do wrong.

Chapter Five

Michael rolled over and looked at his cell phone. It read 3:45. He knew Yolanda was out with Kennedy today to buy decorations for Eddie's upcoming 50th birthday party.

He grabbed the remote to watch PTI on ESPN before he headed home. Yolanda hated sports with a passion. Over here he could get as much ESPN as he wanted. He didn't have to worry about being hassled to do housework, listen to sermons or play referee between Noel and Yolanda. This was his haven of bliss: sports, food, drinks and female companionship.

"Baby, do you want a beer or something while I am in here?" Chantal peeked her head out from the kitchen to check on Michael.

"Yeah, bring me a Bud Light and some of that leftover Rotel dip," Michael called back, glancing briefly at Chantal.

"Coming up in less than sixty." Chantal smiled and then blew Michael a kiss.

Chantal was a twenty-seven-year-old beauty Michael had met at The Silver Slipper. It was a restaurant by day and the busiest strip club by night. As a top tier club, it was patroned by the city's most elite athletes, media personalities, lawyers and doctors. And yes, a few men from church. Michael never worried about being caught there. It was as if all the men had a silent agreement. "I won't tell if you don't."

Michael was gobbling down a T-bone steak with Reggie when Chantal came to their table.

As he swallowed a mouth full of red meat, he looked up to see a pair of perfect white teeth smiling at him. What was even better were the pair of juicy, plump wine-colored lips that seemed to summon all of his attention. Chantal had skin the color of caramel, straight sandy brown hair, with ash blonde highlights that hung to the middle of her back. Her face was shaped like a perfect heart, with a dimple in her chin. She had light brown eyes, with specks of green surrounding the pupils. Her face was perfect enough to give Halle Berry a run for her money. And the face was just the beginning.

Being a dancer, her body was slamming. Long, thick legs with toned calves and thighs. A round derriere, firm and full. Her waist was so small he could almost wrap just one hand around it. To top it all off, she had a heaving bosom. She was a perfect perky D. One look was all it took. She drew him in like pollen to a bee. She had asked him if he could change her tire, which had gone flat in the parking lot. Michael eagerly agreed and she led him to a black Land Rover truck. While he changed her tire, they joked around. She asked if was he married. He said yes. She asked if they could be friends. He said yes. He asked her if he could come over. She said yes.

For the past few months, their time together became more intense. They cuddled after sex. Had serious conversations about their past and future. They met boldly in public for lunch. On more than one occasion, he had stayed at her place almost until dawn. They agreed if things got too serious they would end their rendezvous. The rendezvous was turning into a relationship. One Michael did not want to end.

Chantal brought a tray to Michael with Doritos, a bowl of Rotel dip and his Bud Light. As she sat the tray on the coffee table, Michael playfully swatted her backside. Chantal yelped in mock pain, and then laughed. She sat on the sofa next to Michael. She rubbed his back and kissed him on the neck. Michael turned to Chantal and gave her a long, deep passionate kiss.

"Boy, you may have to call home tonight if you do that again." Chantal laughed.

"I wish. You know the deal though, baby. I'll be back tomorrow. Friday is our day."

"I may be sleep during the day. You know I have to work at the club tomorrow evening. With the ballers in town for the game, I suspect afterward, we may get busy if you know what I mean."

Michael pondered what she was saying. Though he was married, he was starting to get very territorial over Chantal. He hated she was a stripper. He didn't like men feeling on her and getting turned on by his woman. He sighed and sat back on the couch.

"Baby, what's wrong?" Chantal's eyes filled with concern. "You seem bothered. Tell me what's up."

"I can't even trip. I knew you were a stripper when I met you. I'm married anyway, but I can't help but get a little jealous when you go to do your thing." Michael took a swig of his beer. "I don't have the right to tell you what to do. Now, I feel like you are my lady. I don't want all them other brothers seeing what I got at home."

"Baby, I got to do what I go to do. When I get done with school, I'll stop. Besides, since we can't be together, it shouldn't matter. We agreed when we started this to let our outside lives remain the same. Anyway, those fools in the club are getting robbed. You get it all. They get a little. They got to pay. You just get to be my Big Daddy. Don't you think you

79

got the better deal?" She leaned back into a sexy pose on the couch. She put one hand behind her head and rubbed her hip with the other. Michael smiled and leaned over to kiss her when his cell phone rang. He looked at the caller ID. It was Yolanda. Again. He couldn't keep dodging her calls, but he really didn't want to ruin the mood at this moment. "Baby, it's wifey," he sighed apologetically.

"Do you. Take care of home. I'll still be here." Chantal stood up and walked toward the bathroom to give Michael some privacy.

"Hello?"

"Michael, where are you?" Yolanda frantically screamed in his ear. "You need to get home!"

"I'm finishing up a contract in Warrensburg. What's wrong?"

"I got a letter...it's...it's from..." Yolanda started to wail.

"Baby, slow down. A letter? From who?"

"It's him. He wants us to tell the truth. He wants her."

Michael's heart beat rapidly. Without asking for details he knew what was up. A part of the past was coming up for them to face.

"I'm on my way." Michael hung up and searched for his keys. Just as he found them, Chantal appeared. "Is everything all right?"

"No. Remember what I told you about my daughter?"

"Yes. Oh no! She's going to find out, isn't she?"

"Yeah. Call you later?"

Chantal shook her head. "No. Your wife and daughter need you. Call me tomorrow night. Take care of home, baby."

Hearing what Chantal said, he was convicted. To take care of home, home needed his full attention. After all, Michael knew a house divided could not stand.

Pressing Past the Past

Chapter Six

Yolanda paced the floor wringing her hands. Sweat beads popped on her forehead while tears continued to stream down her face. Weeks had passed since she saw Rocky at church so she had hoped she wasn't going to hear from her or her brother. Yolanda was wrong. As soon as she read the letter, she was in emotional turmoil. For years, she'd dreaded the moment when she'd have to face the one fallacy she had carefully built.

Yolanda looked out the front window to make sure Noel hadn't come home. Tonight, Yolanda prayed Noel would miss curfew. She needed time to get herself together.

Yolanda sighed and sat down on the chaise lounge in her office. She re-read the letter that would now cause her life to go in a new direction. She had to prepare herself for the repercussions. While short and to the point, it seemed as if an eternity had passed while reading the letter.

Dearest Yolanda -

It has been many years since we have spoken to one another. I hear you are a new woman and I am grateful. It is refreshing to see God has taken ahold of a life, which was down and is using it for His glory. Having said that, I think you should know my purpose in writing you.

While in prison, I heard the voice of God. I have tried to forget the last night we were all together, but it continued to come to me in my spirit. I know everything I did was wrong. I also know you gained a beautiful daughter out of our mess. For a long time, I believed you and Michael had a child. Then many years ago, my sister Rocky spotted you and Noel at a shopping mall and she brought it to my attention that Noel looked just like our sister, Tina did at her age. I thought she was tripping to suggest I could possibly have a daughter but the more I pondered it, the more I sought answers.

Rocky obtained your mother's information and after many letters to your mother, she confessed Noel was my daughter. I know it bothered you when your mother revealed this truth but with her integrity and your addictions at that time, she felt she had to. I admire Michael for stepping in and being the father I could not be. I thought I would leave it alone. But now since I am a productive member of society, I am ready to meet my daughter. I still want Michael to be in her life but she needs to know her father. As ugly as the conception was, I am determined to make amends. Please find it in your heart to make this transition smooth for her. I must warn you though, I will fight this with everything I have to meet her. Yolanda, find it in your heart to forgive me for my sin against you and then, find the God in your heart to allow a wrong, by all of us, to be made right.

Sincerely,
Terrence Rodney Hudson, biological father of Noel Howard

Yolanda knew he was right. She and Michael concocted a tale to cover up *their* sin but yet they still lived in their sin - a lie. Yolanda knew one day she would have to tell Noel what happened. As the years went on, she grew more cowardly in facing the facts. The facts were simple. A drug deal gone bad led to a sex trade which gave her a baby. Michael only went along with the facade because he was just as guilty in the whole incident.

It was a dismal Friday night. Michael, Yolanda, Terrence and a man named Nicolas were sitting on a rundown couch. There was only the glow of a red light bulb and the faint light of stars from the front windows. They had been playing spades, drinking gin and smoking Newports. Laughing. Joking. Then Nicolas pulled out a gun and demanded $1800 from Michael. Michael didn't think Nicolas was serious. When he yanked Michael up by his collar and put a gun in his mouth, Yolanda screamed. Terrence slapped her across the face and told her to shut up. Michael pleaded for his life and told Nicolas he only had $1,000 on him. Terrence said in exchange for the missing $800, service from Yolanda would suffice. With his eyes, Michael pleaded with Yolanda to go for it and preserve his life. Yolanda was so shaken she did what she thought she had to.

After the incident, she and Michael did not talk about what happened. At the time, he tried to apologize but Yolanda told him to forget it. "I was part of the debt owed, remember? At least everything's over." Or so they thought.

Eventually, they were looking for a period that never came. It had to be Terrence's baby.

Michael's guilt and love for Yolanda caused him to step up to the plate. Although Sable knew the situation, they figured they wouldn't worry about it. Michael would be the child's father and that would be it. Period. They had Noel, dropped her off at Sable's and did what they had to do. Yolanda stayed in school getting her degree and internships. Michael studied and hustled. Because of his street ways, and their addiction, they thought leaving Noel with Sable proved best. When Yolanda got clean, Michael soon followed. So did the open doors of blessing. From a good corporate gig to starting their construction business, life couldn't get better.

The construction business grew as she grew in the Word. Once she and Michael felt they arrived, so did Noel – understandably with a chip on her shoulder.

Now it was time to face the ugly reality. Noel's life was based on a lie. One night of drunkenness, drugs and rage led to a seed, in many ways. The seed of conception. The seed of life. The seed of plots. The seed of pretending. Now it was harvest time.

After what seemed like an eternity, Yolanda heard Michael's voice booming from the front foyer. "Yolanda! Yolanda, baby! Come here, honey." As soon as Yolanda entered the room, she ran into his outstretched arms. He stroked her hair as she silently shed tears on his chest. The tears soaked his shirt. He kissed her head. His arms engulfed her even tighter.

 "What are we going to do, Michael?" she whispered softly. She leaned back and stared into his eyes. "Maybe we should have told her from the beginning."

"Maybe, but we didn't," Michael responded shaking his head slowly. "All we can do is see how he wants to do this. We have no choice. We have to tell Noel. Remember no matter what, I am her daddy. I been loving her since she came out and peed on my basketball shorts."

Yolanda laughed deeply. It put Michael's heart at ease. Michael swooped Yolanda up in his arms and carried her back into her office. He laid her on the chaise and stroked her arms.

"We can make it through this. We've made it through worst situations, Yo."

She nodded her head in agreement. "How do we break this to her? Do we meet with him first or what? Do I need to tell Pastor?"

Michael got agitated. Here they were discussing a serious family issue and again her church image comes up. He stood up and folded his arms against his chest. "First of all, what does Pastor Griffin got to do with this? Pastor man don't pay no bills here. We have a God we are accountable to and a Bible to aid us. So why do we need to confirm anything with him?"

"Michael, don't be stupid! You know a revelation like this could threaten my position at the church. And, Noel's lifestyle is at stake. This could devastate her."

"Noel. Yes, she is my concern. Your position is not." Michael paced the floor. "This happened in your past, not now. If any of them hypocrites got something to say that shows you where they're coming from. Besides, if your position is based on a pure past, you need to go now. You got a past. Get over it and move forward with your life. Stop looking for them to affirm you."

"I don't make the rules. I just live by them, Michael," Yolanda said in a soft dry voice. "I agree with you, but at the same time understand where I'm coming from. If this leaks out, it could appear as if I purposely hid it from everyone."

Michael laughed. "Fool, you did! What did you expect, Yolanda? Hope it would never come up? We'd never have to face this? I mean what is done in the dark does come to light."

"I don't appreciate you calling me a fool," Yolanda scolded. "And, what's wrong with you? You look like you saw the devil fly through here."

"Nothing...nothing..." Michael stammered. "This has just thrown me off, that's all. We'll meet with Terrence first, and then talk to Noel. Be prepared. She's going to explode on this one, baby."

"I am already praying up for it. If He be for me, He is more than the world against me, right?" She was trying to convince herself that everything would be fine. "Let's pray, baby. I feel like this is something we need to approach the Lord together on. We need to collectively draw from His power."

Michael reluctantly walked over to the paisley covered bench where they often knelt together. After the sin he was just into, he felt too unclean to pray. He knew if he did not oblige, Yolanda would question his lack of desire to pray and it would become a three-hour battle.

When Yolanda knelt beside him, he wrapped his arm around her waist. He glanced at her pretty face, free from worry. It was as if the peace of God transformed her countenance to one of calm, beauty and confidence.

Yolanda kissed him on the cheek and prayed.

Chapter Seven

The Faith Festival at church had kicked off at noon and still had eight long hours to go. Kennedy was one of the first to set up this morning. She helped vendors get to the right booth, coordinated with the kitchen staff on when to serve breakfast and lunch and then assisted in the parking lot to aid in getting cars situated. Needless to say, her being there made her husband beam with pride. He watched her every move and occasionally gave her winks and smiles of affirmation. Before she left to take a break, he pulled her close and whispered tenderly in her ear, "I am so blessed to have a woman as beautiful and giving as you. I love you, Kennedy. Thank you for what you've done today."

When she pulled back to look at him, Kennedy saw a look of contentment on his face. Gone was Deacon Stone, the had-to-be perfect church leader, ready and willing to impress at all costs, she saw a little boy looking for confirmation of being appreciated and having his love reciprocated. Kennedy's heart was so overcome with emotion she almost cancelled her afternoon rendezvous with Marcus.

Almost...

✝✝✝

A while later, Kennedy found herself in the warm embrace of Marcus, after another tiring tryst. She and Marcus had done the usual: a little conversation, a little bite to eat and a whole lot of physical activity. Today, Kennedy stayed longer than usual in their suite at a quaint inn right outside the city.

Kennedy looked at Marcus' chocolate back rippling with muscles as he headed to the shower. Being with him was so different from her balding, aging, weight gaining, boring husband. Kennedy never fell for Eddie for physical reasons. He was a knight in shining armor to her. He had respected her desires. Prayed with her through her problems. Listened to her life story, the good, bad and downright nasty. After knowing her past, he seemed to actually accept her as is - defects and all. As years went by and his pew sitting turned into service, things changed between them. It had always been Kennedy's dream to have a Christian husband regardless of her inner struggles. She knew she believed in Jesus. But she also knew that her carnality in sexual sin had always been an issue. She thought by marrying the first genuine Christian man she met, it would curb her problem. And it did, until recently.

Kennedy tried to convince herself having a godly man was more important than having her sexual needs fulfilled. The harder she tried to convince herself of the fallacy, the more she found herself needing physical affection. She never dreamed she would actually fall into temptation and commit adultery. Watching her lover's nude silhouette behind the shower door, her mother's voice came to her, *Chile, you got to cast down them imaginations that ain't from God. The world calls it fantasy. God calls it sin. If you can't tell someone what you thinkin' about, you don't need to be ponderin' on it.* She never cast down the imaginations that roamed through her head. Now she was falling into a situation that could mess up her whole life.

Kennedy sighed and slowly dragged herself out of the bed. She decided to wash up and later soak in her tub. She grabbed her burgundy lace bra and matching panties, then walked into the bathroom. She pulled back the shower door to tell Marcus she was about to head out.

Steam filled the bathroom as Marcus soaped himself down in the

90

scalding water. When Marcus noticed Kennedy had opened the door, he jumped slightly.

"Girl, you letting out all my steam." Marcus hollered, with a playful grin. "Why you staring at a brother like you've never seen nothing like this before? My bad. You haven't." He laughed at his own joke.

"Ha-ha," Kennedy replied dryly. "You all right. You okay for something to do, but uh, you not the world's greatest lover." She smiled slyly at him while batting her eyes.

"Please," Marcus huffed. "Had you climbing the walls. Shoot, you took almost a two-hour nap when it was over. So yes, I am all that."

Kennedy agreed. Even though she tried to convince herself it was just a sex thing and she could stop anytime she wanted, she was beginning to need Marcus. Her body craved his, even when she was with Eddie. Marcus felt like an overnight addiction, one hit and she was hooked.

"I'm going to get dressed and head back over to an event. I can't be missing too long." She leaned in and gave him a deep, lingering kiss. He wrapped his wet arm around her waist and pulled her close. Water fell on her hair, drenching it as the smell of hairspray filled the small space. Kennedy jerked her head back. "Boy, I can't be going nowhere around my friends and family with my hair all wet!" She quickly stepped out of the shower and shook her hair. She decided it would be safer just to brush it into a chignon.

Marcus peeped his head out of the shower. "Sorry, baby. Didn't mean to get you all wet." He looked at her with a seductive stare. "Girl, get out of here before we both end up right in this room and not where we should be." He closed the door.

Kennedy lingered at the sink. She knew what she should do. She needed to get dressed and get the heck out of there. But, she didn't. She headed back to the shower.

✝✝✝

"Minister Howard, have you talked to Kennedy yet? She should have been here by now." Deacon Stone wiped his sweaty forehead. The heat got to him while he was helping one of the vendor's barbeque. He wiped his hands on his apron before pulling out his cell phone. He flipped through his received calls log and fumed, "She hasn't even tried to call me."

Yolanda admitted it was awkward between her and Kennedy that afternoon. She'd been aloof when Yolanda tried to find out where she was going. Kennedy seemed agitated when Yolanda jokingly said, "What? You getting your creep on and that's why you can't let a sister roll with you?" Kennedy rolled her eyes at Yolanda and walked away, leaving Yolanda puzzled. Normally, Kennedy would crack a joke back and they would end up laughing. When she later tried to call her, Kennedy's phone went straight to voicemail.

"Deacon," Yolanda solemnly began, "Earlier she let me know she was going to...to...get some rest and run around. She'll be here soon." Yolanda silently asked God to forgive her for the small lie she told. She felt sorry for Eddie. She knew how proud he was of his wife and to have her gone for more than three hours at a church event upset him.

"Can I ask you something?" Eddie questioned Yolanda. "And I need for you to be honest too."

"Preacher honest or street honest?"

"Which one is to the point?"

92

"Street. Preacher honest means I have to make it sound nice."

"Okay...I got you. Does...is Kennedy happy with me?" His forehead wrinkled with concern. "I mean...lately, she seems as if she could care less about anything I say or do. I even miss our fights about mama, cooking, church and love..." Eddie stopped mid-sentence. He was curious about how much Kennedy had told Yolanda in regards to their home life. He had hoped that the sex issue wasn't a topic of conversation but with girlfriends, he could never tell.

Yolanda gave careful thought before opening her mouth. Kennedy had more than hinted about her problems with Eddie. First, it was the fact he spent more time taking care of church business than her. His nosy mother had always been an issue. Yolanda didn't find out about her lack of sexual satisfaction until a few weeks ago. In her spirit, Yolanda believed Kennedy found an outlet to fulfill her sexual need. She prayed Kennedy would resist temptation but her avoidance of Yolanda and now Eddie's conversation raised alarm within her. *Lord, I don't want to hurt him or cause problems with Kennedy and me. What should I say?*

"Eddie, I don't know what Kennedy feels. I have been pretty busy lately and we haven't had a chance to play catch up," Yolanda responded.

Eddie look puzzled. He thought the two of them hooked up at least once a week to do lunch. He hadn't heard Kennedy mention anything about Yolanda of late, but she also hadn't given him any hint that they weren't communicating. "I thought you all did lunch once a week. In fact, last week she told me she was with you one afternoon."

Dang! She used me as a cover and didn't even tell me. "She probably was..."

Eddie abruptly cut her off.

"What do you mean, 'probably' was?" His voice was thick with anger. "Now, look here preacher girl, you haven't been a saint all your life. Don't play innocent with me. You up here trying to lie for her. You're probably the one that put her up to whatever sin she's in. I know you and your husband might be into some of that freaky-deaky sleeping with other couples and everything. You see, my family is a family of the Lord and we choose purity in our household. You better tell me what you know before I really got to check you."

"Check me? You need to check yourself! If you were doing your husbandly duty instead of running around letting these so-called church people use you, you would know where your wife is." Yolanda looked him over from head to toe and shook her head. "In fact, do you even know what pimping is?"

Eddie furrowed his eyebrows. "What you mean do I know what pimping is? How should I? I ain't never been a gigolo. I mean I was a hot-blooded lad. The ladies did love some Eddie before I became a deacon, but I ain't ever got paid for my past sexual prowess." Eddie actually had a grin on his face. He seemed proud of his past conquests.

Yolanda was astonished at Eddie's arrogance and ignorance. "Pimping is when people come looking for something never to give anything in return." Yolanda paused and took a deep breath. "You allow all these people to take from you. They take your time, your energy, and your commitment. What do they give you in return, Eddie? I mean, *lead deacon*? You allow them to take priority in your life then you put your wife on the back burner. You're being pimped by church folk who want all you've got to give and you foolishly do it." Yolanda rolled her eyes as she pivoted away. *I still got one more thing to get off my chest.* She turned back around and faced Eddie with her hands planted on her hips.

"You think you know something about my household? You up here chastising me like I'm your child. I have a heavenly Father that can chastise and rebuke me, not some wanna-be-on-top church deacon who needs to go through marital counseling before trying to help anybody else. As for my husband, all you need to know is he is doing everything to take care of me, which is more than I can say for..." Yolanda caught herself before she went any further.

Eddie's chest heaved from his heavy breathing, enraged at the mere thought of what Yolanda tried to insinuate. "All you can say for what? You trying to say I don't take care of my woman? Get out my face with that nonsense. I'll call the board and have you put out of here. Do you understand me?" Eddie stepped so close to Yolanda, she could see the deep, oily pores on his face. She thought about shoving him in the chest but knew she would never live that down.

Yolanda stared at him without blinking and stepped even closer to him. Although her voice was soft, it had such force and power Eddie stepped back with each word that fell from her lips. "Deacon, God called me. Not you. No weapon that is forged against me will prosper. In fact, He says, 'Touch not my anointed and do my prophet no harm.' So you can run to the board and try to exercise the power you think you have. Please remember this, because you chose to follow the way of men and mama pleasing, you are walking in nothing but foolishness. Stop pretending to have this holy power to do what only God can do."

Yolanda took a drink of the soda she'd been holding. "You think you have some sort of favor with God because you're the lead deacon. You have your reward in titles and recognition. I have mine from God." She leaned in to whisper Eddie's his ear, "Find the truth, Eddie. The truth will set you free." She then strolled away.

Eddie thought about what Yolanda said. *I guess the Lord did call her. My bad, Jesus. Shoot, she even threw me some stuff that sounded like it's actually from the Bible.* Eddie's own thoughts convicted him. If he spent more time with God instead of trying to just work for God, he would have known what Yolanda spoke was from God for that moment. Words that stabbed at his heart and conscience. Eddie sighed and walked into the chapel to pray.

When Eddie walked into the main sanctuary, he went to the altar and prostrated himself on the floor. *The truth will set you free* permeated his spirit. "Lord," Eddie prayed. "I need to know the truth. I need to really know You. All these years I have been working for You and now I doubt that I know You as well as I thought. As I seek You again, reveal to me the truth about everything in my life. Show me the truth about myself, my place in this church and even my wife. Lead me in the way You'd have me to go. In Jesus name, amen." He sobbed. Eddie craved acceptance all his life. When he became active in the church, people applauded and recognized him. He thought he had finally arrived. But now Eddie was confused, broken and alone.

Of course, being a man, Eddie knew he would never admit it to anyone. He enjoyed the facade of being a strong church leader with a gorgeous wife, beautiful home and material riches. His boys gave him props on everything he seemed to have. On the outside, Eddie was prosperous. Inside, Eddie felt wretched, pitiful, poor and naked.

Eddie felt a hand on his shoulder. The touch was warm. He was a little nervous to open his eyes but was curious, and embarrassed, as to who may have seen his emotional outburst to God. Eddie sat up on his knees. Next to him was the very one he had attacked. Now she was there to comfort him.

Yolanda smiled at Eddie and handed him a tissue. "When God reveals what you need to see, be attentive. Do not take anything He shows you for granted. Though it may appear to throw you off track, please know that nothing surprises God. No matter what happens, He can work it for good if you let Him. Be prepared to disclose what has been secret. And be willing to do what He would have you to do," Yolanda warned. She grabbed his hand and held it looking into his eyes.

"Man, Minister Howard. How...why did you come in here? Especially after how I talked to you. Why did you come to help me?"

"Because I listen to God, not myself. If I listened to me, you would have had Coca Cola all over that bootleg Gucci shirt."

"Bootleg?" Eddie asked. "Please! I bought this from one of my boys. He had a bunch of them he bought from the Gucci store online. He works for a third party retailer and then sold them to me and some of the other deacons."

"Please. You mean Ethan? Ethan got them off the back of a truck dropping off hair at the beauty store. Since when can you buy Gucci in bulk online? He got those from the hair store, sewed a fake label on it and you old fools fell for it. That's why the fifty and over need to stick with the old men gear."

"Old men gear?" Eddie asked, looking puzzled.

"Yes. Stacy Adams shoes. Knee socks with sandals. Long shorts with loafers. Don't act like you don't know." Yolanda pursed her lips together. "Please, deacon. You've been a fashion felon before."

They laughed and stood. "You got jokes? Okay. I'll let you slide one in." Eddie looked down and sighed. He peered at Yolanda, "So my little breakdown is between us, right? I'm a manly man. You know I can't let everyone know I was bawling like a girl."

"Your secret is tight with me," Yolanda assured him. "Besides, it's not girly to cry. Jesus wept and He was all man."

Eddie grabbed Yolanda and hugged her close whispering, "I'm sorry," in her ear over and over.

✝✝✝

As the sun went down, Pastor Griffin made the announcement that it was time to go in for the musical part of the day. The mass choir would sing three selections and the Faith Festival would close with a sermon from Minister Leems.

As Yolanda headed toward the building, she heard someone call her name. She quickly spun around to find Kennedy chasing after her. Looking flustered but beautiful, Kennedy held her arms outstretched to her friend.

When she caught up with Yolanda, she engulfed her in a bear hug and kissed her cheek. Yolanda was flabbergasted. Earlier that day, Kennedy was in such a funk. Yolanda was curious as to why the change of attitude.

Sensing Yolanda was still pretty miffed about their earlier encounter, Kennedy immediately apologized. "I'm so sorry about earlier. I was hot, tired, and suffering from PMS. But a quick break with myself made a world of difference." Kennedy smiled broadly. She looked not only rejuvenated but...

In love.

Yolanda recognized her aura from the past. When Kennedy first hooked up with Eddie, her joy was almost unbearable. Kennedy had not appeared this radiant since that day many years ago. It was odd. Kennedy recently revealed the problems in her household, but hadn't

98

looked that exuberant in years.

Yolanda decided not to rock the boat with questions. Besides, after her incident with Eddie, she felt compelled to be concerned for him. Even though she knew loyalty to her longtime home girl was a priority, Yolanda felt like Kennedy was not only playing Eddie, but also playing her.

"What's wrong with you?" Kennedy quizzed Yolanda, still grinning. "You looking at me all cross-eyed. Are you mad at me?"

"No," Yolanda said quietly. And it was the truth. Confused? Yes. Disappointed? Extremely. Anger had no place in her heart for Kennedy. She discerned something was different in her friend's life, but thought it would be best to remain quiet. "We're about to start the musical part of the show. Let's go be seated."

"Okay," Kennedy happily chirped. "So how was everything today? Not like it could be different from anything else we do. We pray, eat, sing, and gossip. So I know I didn't miss much." She reached into her purse and pulled out her Altoids. "Want one?"

"No."

"Yes, you do. Here," Kennedy insisted.

"Oh, so you trying to tell me my breath is kicking?"

"No, I am telling you I can tell you ate chitlins earlier." They burst out laughing as she slipped the Altoid on her tongue. Yolanda put her arm around Kennedy's waist and pulled her close. Kennedy, almost a foot taller, put her arm on her friend's shoulder and hugged her tight.

"I miss you."

"I know." Kennedy's smile faded and sadness filled her eyes. "When you are ready, let me know."

Kennedy nodded and they headed into the sanctuary. Even though Kennedy said nothing verbally, the silence was loud.

Kennedy had a secret. In due time, she would tell Yolanda. Until then, Yolanda would pray for her and Eddie. The events that happened today made Yolanda momentarily forget about her own dilemma. There wasn't too much she could do about either one. She would pray for wisdom, power and strength.

Without doing so, she knew she couldn't face the past she worked so hard to forget. *I got to press on. Face it and press on.*

✞✞✞

After the altar call, members of the church mingled amongst themselves. Eddie stood with Yolanda and Kennedy. They were interrupted by a loud female voice everyone loved to hate.

Monica.

"Hey y'all." Monica belted out as she sashayed toward them. "The night is over and I am spent." She paused looking at Kennedy and Eddie. "So nice to see you, Sister Stone. The only woman I have seen Eddie with lately is his momma. I thought you ran off with another man or something." Monica laughed at her own tasteless joke while Yolanda shook her head, embarrassed for her friend.

"Minister Caine," Yolanda began. "Don't you think that was a little out of order?"

100

"Girl, please. It was just a joke. Besides, I haven't seen Kennedy here except on Sunday mornings now. I just thought it was odd one of our ministry members and employees would have to attend all functions with their momma when they have a spouse."

Eddie rolled his eyes and prayed for God to send a whirlwind and carry Monica off in it. For a minister, he found her to be tacky, loud, abrasive and a hood rat. Kennedy smirked at Monica.

"If that's true, then how come no one at this church has ever seen *your* husband? A man should be a covering for his wife, and from the looks of it you're pretty naked. You...a *minister*...should have her man at her side. So why is it we never see this man?" Kennedy was being sarcastic but she loved to see Monica get stumped for once.

"Well, he...he...uh...he has to be on the road a lot for the type of work he does. And one day, when he is not being the busy executive, perhaps we can all get together and do the couples thing." Monica smiled nervously as her face became flustered with embarrassment.

Yolanda almost felt sorry for her. Almost. For a woman of God, Monica could be really crass. To see her get a taste of her own medicine was a delight. "In fact, let's plan on seeing you all at Eddie's 50th birthday bash." Yolanda suggested.

"Eddie, I didn't know you were about to celebrate a birthday." Monica quipped. "The big 5-0, huh? Who would have guessed?"

Eddie beamed, thinking she was insinuating he looked younger than he was. "Yes, people often forget I am a little older than I appear," he bragged. "Didn't realize I was creeping up there, huh?"

"Actually," Monica dragged her words out slowly, "I thought you were a little...older. Especially when your hair line started receding back."

101

"Minister, watch it." Kennedy warned. "That's my man you are talking about."

"Yeah, well. If he is free, you'll see us. My husband is so fine you all won't believe he is real." Monica chuckled.

"We'll believe it when we see him," Eddie retorted. "Been here for four years and nobody has seen him. I pray he's real."

Yolanda, Kennedy and Eddie busted out laughing, while Monica hurried off, rolling her eyes.

"We were wrong for that," Yolanda admitted. "She had it coming, though. Always sticking her nose in somebody else's household."

"No one even knows her husband's name." Kennedy exclaimed. "I don't know what kind of marriage they got but when you don't hear somebody talking about their home life, usually it's because it's not right." The three of them nodded in agreement and went off to conclude their evening. Between outbursts, tears, praying, and Monica, the evening had worn Eddie and Yolanda out.

For Kennedy, she was worn out from her afternoon and the guilt that was slowly creeping back into her heart and mind.

Chapter Eight

Yolanda and Noel sat at the kitchen table having dinner in silence. As they munched on fried chicken, macaroni and cheese with greens, each of them seemed consumed with their own internal issues. Yolanda thought about how to approach the situation with Noel and the identity of her real father. Noel wondered where her father was--again-- and when Daryl would call her back.

"Where's Dad?" Noel asked. She watched her mother closely to see her reaction. Her mother often wore her feelings on her face. She had noticed her father was out more than usual lately and when he was home, the two of them fought. Noel was beginning to think either her mother was running him off being the Perfect Preacher or he was creeping. Either one would not surprise Noel. Her mother's determination to appear flawless was nerve-racking. *But still, Daddy should either pee or get off the pot.* She didn't want to see her mom hurt if her dad was tipping with some tramp. Regardless of their disagreements, she was still her mother.

Yolanda sighed before she answered. She got tired of making excuses for Michael. Even though she had no proof that he was fooling around, her spirit confirmed something was out of sorts. "I don't know, honey," she admitted. Yolanda looked intently at Noel as her daughter studied her mother's face.

"What?"

"Nothing. You just seemed so distracted lately. Are you guys okay?"

"Yes," Yolanda answered quickly. "We have misunderstandings just like anybody else but he's my husband. We'll work through it."

"Mama, keep it real! I love Dad but the way he comes in and out of here, gone from sunup to sundown, you can't tell me the brother is working on 'projects'. A project chick perhaps." Noel laughed at her own joke until she noticed her mother frowning at her. "My bad, Mom. That was a joke."

"I know, but a very tacky one," Yolanda said harshly to Noel. "Clean up the dishes for me. I'm not really hungry." Yolanda pushed herself back from the table and walked out of the kitchen.

"Mom! Hey, don't walk away from me. Let me talk to you."

Yolanda slowly came back to the table. "What do you want to talk about, Noel? How strict I am? How I'm running your father off? Or what a liar I was? What Noel?" Yolanda raised her voice in anger. Tears started to fall. She sat down and laid her head in her arms. Noel scooted closer to her mother and rubbed her back. She had never seen her mother break down like this. Until recently, she seemed so emotionally unattached. It was like living with the Tin Man from the Wizard of Oz. Noel's heart went out to her. She could feel her pain in the sound of her sobs.

Yolanda pulled herself together. "No matter what, always remember I love you. Everything I have done may not have been right, but I always thought of your best interest. Keep that in mind...okay?" Her eyes pleaded with Noel's for understanding.

Noel nodded. She meditated on what her mother said. *I knew it. Something is about to go down or come into the light. God, help me to take it.* Noel smiled at her mom. "Let's go to the show. My treat."

104

"How? I'm the one that gives you your money."

"Oh. That's right." Noel laughed. "Give me cool points for the offer."

Yolanda stood and laughed. In spite of their many battles, right then, waves of love flooded through Yolanda. This was her seed and she was determined to see a great harvest in her life. Yolanda pulled Noel into her arms and held her as if it were the last time.

✟✟✟

Michael rolled over and looked at the digital clock. It read 11:15 p.m. He was trying to wait for Chantal to get home. He had made up his mind to cut her off for good. Although she was beautiful and the sex was amazing, he couldn't risk ruining his home life. He knew when the real identity of Noel's father came to light, it would cause disruption. Still, he was determined to stay committed to Noel as the only father she ever knew.

Michael heard a car door shut and realized the moment had come. He braced himself as he heard Chantal enter the front door. She stepped in the foyer, smiled at Michael and slid out of her coat. *Dang, even in a sweat suit that girl got body.* She came toward him with her arms outstretched.

Michael fell into her embrace and squeezed her close. She kissed his neck and pulled away. She started walking toward the bedroom. Michael followed.

"Baby, I can't wait to get my degree so I can quit." Chantal pulled her hair into a ponytail and undressed. "Hand me my yellow night shirt, please." Michael tossed it to her. She slid into it. "I mean these old greasy men are getting on my nerves. The money is so good though..." Chantal stopped mid-sentence as she noticed Michael's stern look on his face.

"Is something wrong?"

Michael sighed and sat on the bed. "Sit down, Chantal," he began quietly. "We always said when things got to be too much we would walk away. I've prayed about it and it is time to close this chapter of my life."

Chantal scooted closer to him. "Wow. I wasn't expecting this. I figured the day would come. I just didn't know when or how." She kissed his cheek. "I'm going to miss you."

"I'm going to miss *you*, baby. I need to do right by my wife and help my daughter get through this new transition she'll be facing."

Chantal nodded. "I understand, honey. You need to be there for them." She smiled broadly. "Don't worry about me. I'll be all right. You just take care of business. And thanks for being here for me."

Michael stood, feeling relieved for the release of this burden. "I'm going to go ahead and step. If I don't, I never will."

"Go, boo. Go to your family." Chantal stood and hugged him one last time. When Michael pulled himself out of her embrace, he dropped the key to her place on the dresser and left the room. Chantal heard the front door close behind him.

She went to the bathroom and lifted her shirt. She noticed the subtle changes taking place in her breasts. They were beginning to swell as her hormones fluctuated. She rubbed her belly, which was still flat. She figured within the next three months she'd be receiving enough support to not work at all. She pulled her shirt down and smiled.

Michael may have been free from her but not the seed that had been planted a month ago. A booming business and a wife who worked for the biggest church in the city – yep. She was about to get paid.

Michael stumbled into the house a little past midnight. He noticed the light of the television from their master bedroom. He walked up the steps and stepped into their room. He marveled at what he saw.

Yolanda was lying in bed with Noel lying on her chest. They apparently had been cuddling as they watched television and fell asleep. Seeing them fight more than cuddle, Michael felt overjoyed to witness them acting in love instead of acting as enemies. He kissed Yolanda's cheek and stroked her hair. Her eyes fluttered open. She smiled slightly at Michael as he leaned in to whisper in her ear.

"I am here, baby. I am right here, now and always." Like the prodigal son who had run off, he was coming back home.

Chapter Nine

It had been several weeks since Kennedy and Yolanda had their weekly lunch meeting. Deciding they needed a change of scenery, the two met at an upscale day spa for a day of pampering and catch up.

They lay wrapped in seaweed and hot towels as heat immersed their bodies. As they lay alone in the room to relax for a half hour, the two closed their eyes and sighed deeply.

"Girl, if I knew some seaweed could feel this good, I would have taken some home from our trip to Florida, okay? I needed this, honey."

"Trust me, I know how you feel," Yolanda closed her eyes. "I need all the stress relief I can get. You know we're going to have dinner with Terrence."

Kennedy sprung up. She jerked her head to face Yolanda. "So dang, you mean you all are getting together for dinner like you at Big Mama's house from Soul Food? How in the world are you going to explain the fact that this man Noel has never seen is her dad over mac and cheese, and catfish?"

"I don't know what you expect me to do." Yolanda cried out in exasperation. "I called him Wednesday and we just decided to put it all out there. I pray she'll take it in stride."

"Come on, Yo. The girl has no idea Michael isn't her father. She was conceived in a sex sale. I don't know how you expect her to take it in stride."

"Look, I need your support. I already know how bad the situation is without you reiterating it. Besides, I gave it all to God and I know He will work it out."

"Too bad you didn't give it to God in the first place," Kennedy said, shaking her head. "If you had, you wouldn't have spun this web of lies. Look, I love and support you to the utmost but how do you expect her to act?" Kennedy could not believe Yolanda was naive enough to think Noel would receive this startling revelation without major drama. "She grows up with her grandmother, occasionally with her real mother and thinks the man she has known all her life is her father, right?" Kennedy paused. Yolanda didn't respond so she proceeded. "Her real father is an ex-con who had sex with her mother to settle a drug debt. Somehow, Yo," Kennedy added with sarcasm in her voice, "I don't think this will be like a Cosby show reunion. I believe in the power of Christ but I know you reap what you sow."

Yolanda opened her eyes, now irritated. She knew Noel's reaction was going to be a torrid event. At the same time, Yolanda thought Kennedy had some nerve considering the skeletons living in her closet. "The last thing I need is you judging me when you can't admit: one, you have a sex problem and two, your own household is a funked up mess. Who are you to say *anything* about what I sow?"

Standing, Kennedy stripped off her towel. Buck naked except for dried seaweed, she was ready to rumble. *No, she didn't go there. She doesn't even know what she's talking about.* "Girl, you haven't been a preacher all your life. Shoot, I'll be surprised if you make it a full ten years. You don't live in my household and as far as me having a *sex problem*, at

110

least I never sold it!"

Yolanda couldn't believe her ears. *This heifer went there? Lord, I know I haven't been a preacher all my life so hold me back.* Yolanda jumped off her massage table and dropped her towel as well.

"You may have never sold it but you gave it away for free, which is just as bad," Yolanda retorted. "Don't try to make like one is better than the other. The truth is you and I have both walked some crooked streets." She tried to calm herself. "Neither of us is innocent, Kennedy. I need your help not your judgment."

Kennedy pursed her lips. "You gave me the right to judge you when you brought me into your lies. You had me in on this charade, so how do you expect me not to judge you?"

"Wait a minute, Sister 'I Get My Creep On and Freak On'! Just because you haven't directly told me your dirt, don't mean your stuff don't stink. Running off for hours at a time. Using me as a cover and not even telling me." Yolanda brought her voice down a notch. "Look, we need to end this conversation before we both say something we regret."

"Oh no, honey," Kennedy rolled her neck in true sista-girl style. "You went there so let's take it home, baby. What you mean I 'used' you as a cover? And what you talking about me gettin' my freak on? I ain't never been a tramp. Believe that!"

"You try to play the innocent role but who you fooling? Your husband came to me talking about how you and I were together and everything. You weren't with me and considering I'm your *only* friend, I know you had to be with some guy."

Kennedy's eye narrowed. "What did you tell him?"

111

"Nothing. I hadn't talked to you that much until the Faith Festival."

"Really?" Kennedy asked suspiciously. "Hmmm, because this fool started leaving scripture cards all over the house. Like the one about not defiling the marriage bed and adultery is sin. I woke up to him laying hands on me praying."

"Well, maybe God gave him divine revelation because it wasn't me," Yolanda smirked.

"Kennedy, I hate to break this to you, but God talks to everyone. You act like you have His private two-way and He only tells you things. Face it, Ken. He is a man of God. He makes his mistakes and all, but God can speak to him to help him discern what is up with you." She shook her head. "Whoever this brother is, he got you so caught up you dancing or sexing rather with the devil. You falling right into a pit you will have to lie your way out of. If you're really the woman of God you believe yourself to be, you'd end this mess and repent."

All of a sudden Yolanda felt a crushing blow to her mouth. A red river of blood infused saliva ran down her chin onto her towel. The pain was searing. Her teeth had cut her bottom lip from Kennedy's punch. She was stunned. Her best friend had busted her mouth. As blood poured from her lower lip, Yolanda froze. Everything stopped.

Kennedy was so livid she didn't realize she had punched her best friend. Listening to Yolanda's depiction of her caused a tidal wave of anger throughout her entire being. She hadn't planned on hitting her. Everything happened so quickly and she could not take it back. Her home girl since childhood. The one with whom she shared every secret. Her ace who helped her buy her first good bra. The one who told her the truth about herself that she was living a lie and caught in a web of sin. Kennedy stood, her nostrils flared with anger. Heart convicted by

112

the harsh reality of what Yolanda said. *Should I say sorry or just leave the room?*

Before she could make a final decision, the sting of a palm hit her left cheek. *No, Preacher Girl did not just slap me!* The blow of Yolanda's hand caused Kennedy's face to immediately start swelling.

Yolanda stepped closer to Kennedy. "I may be saved but the street side of me could not let you disrespect me." In decibels, she was soft but there was rage in every word she spoke. "How dare you hit me like I'm some criminal attacking you. Better yet a stranger." Yolanda started to weep. "For years I listened to you tell me how messed up my life was. I received the truth from you. I may not have wanted to face it, but never did I physically harm you."

Kennedy held her bloated cheek, walking away from Yolanda. "Oh, so now you gonna turn your back on me? I'm up here bleeding and crying while you want to turn away from me?" Yolanda's voice rose. She took the towel off her body and threw it at Kennedy.

Kennedy spun around. "Maybe you didn't hit me first. So I was out of line. But you attacked me verbally. You talked to me like I'm some nasty tramp. You don't know what I am doing or why." Now Kennedy was crying. "In fact, you don't know anything about what's going on in my house." Kennedy rubbed her swollen jaw. "Look, I got a situation on you can't even relate to. I can't deal with this right now. I don't need you judging me. You are not perfect. You never will be. Face the fact. Everyone still sees you as the same Yolanda, except you."

Yolanda could not believe her ears. She shook her head furiously. "No, Kennedy. I am not the same and that's your problem. And what *everyone* are you talking about? Your husband? Your mother-in-law? Who?" Kennedy hung her head. "You can't answer me because you're trying to conceal your sin by pointing out my *old* sin. If you can't accept

113

I'm a new creature and right now you are a backsliding one, maybe we need to end this facade once called a friendship."

Kennedy rolled her eyes. She picked up the towel lying at her feet and threw it back at Yolanda. "Catch this," she snapped. "I'm throwing in the towel."

Right then, a massage therapist came through the door. She stopped in her tracks. Her mouth hung open. Yolanda stood there naked with seaweed on her body and blood seeping from her lip. She walked closer to the duo, noticing Kennedy's left cheek was twice the size it should have been and purple. "What the..." The therapist was too stunned to speak. "I guess girl's day out is over," she managed to whisper.

"No," Yolanda said curtly. "The whole thing is over." She grabbed a robe off a stool and wrapped it around her body. "I'm washing this off and washing my hands of this situation. I love you, Ken. But love isn't supposed to hurt. Love delights in truth." She walked to the door. She glanced at Kennedy one last time before allowing it to shut behind her.

Yolanda headed toward the spa shower. A sharp sting went through her chest. *It's probably my nerves,* she thought as she writhed in pain. Her body hurt but her heart was in more pain at the loss of her friend. She silently prayed for Jesus to deliver Kennedy from her past issues that plagued her and the new ones chasing her.

✢✢✢

Kennedy pulled her Beamer into the garage. She shut the door then happened to look into her rearview mirror. Her cheek, even with the heavy matte foundation and powder was noticeably bruised and swollen a bit. "Snap! How am I going to explain this?" She paused before stepping out of her car, whipped down her long ponytail and arranged her hair to fall over the side of her face where Yolanda's imprint was visible. She'd leave her hair down and sleep on her left side. *Lord, please let the swelling be gone by tomorrow.*

Kennedy walked into the family room and noticed a dim light from down the hall. She thought she would blow him a goodnight kiss and head to bed. Even though it was only five o'clock, Kennedy couldn't afford for deacon-man to notice her bruise.

Kennedy gently tapped on the door that was slightly ajar, leading into his study. Eddie looked intently at his black leather Bible with his forehead scrunched up as it did when he was in deep thought. He glanced at her and smiled, showing the dimples she had loved so much at one time. Kennedy felt a wave of guilt rush over her since he appeared genuinely happy to see her. He closed his Bible, laid his glasses on the table and practically sprinted to Kennedy.

He grabbed her close in a warm and tender embrace. Kennedy, taken aback, forgot about her bruised face and felt her arms automatically embrace his neck. She inhaled deeply the soft scent of his Issey Miyake cologne she had turned him on to years ago. Though they were silent in their intense embrace, various emotions flooded through the couple.

Kennedy pondered if her affair with Marcus was worth hurting the man she had loved so much at one time. She started to wonder if God could restore the love and attraction, in spite of the current situation. Eddie firmly grabbed her perfectly round bottom and squeezed tightly.

Kennedy jumped slightly. She was astounded. Eddie hadn't touched her with true passion in six months. She pulled back and searched his eyes for understanding. When their eyes locked, they leaned in closely to one another and kissed passionately. Forgetting about Marcus, her bruised face and the events of the day, she willingly responded to her husbands' passion. While they kissed long and hard, Kennedy felt her body being lifted up. Eddie held her in his arms and rushed down the hall to their bedroom, he kicked open the door and threw her on the bed. Kennedy was amazed, shocked and turned on by his aggressive behavior. Clearly something she was not used to. The minute they wrestled out of their clothing, the phone rang. She pulled away from Eddie expecting him to answer the phone. He looked anxiously at her.

"What?" she said, exasperated and out of breath. "Don't tell me you are going to actually answer your phone."

"What are you talking about?" Eddie glanced at the cell phone on the couch next to them. "*Your* phone is ringing. You want me to get it?"

She wanted to grab the phone before Eddie could get to it. *What if it was Marcus?* She panicked and froze when Eddie nonchalantly snatched up her phone.

"Who dis?" he bellowed, sounding more ghetto and hood than his normal pristine deacon's voice. "Who? Naw, you got the wrong number, player." He threw the phone back down on the couch. Eddie took off his undershirt and hovered over Kennedy.

Kennedy was shaking. She was paranoid about the close call that could have made her world come crashing down. "Who...who...was it?"

"Some brotha asking for a Marsha Browdy...whatever he said. He wasn't looking for you. He called anonymously too. Probably a solicitor." He leaned in closely to Kennedy and kissed her lips gently as he continued to disrobe her. Kennedy knew all too well it was Marcus. She was grateful God did not let her get busted. Or maybe it was a warning to stop now.

I'll worry about everything tomorrow. I just want to enjoy tonight.

116

Kennedy told herself as she enjoyed her husband pleasing her with a passion that even Marcus could not compete with.

At least not in the moment.

✝✝✝

The early morning sun filled the whole room. The bedroom window was slightly open as a crisp, summer breeze gently flowed in the room, brushing across Kennedy's bare face. The sun pierced her shut eyes so she lifted her head to see the clock. It was six a.m. She looked over at Eddie who was knocked out. *I guess our little tryst took a lot out of him.* She smiled slightly at the memory of their passionate encounter. Though Kennedy felt physically satisfied with her husband's performance, she still wondered what Marcus was up to. Kennedy slowly crept out of the bed and tiptoed to the chaise lounge where she dropped her phone before climbing into bed. Not wanting to wake Eddie, she grabbed it and headed to his study.

She sat down on the burgundy chair where she had spent many a morning praying and meditating on the Word of God. A wave of guilt washed over her conscious.

Yes, at one time this was My time. Now, you are using it to gratify your flesh. Staring at the cell phone in her hand, she knew for certain she'd heard the voice of the Lord. Though not audible, her entire being shook on the inside while she pondered what she'd been up to for the past few months. Though Kennedy had a secret promiscuous lifestyle in her earlier years, she had made a vow to God when he sanctified her through marriage that she would keep herself pure. Yet, she'd committed a heinous sin against the Lord and her husband by defiling the marriage bed.

Kennedy got down on her knees, for the first time in weeks. She had always had a close relationship with God even through her struggles

117

with sexual sin. She had never *not* prayed. After getting caught up with Marcus, she felt a wall come between her and the Lord. Suddenly, Isaiah 59 came into her spirit.

Surely the arm of the Lord is not too short to save nor his ear too dull to hear. But your iniquities have separated you from your God; your sins have hidden his face from you, so that he will not hear.

Instantly, Kennedy knew she could not continue her affair with Marcus. She thought about how she could have been busted last night when he called her phone. Yes, he pretended to have the wrong number but what if Eddie suspected something was going on? Was an illicit sexual affair with Marcus worth the estrangement from God? An embarrassing divorce from Eddie? And would she be happy?

No, she would not. Kennedy wanted her God back and she wanted to be free from sexual sin for good.

She pulled her plush pink robe closed and prayed to the Lord. Tears streamed down her face. She felt a burden lift from within her. She determined not to contact Marcus anymore. Besides, they had made an agreement that when they were too wrapped up in each other they would walk away. No questions asked. Kennedy pondered whether or not to call him and break things off but something inside of her shouted, *No, flee from immorality.* Kennedy brushed it off. She believed she was strong enough in the Lord to make a clean break from him. She stared into space, rehashing memories of their time spent together. Her phone vibrated. She picked it up and looked at the caller ID.

Anonymous. It was Marcus.

Though the conviction of the Holy Spirit tugged at her to ignore his call and change her number immediately, Kennedy was conflicted. She knew it would take more than one good night of sex to restore and strengthen her marriage. But she realized in order to do so, Marcus would have to go. Kennedy got off her knees and sat back on the chair. Her phone had stopped vibrating and the voicemail indicator was on. She picked up her cell phone and checked her message.

"Hey, baby. It's Marcus. Look, I am going to have to cancel our evening. My wife is sick and needs me to help her out. She really needs a quick recovery because her weekend is filled with obligations. I sure hate we are missing our Friday night date. I'll make it up to you. I promise. I called you last night but your man answered the phone. I wanted and needed you so badly but I guess he can have a little of you too." Marcus had chuckled and then hung up.

"What do you mean he can have me too? After all he is my husband. Shoot." Kennedy made a vow to check him about what he said. Especially since she was kicking him out of her life for good. He was fine and their relations were *amazing* but Kennedy missed God.

Right now, the fear of God was more powerful than sex for Kennedy.

Pressing Past the Past

Chapter Ten

Yolanda grabbed her MAC Studiofix and touched up her make up before she and Michael headed out. They were on their way to meet Terrence to discuss how and when they would break the news to Noel about him being her father.

Michael veered left onto a hilly side street. He and Yolanda were trying to see the address to the house where Terrence lived. It was a part of town the two of them didn't travel in much and they seemed to be going in circles.

"Michael, it has got to be the house on the hill. None of these match the address he gave us." She hated riding with Michael when he didn't know where he was going. He insisted on finding his destination without help from anyone else even if it meant driving around for hours on end.

"It can't be his crib. How in the world could he have a house like that? I mean, he's a felon. Unless he had some drug money under wraps, there's no way it's his. Deep down Michael had hoped to see Terrence living in a shack. He could not grasp the idea of him being successful. Normally, jealousy was not a part of Michael's character but the last thing he needed was for the father of Noel to be at his level. Michael thought he needed leverage to keep Terrence distanced from Noel.

"Wait! I see the numbers on the mailbox. 12576. Yep, here it is."

Yolanda was shocked at what her eyes beheld, a peach stucco and brick house on a hill, surrounded by a beautifully landscaped yard. Perfectly squared shrubs surrounded the house, along with salmon colored rocks gracefully outlining the circular curve of the driveway. It was easy to see the home was about three stories, with wide windows overlooking the rest of the neighborhood. *Not bad for an ex drug dealer*. She was actually relieved to see the biological father of her child had made something of his life.

"You ready?" Yolanda asked Michael as he turned off the car. She thought his face looked strained. "Do you want to pray before we go in?"

"No, I'm good. Me and Jesus already got this handled, Rev. Let's see what this cat got to say." Michael got out the car and slammed the door without even looking at Yolanda. Yolanda followed him up the stairs and rang the doorbell. She saw a figure faintly walking to the door. When the door opened, she had to catch her breath.

Terrence looked younger than she remembered. He had on a Nike jogging suit and a backwards baseball cap. His teeth looked like perfect pearls against his dark, almost blue-black skin. He had deep dimples, like Noel, and thick eyelashes that would make any woman envious. He smiled at them and reached out to shake Michael's hand.

"Big Mike," he bellowed in a deep baritone voice. "You looking good man. Great to see you."

Michael grunted and half-heartedly shook his hand. "Yeah, whatever. Let's just cut to the chase."

Terrence clasped his hands together and shrugged. "Okay. Yolanda, you look breathtaking. Got that holy woman glow on you." His eyes met hers and her heart fluttered. She didn't know if it was out of nervousness or what. *Lord, I know I cannot be taken in by a man who practically raped me*. She felt the Lord say in her spirit, *All of you were in*

122

sin so you cannot cast the first stone. She reached out and shook Terrence's outstretched hand. "Thank you," she muttered, slightly stuttering.

"My bad. I'm being rather rude." He stood back and held the door open. "Come on in. Make yourselves comfortable. Dinner should be ready soon."

"Look," Michael stood perfectly still in the doorway. "This ain't no family reunion, partner. I just wanna see what it is you want with my wife and daughter so we can get to steppin'." Michael crossed his arms over his chest and looked sternly at Terrence. He rocked back and forth on his heels. A move he did when he was ready to fight back in the day.

Yolanda could understand the offense Michael felt by an old enemy reappearing in their lives, expecting amends to be made instantly. Yet deep in her spirit, she had peace. Peace which passed human understanding.

Terrence began softly, "Michael, we've been standing here saying nothing for about ten minutes. I know this is a lot to take in at once but just...just give me a chance." Terrence looked down at the marble floor of his hallway so they couldn't see the tears forming in his eyes. "Try *with* me to make this whole thing...right."

Michael reluctantly stepped into the foyer. Yolanda followed behind, surprisingly eager for the conversation. Something about Terrence seemed endearing, humble and *real*. She believed she could look beyond their rocky path and come to terms with the truth. Terrence was her daughter's biological father - no matter how ugly the conception.

Terrence smiled at them both, relieved that God answered his prayer of opening their hearts to hear him out. "Follow me into the kitchen," he

123

said and headed down the hall.

Michael grunted as he grabbed Yolanda's hand, and practically dragged her behind him. "Baby, I'm right here. You don't have to push, pull or drag me. Slow down."

Michael cut his eyes sharply at his wife. He made a mental note to check her later about trying to call him out in front of Terrence. They walked through a large living room. African art hung on the walls, and then they arrived in the kitchen. Chrome fixtures were everywhere. The kitchen looked like something from some cooking show Yolanda watched on the Food Network. There was an island in the center of the kitchen with a black marble counter top and a long wood kitchen table. Looking at the gorgeous home Terrence lived in made Yolanda question whether he was up to his old tricks.

"Please have a seat," Terrence nodded toward the high back, black leather chairs that surrounded the round polished cherry wood table. Yolanda smiled and sat down. Michael rolled his eyes, unenthusiastically following suit.

The aroma of roasted chicken filled the air when Terrence opened the oven. He set the chicken down on the stovetop and got plates from a cabinet above the sink. "So," Michael began with a hint of laughter in his voice, "You used to cook drugs, now you a regular Chef Boyardee, huh? Was culinary one of your skills you picked up in the joint?" Michael cocked his head to the side as he waited for Terrence to answer.

Yolanda's face flushed with embarrassment at her husband's behavior. "Terrence, I had no idea you were so good in the kitchen. You kind of like a black Emeril, huh?"

Terrence smiled gently and shook his head. "Actually, Michael is correct.

124

In jail, I learned three things. I learned I did not want to ever go back to jail. I did kitchen duty and learned how to cook. And I learned who could forgive all my sins and make me a new creature." Yolanda noticed his eyes tearing up and empathized with his emotion.

Michel, however, wasn't buying it. "I'm not impressed. Everybody finds Jesus in jail. Question is, have you kept Him since you got out?"

Terrence walked over to the kitchen table and stood before Michael. He faced him dead on. "No, I have not. Jesus has kept me since I met Him in jail." He sat down next to Michael. "Look brother, I know who I am may be a surprise to you. I wasn't even expecting you all to be open to meeting with me." He paused. "You can discredit me or even deny the new man you see. However, don't disrespect my relationship with my Lord. We all fell short and sinned together...willingly. The only difference is my sin caught up with me in a jail cell. How about you?"

Michael stood. "Who you talking to?" He pushed the chair out of his way and stepped closer to Terrence. "While you were in jail getting to know Jesus, I was raising your daughter as my own. She loves me like the only father she has known. Now you think because you got a little Jesus, can grill some chicken and got a fat crib you can just come in and demand a relationship with her?" Michael shook his head and crossed his arms over his chest. "It don't work like that, player."

"I understand your anger." Terrence stepped about an inch closer to Michael. "Man to man, I am trying to make right of a wrong situation. We never should have kept her in the dark for this long." He turned and walked back over to the counter, where the food set. "God has been wrestling with me over this for three years now. I have to be obedient to walking in the truth. I've had nightmares about this." Terrence's eyes pleaded with Michael. "I cannot apologize or repent enough for what went down, but what I can do is face the truth and my responsibility. Can you let me do that?"

125

Michael threw his hands up in the air in exasperation. He sat down at the table and buried his face in hands. "Go on, man. What you wanna do?"

Terrence sat down and looked at both Yolanda and Michael, his eyes slowly sinking into theirs. "How can we, as her parents, reveal this to her in the least painful way possible?"

Yolanda spoke up quietly. "What exactly are we talking about? Do you want partial custody or what?"

Terrence sighed. "No, I could never just uproot her from the two of you whom she has known all her life." He shook his head slowly. "Did you adopt her, Michael?"

Michael's heart thumped rapidly. He was nervous. He never thought Terrence would show up in their lives again. "No," he said sorrowfully. "We never expected..."

Terrence held up his hand. "I know. To see me again. I don't want to disrupt her life. I just want her to know the truth and give her the option to get to know me."

Yolanda looked down at her lap. Her eyes brimmed with tears. "Back then was such a horrible time in my life. Noel was a beautiful result of it, but I don't want to put her through any more pain, Terrence."

"Well," Terrence said as he stood up. "Let's go to the Lord in prayer right now and let Him lead us." He walked over to a cushioned wood bench covered with soft black pillows. He knelt down and looked over his shoulder at Yolanda and Michael. "Let's agree on this."

Michael pushed himself away from the table and stood. His eyes filled with fury, he snatched his car keys. "You know what? I'm not in a praying mood right now. Yolanda, you can touch and agree with this fool if you want to. I'm going to the car." He promptly turned and headed toward the foyer.

Yolanda was torn. She agreed with Michael. This was too much to take in at the moment, but she was tired of living in a lie. She wanted the truth to set her free. However, she was more fearful of walking in the truth than facing it. She slowly stood and walked over to Terrence. "I love my husband. He loves my...his...our daughter. He's hurting. Give him some time to come around."

She knelt beside him and he put his arm around her back. Yolanda tensed, thinking about the last time he touched her. Terrence felt her tension and understood. "Yolanda, I may have touched you once with violence...I promise... never again," he said firmly. "I understand how Michael must feel, but let's try to see if we can do the right thing." Yolanda gazed at the gentle smile that emerged on his full lips. Almost in a daze, she grabbed his hand as they bent their heads ready to acknowledge the only one who could help them.

An awkward silence loomed in the car as Michael and Yolanda headed back home. Yolanda was still in awe over how Terrence truly seemed like a new man. *After all, if any man be in Christ, he or she is a new creature. I am. So can't he be as well?*

Yolanda looked at Michael as he entered the expressway. He appeared to have a lot on his mind. Of course, they both had a lot to think about as they finally had to face up and tell Noel who her biological father was. Still, Yolanda discerned there was more going on with Michael than she knew. She hoped he would open up and tell her what was on his mind.

"Baby, how you doing right now?" Yolanda asked tenderly. "I know this is a lot to deal with. You know if we let God lead, everything will work out."

"Sounds easy – until it's done. In a perfect world, we could tell Noel, she'd meet him and the ending would be happy through eternity. Forgive my cynicism, but I think some more bombs over this Baghdad we created will drop."

Yolanda put her hand on Michael's knee. "I know there is more to this than us telling Noel and hoping she'll receive it. I am ready to walk in complete freedom. Sometimes in freedom there is pain. I am willing to feel it, if this means a new beginning."

"Even if our daughter ends up hating us?"

"She'll hate us worse if we put it off and let someone else tell her."

Michael took a deep breath. "All right." He paused. "Let's prepare to do this soon. I can't take any more surprises."

Chapter Eleven

"Happy 50th birthday, baby!" Kennedy shouted louder than anyone in the crowd. The rented ballroom overflowed with church and family members, along with the aroma of Eddie's favorite soul food and the sounds of the Temptations. Eddie was the epitome of pride, beaming at his gorgeous wife. Over the past week, things between them had changed significantly. They had been more physically affectionate and even talked like they used to. The discussions went beyond church business and the "how was your day" context. They talked about their hopes; those met and those still waiting to be fulfilled. They cuddled at night. And the sex? It could make Kennedy forget Marcus for good.

Kennedy held up her glass of sparkling cider, kissed Eddie on the cheek and made a toast. "Here's to the top notch man in God's master plan, who has held my hand and is still my man." The crowd cheered as Eddie gave Kennedy a long, passionate kiss, soliciting howls from the crowd.

"Fifty ain't half bad when you got a lady like this." Eddie hollered. Men in the crowd gave wolf whistles in jest, while the ladies laughed at their antics. "Thank you all for being in our lives. It's moments like these that remind me to keep my focus on God, family and then the work of my hands." Everyone clapped then continued to party.

Kennedy walked out to the back deck where she noticed Michael. She didn't see Yolanda with him. Michael caught her eye. Kennedy waved him to where she stood.

"Hey, girl!" Michael walked over and embraced her. "You Stone folk know how to throw a party for sure. How you doing, lady?"

"Good, good. I don't see Yolanda. Where is she?"

Michael shook his head. He looked unsettled. "She'll be here in a bit. She was at home resting. She had a migraine and was talking about being short of breath. I think she's stressed."

"Wow, I hate to hear that. We'll definitely intercede." Kennedy paused. "You know she and I had a disagreement, to say the least."

"She didn't mention it but I knew something was up. I haven't heard y'alls cackling phone sessions. You want to fill a brother in?"

Kennedy knew she needed to make things right with Yolanda but wasn't ready to admit to anyone she had strayed outside her marriage. In fact, she pondered if she would ever utter, "I cheated on my husband" to anybody.

"I can't get into details, Michael. Please let Yolanda know I heard her. And I love her very much. Okay?" Kennedy turned on her heel and went back in.

Michael's curiosity got to him as he wondered what could have possibly gone down between those two. They had been dubbed "the dynamic duo" for years and couldn't imagine their friendship ending abruptly. *Oh well, if she wants to tell me she will*. He decided to take advantage of all the good free food before heading home to take care of his number one concern - Yolanda.

✝✝✝

Yolanda showed up as the party began to wind down. Kennedy had wanted to approach her, but she was so aloof she decided to wait. Kennedy was helping the hotel staff prepare to present the cake when a

130

familiar voice disrupted her peace.

"Hey everybody! Don't tell me the party is over." She spun around to find Minister Monica Caine sauntering through the door. "When you all were in the world you partied all night. Now you want to get sanctified and shut it down at nine." Monica laughed loudly then walked over to greet Kennedy.

"So, where's the birthday boy?" Monica gave Kennedy a quick, forced hug.

"He's around here somewhere," Kennedy responded dryly. "Good to see you. Where is your fine husband you were bringing? Shoot, does he even have a name?"

"Whatever. For your information, he's parking the car. And when you see my boo, don't be mad," Monica teased. "There he is. Baby! Right here." Monica belted out as she waved to a man in a black polo top and aviator glasses. From a distance, Kennedy wondered if he actually went to the church, as his appearance looked familiar.

"Baby, this is Eddie Stone's lovely wife, Kennedy. Kennedy meet my husband," Monica said in a singsong voice. "Take off your glasses, baby."

When he did, his eyes locked with Kennedy's. She thought her chest would explode.

Monica's "baby" had been her Marcus.

Marcus, if flustered, did not show it. He reached out to shake Kennedy's hand and said, "Nice to meet you. My name is Marcus. Feel free to call me Marc. Such a great party you all have going on. Didn't know church folk could kick it like this." He turned to Monica and the two of them

131

laughed. She pulled him close and gave him a passionate kiss. Kennedy was dumbstruck. She realized she had better say something or Monica may wonder why the unusual quiet.

"Nice to meet you as well," Kennedy stammered nervously. "We were beginning to think Monica made you up." She wished it was a bad dream but Kennedy knew this moment was real and inevitable. She just didn't expect it to come like this.

Monica rolled her eyes. She rubbed Marcus' arm, "Baby, they seem to think you got to be all up in the church by my side because I work there." She paused and looked pointedly at Kennedy. "Some people's spouses spend more time at church than with their mate. I like to do what I do there and then come home to you." She pulled him to her and nibbled on his ear. As she did Marcus looked at Kennedy with an expression of surprise, and if she wasn't mistaken, a little embarrassment. He freed himself from his wife's possessive grasp, "Well, baby, every couple is different. Let's go over to the food. It looks great." Monica took him by the hand and dragged him away. She glanced over her shoulder. "Bye, lady." She called cheerfully to Kennedy. "Find your birthday man."

Kennedy was in a trance as they walked off. Not that she was jealous or even wanted to hook back up with Marcus at this point. For starters, his wife was a former gangbanger - gone preacher. She was sure if Monica found out, Kennedy's life could be at stake. Saved or not, Monica was known to have some fight still left in her. Kennedy valued the beauty of her face, and her life. Just knowing who Marcus' wife was, was the confirmation she needed to walk away.

Secondly, she honestly didn't think her dirt would come this close to catching up with her. If this was not a sign from God to get it right, she didn't know what was. How coincidental. The man she creeped with not only showed up at her husband's birthday party but with a minister from her church. *This is so messy. This is worse than an episode of Basketball Wives and Real Housewives of Atlanta combined.* Kennedy shook her head. Inside, she prayed a prayer of thanksgiving to God. She didn't think it was really kosher or holy to pray a thank you for not getting busted, but still. God had to be looking out for her.

Yolanda was in the corner talking to one of Eddie's cousins when Michael spotted her. He walked over and kissed her on the cheek. "Glad you're feeling better and decided to come. They are getting ready to serve the cake. I know how your sweet tooth is so come on, lady." Yolanda excused herself from Eddie's cousin. They headed toward the patio area, right outside the ballroom. As they pushed through the crowd, they ran smack into Kennedy, who was holding a plate of shrimp skewers.

"Our bad, Ken!" Michael helped her balance her plate. "I had no idea Deacon could kick it like this." He and Kennedy laughed loudly, while Yolanda stood silently watching their exchange. He sensed she was irritated. He imagined her and Kennedy would start jonsesing on one another, as they always did. But, it didn't happen. Instead, Yolanda walked off.

Michael knew something serious had to go down for Yolanda to react the way she did. He smiled at Kennedy and said, "Hey, you know…" He was speechless and for a moment regretted opening his mouth. "Whatever it is, it'll work itself out."

Kennedy looked at the floor to avoid Michael seeing the tears gathered in the corner of her eyes. "I hope so," she whispered. "Can you ever mess up so bad you can't change it?" She didn't mean to utter it aloud nor did she expect an answer. Much to her surprise, Michael spoke up.

"Well, for every mess up, there is a consequence. Yet, there's always a chance for reconciliation. There may be some hindrances. It may even take a while, but as much as it is up to you, try to work it out." He sensed his words would come back to haunt him.

Kennedy seemed to lighten up at the suggestion. "Yeah, your wife is saved and knows those who are forgiven much loves much. She also knows God says to forgive." She paused. "Will you pray for us?" Michael wasn't used to getting prayer requests. While he wanted to really find out what was wrong between them, instead he just said, "Absolutely." He reached over to hug Kennedy when he heard her say, "Now who is *that*?" As she pulled back from his embrace, a frown had formed on her face, replacing the tender moment.

"What?"

"I know Monica brought her hubby, and that's fine. But, why did her dude bring other uninvited guests? That's so tacky. He brought his little sister or somebody."

Michael glanced to see who Kennedy was agitated with. When he saw, he had to keep himself from running out of the room.

He never thought he'd see Chantal outside of their former rendezvous. But, there she was chatting with Marcus and another church member. Michael knew there was always a chance he'd get busted. But he never expected the day to come now in the presence of his wife.

Lord, have mercy...if it's not too late.

134

Chapter Twelve

Yolanda stood outside and stared at the stars. She wondered what the outcome would be in her life with Noel, Michael, and ministry. "Lord," she said aloud as she looked at the Big Dipper, "I don't know what is going on, but You know all my days before one of them comes to be. Help me to trust You, Lord." A gentle wind brushed against her face, like the fingertips of God letting her know everything would be okay.

Yolanda decided to go back inside and say good-bye. She had had enough of a party for the night. As she headed toward the hotel lobby, she noticed a young woman sitting on one of the couches with her hands over her eyes. She rocked back and forth in the soft-pillowed chair quietly crying. Yolanda allowed the Lord to use her to comfort a sister in need.

She walked slowly toward her. As Yolanda approached the chair, she tapped the lady on the shoulder. "Excuse me, I noticed you over here. You seem to be upset. Can...can I pray with you or talk with you?" The fluorescent lights of the hotel accentuated the woman's stunning features. She was beautiful. When she smiled at Yolanda, a deep dimple appeared in her left cheek, along with a cute cleft in her chin. She pulled her long hair back and sighed.

"Thank you. I could really use some prayer. I am about three months pregnant and don't know what to do." She looked down.

"I see," Yolanda carefully began. "Well, God knew the little one in your womb even before the world began. When your baby was formed, God knew what He was doing. He made you a mother on purpose, for His purpose." Yolanda paused. She hated to be so "preachy" to people she didn't know, but for some reason, Yolanda believed she was led to minister to her. She seemed receptive, nodding at Yolanda.

"Thing is, I'm not really with the father. In fact, he's older than me and has his own family." More tears filled her eyes. "I was wrong to ever become friends with him, but he seemed so unhappy. I just knew he'd file divorce papers." She looked at Yolanda, desperation on her face. "What do you do to correct something like this? I don't want my child's life to be a lie."

What she said hit Yolanda hard. It was the confirmation she needed to correct the web of deceit she had created in her own daughter's life. Yolanda regained her composure. "We all make mistakes. Even parents who mean well get caught up in their own desire to save face. And then later, the children have to pay the consequence for their parent's actions. Have this baby and tell them the truth." Yolanda paused. "All you can do is repent for your wrong and trust God to work it out. He's not mad at the baby nor will He withhold His love from you. And trust...the man who's responsible, God will deal with him. Not only did he break his vow to his wife, he deceived you." A wave of righteous anger flooded Yolanda's being. It was as if she was the one wronged.

The young lady wiped her eyes with the sleeve of her jacket. "Can I hug you? I was feeling like it was the end of the world, but you really just gave me hope." Yolanda smiled and opened her arms. The two embraced.

"Hey baby, you ready?"

Yolanda turned around. Michael stood behind her, looking very...odd. She couldn't put her finger on it, but sensed an underlying current of hostility, surprise and even shock. She wondered if the Spirit was trying

136

to let her know something. She snapped back to reality answering Michael, "Yes, honey. I was just giving some encouragement to my young sister." Yolanda realized they never even exchanged names. "I'm sorry, dear. We got so caught up, we never officially introduced ourselves." They both laughed, as if they'd known each other for years.

"My name is Chantal." She smiled cockily at Michael, unbeknownst to Yolanda.

"I'm Yolanda Howard and this is my husband, Michael." Michael stood there, with a hard look on his face, not bothering to shake the hand Chantal had extended to him. Yolanda nudged her husband. She couldn't believe he was so rude. "Hello," he said very coolly, limply shaking her hand. He turned toward Yolanda, "I know we took separate cars, but let's go *home*." He put extra emphasis on the word "home" and looked sideways at Chantal as he said it. Yolanda wondered what his deal was.

"It was nice meeting you, Chantal. I hope I gave you some encouragement to help you."

"You did!" Chantal answered, excitedly. "You ought to be a life coach or something. You make me want to talk to you all the time."

Yolanda laughed. "Well, give praise to God. I am no life coach but I am a minister at New Life Worship Center. You should visit if you don't have a church home."

"Oh! No wonder you look familiar. That's my uncle's church. Pastor Griffin."

Yolanda giggled with Chantal. They hugged like two old high school buddies. "I'm not preaching this Sunday so look for me. I'd love for you to sit with me and my family. Here, this is my cell. When you get there, shoot me a text and I'll make sure to get you seated with us." Yolanda hugged her once more, and then turned to Michael. "Okay, baby. Follow me to the car. I'm exhausted."

"Uhh, yeah." Michael muttered. Flustered at the exchange between his wife and girlfriend, he followed Yolanda out. He didn't even look back at Chantal.

When Michael got to his car, he took a deep breath and laid his head on the steering wheel. Yolanda had already headed home. Someone tapped on his window. Startled, Michael jumped straight up and almost hit his head on the ceiling of his car. He glanced to see who it was. Much to his surprise and dismay, Chantal was standing there. She smiled smugly at Michael knowing she had one-upped him.

Michael reluctantly rolled down his window, "What do you want?" As much as he dug Chantal, he was seething that she had the audacity to take his wife's number knowing who she was. Plus, he had a hard time dealing with the fact she never informed him Pastor Griffin was her uncle.

"Well hello to you too, boo! Why you got your drawers in a bunch? I'm the one who should be mad. Had me all up in there accosted by your wife." She paused. "How do I know she wouldn't have 'heard in the spirit' as the preachers say I was bangin' her man?"

Michael never believed in hitting a woman, but Chantal was playing a dangerous game and he was boiling. "Look," he looked around to make sure no one saw them talking, "I don't care what we had going on, she's still my wife." He looked down and sighed. "Man, I can't...I can't do this. She may not be perfect, but she is my *wife*." Out of nowhere, his eyes fell to her heaving bosom. He relented as he thought about waking up on them so many times. *Dang, she fine.* Then again, was fine worth the

138

pain he would cause his family or the loss a divorce could cost him?

Chantal looked him directly in the eye. She stuck her head in through the car window. "I know," she said softly. "From day one, your marriage was never a factor. But what is this? You come and complain about being a preacher's husband. You pretty much said you're with her out of guilt."

"Hold up." Michael said with such sharpness Chantal pulled her head back as if she'd been slapped. "I told you that, as a friend, because of how I was feeling. Not for you to try to use against me later." He was silent for a moment. "I do care for you, Chantal. There is no question. You are sexy. You are fun. You make me forget my everyday struggle. On the real though, I can't keep doing this. Tonight was a sign I have gotten away with much. Even I know God ain't gonna let me slide." He reached out and grabbed her hand. "Baby, it's time for me to back out, for real. I shouldn't have let it get this far but knowing how this could have went down... Naw. Brother got to get right." He dropped her hand and she backed away. "I'll miss you, but I have to roll. And throw away her number. Leave her...me...us...leave it alone." Michael put his car in gear and tore off down the street.

"Oh, okay," Chantal said, as she rubbed her belly. "I see. You wanna go down this road? It's not gonna go good. Not at all." She looked at Yolanda's card and knew they'd see each other again.

Yolanda tried to study her bible but her mind kept drifting off. She was certain Michael wasn't just agitated by her going into "preacher mode" at Eddie's party with Chantal. She knew sometimes it infuriated him when they weren't at church and Yolanda ministered to random people she met. At first, Yolanda wrote off his annoyance as just that. However, the more she replayed the scene in her mind – his coldness, the inability to look Chantal directly in the face, the fidgeting while Yolanda interacted with her...Yolanda didn't want to read too much into it. After all, she was at least a good ten years his junior. Where would he know her from? *Heck, she can't be too much older than Noel.* She wanted to give Michael some credit. What would he be doing with a young sister like Chantal?

Yolanda knew no matter how she tried to ignore it, there was a reason why her husband acted like he did. She hoped it wasn't what she thought it could be. Or maybe it was a past interaction. After all, Chantal was expecting.

Yolanda sat straight up. A bright neon sign went off in her head. "Oh my gosh," she whispered. She remembered Chantal saying she was indeed pregnant by an *unhappily married man.* Was the unhappily married man *hers? Surely not, sweet Jesus.* She decided all she could do for now was hope and pray.

Yolanda knelt by her chaise, buried her face in her hands and prayed. She figured whatever had been done she could do nothing about. *Besides*, she reasoned, *you can't have a testimony without a test.* She knew now she'd see if her words were just talk or her walk.

And Yolanda was scared.

Chapter Thirteen

Kennedy was exhausted from the night before. After all the guests left, she and Eddie had spent some quality time, talking, making love and watching the dawn arrive in a hotel suite. She knew he would not miss church, regardless of his two-hour nap. She was surprised he let her sleep in. She was glad, and not just to have a Sunday off from the whole "churchy thing". She wanted some time to think about the mercy God had granted her.

Yes, she recognized the sin she got caught up in, but was grateful it was over. Learning her previous lover was the husband of one of the church ministers especially made Kennedy relieved they were done. Not just any minister, but Gospel Gangster Monica Caine. Kennedy imagined Monica's reaction if they'd gotten caught before she broke it off.

Kennedy tried to force herself out of bed. She found herself wrought with nausea. "Man, I must have eaten too much last night." When she stood up, she felt dizzy and plopped back down on the bed. She thought maybe the overindulgence of food and then lack of sleep contributed to her feeling sick. She hoped it wasn't food poisoning. It'd be so embarrassing if folks got sick from their party.

Kennedy slowly laid back down. Maybe the sickness would wear off. She also wanted to forget the emptiness she felt. Yes, things with her and Eddie were good. Although she repented for her sin, the lack of confession to Eddie plagued her. Yes, she'd risk losing her marriage. But could she really go through life as if it never happened? She could try, but she wasn't sure if she was the type who could brush it under the rug.

Kennedy tried to ignore the gurgling in her stomach but suddenly felt all of last night's food coming up her throat. She raced to the bathroom and made it just in time. She hadn't vomited in years and couldn't understand why she was so sick. After ten minutes, Kennedy managed to clean herself up. As she looked in the mirror, she noticed something. She removed her robe and wondered had she gained weight. Her breasts looked about a half cup larger, which they normally did before her period.

My period...

Oh, no! She tried to remember the last time she had a cycle. Her and Yolanda were in sync with one another but the last thing she was going to do was call and ask when her last period was. Kennedy was excited and scared. If she was pregnant, this would surely secure her bond with Eddie. For years, Kennedy had enjoyed the freedom of being married to a man who made a nice living, doing what she wanted, and having nice things. Even though he was twelve years her senior, it wasn't too late for kids. Kennedy planned how she would use the story of Abraham and God's timing if he argued he was too old.

Kennedy decided she'd take a test first. Since she and Eddie had only recently been intimate, she figured she couldn't be more than two months, maybe three. She was glad she'd stopped drinking. The thought of becoming a mother gave her a sense of excitement – despite throwing her baby wishes away years ago. *Funny how things turn out, I decided not to have kids due to our issues and now, the former baby dream is the real deal.* Once again, Kennedy found herself grateful God would bless her with a baby even after all her sin with Marcus.

Marcus.

Kennedy reasoned she wouldn't tell Eddie about Marcus since they

142

were adding a new addition to their family. *After all, it's over so I may as well move on.* She longed to call Yolanda and share the good news. Maybe the baby would be a way to mend their relationship.

Kennedy felt a little lightheaded and decided to nap until Eddie came back. She wouldn't tell him yet, but the thrill of bringing a baby into their world lifted Kennedy's spirit. She felt redeemed. Complete. Determined.

Determined no one would ever hurt her child.

Determined to not let the stronghold of sexual sin or perversion touch her offspring.

Determined to be a Hannah – a woman who would commit her child unto the Lord for His purpose.

Yes. She was determined and destined for the gift of motherhood.

Kennedy wanted to go get an early pregnancy test right away but she was so tired. She eagerly anticipated Eddie's reaction. Would he be nervous? Exhilarated? Ready to bring the pitter-patter of little feet into their big but childless home? As she pondered these things, Kennedy put on her gown and returned to bed. This time, her sleep was indeed sweet.

Pressing Past the Past

Chapter Fourteen

Michael, Sable and Yolanda rode in silence to meet Terrence at the Bistro for brunch. They would decide how and when they would sit down with Noel to tell her who he was. Michael could not focus. For one thing, Sable insisted on bathing herself in Chanel No. 5, which he thought was discontinued. Then she kept talking and talking.

"See, we need to make sure this fool understands where we coming from." Sable folded her arms over her heaving bosom. "I mean, I'm glad Jesus done saved you, but don't come demanding how we going to raise our daughter."

"Mama!" Yolanda's nerves were on edge and she kept having pains in her chest. She wrote it off as indigestion and the headache as allergies, but her mama didn't help. "All we need you to do is sit there. I don't know why he wanted you there, but he did. Please let Michael and I do the talking. And for the record, Noel is *our* child – Michael and me."

"Amen." Michael said, surprising himself.

"Technically, she is you and *Terrence's* child." Sable had a smug look on her face. "I mean it's nice that your husband stepped in but that's the least he could do since…"

"Hold up." Michael's baritone voice filled with fury. Sable jumped and immediately clamped her mouth shut. "I *wanted* to take Noel as my own. I love her like she came from my seed. And the whole 'least I could do' stuff, I didn't do it out of guilt. I love *your daughter*." Michael pulled into the parking slot and slammed the car into park. He turned and glared at Sable, whose eyes were open so wide Yolanda thought she was about to bust a cataract. She was grateful for Michael. His commitment and love for her and Noel was one of the biggest blessings in her life.

"Just to make sure the conversation is led by God, let's pray for Him to lead us. Okay?" She looked at Michael. Her eyes pleaded with him to oblige. She knew prayer would be the only way this could go off without...well...him going off. He sighed, bowed his head and grabbed her hand. Elated, Yolanda prepared to pray. "Heavenly Father in the name of Jesus--"

 "We bind the enemy right now! We ask that you not let this Terrence come back to get our baby. Lord, I know my daughter has been forgiven for her ho-ish...I mean, whoremongering ways. I know she used to smoke dope to get high but now she's high on you." Sable waved her hand in the air, shaking her head back and forth. She snatched Yolanda and Michael's hands apart, grabbing each one of them by the hand. "And Lord, just like Adam let the serpent talk to his wife Eve...I mean the man was right there. Right there, Lord!" Yolanda flinched as her mother shrieked and shook. *What in the world, Lord?* She silently prayed her own prayer on what to say while asking God to silence her mother. Yolanda glanced at Michael as he rolled his opened eyes at Sable's dramatics.

"Lord, Michael didn't let the devil tell his wife to eat the fruit..." Sable softly said, giving Yolanda hope that the prayer was going another

146

direction. "No, Lord. He didn't." She paused. Then, at the top of her voice she hollered, "He just let the devil screw his wife for drugs and then this beautiful baby was made. Yes, Lord! You know that's what happened. But You said in Your Word all things work together for good," she paused again to fan herself and rocked back and forth. "For those who love You and are called according to Your purpose. Do you love Him, son? Do you love Him?" Sable took her hand from Yolanda and grabbed Michael's face.

Yolanda could see he was two seconds from cussing her mother out. Before Sable could say anything else, Michael surprised Yolanda. The look of rage in his eyes died down. He simply said, "Lord, have Your way. In Jesus name, amen." Michael calmly opened the door and walked into the restaurant.

Yolanda sat stunned. She almost asked God who was that man and where did her husband go. The Michael she knew would have told Sable where to go and rest assured it would be nothing short of hell itself. She breathed a sigh of relief before turning to her mother. "You know you was wrong, right? Who prays like that?"

"Well, the Lord knows my heart so I went ahead and prayed what was in it." Sable pulled out her lipstick and painted her mouth. She pursed her lips and checked herself out in the rearview mirror. "I still look good, girl." She smiled at Yolanda. "Let's go in here and lay this man straight, cuz what he ain't about to do…"

Before Yolanda could hear the rest, she simply got out of the car, closed the door and straightened her jacket. "Here it is, Lord. I knew the day would come. Just help me get through this." Yolanda figured if she could make it through this, anything would be possible.

"Come on, girl! Let's get ready to rumble." Sable pumped her fist and then broke into a light jog toward the restaurant doors. Michael looked

147

at his mother-in-law like she had lost her God-given mind. He shook his head as held the door open for her. He mouthed at Yolanda, "That is your mama." Yolanda had to laugh. She was mad her mother was acting like it was a WWE match instead of the moment of decision that would change their lives forever. She figured laughing would keep her from crying.

At least for now.

✝✝✝

Once inside, the hostess came over. The smiling petite blonde looked as if she was expecting them. "Good afternoon, Howard family. Mr. Hudson and his guests are seated in the back room. If you will follow me."

"Guests?" Michael huffed. "We're not supposed to be talking to nobody but him. Shoot, we shouldn't be having our *guest* either." He looked pointedly at Sable.

"Chile, please. You think I'm going to let this hood rat come up in my mix and just take the baby I raised?" She rolled her eyes. "He got another thang coming."

"Mama!" Yolanda said loud enough that nearby patrons turned to look. She softened her tone. "Let us handle it. We are glad you raised her when we couldn't, but we got this." Yolanda silently prayed, *Holy Spirit, please step in and steer this conversation in the way it needs to go where truth and peace will rule.* She felt more at peace.

Terrence was dressed to the nines. His white teeth, which were obviously veneers since he had a full grill back in the day, stood out against his chocolate skin. He had the sexiness of Idris Elba, with his goatee neatly trimmed. Swag surrounded his being. He had on a

148

Michael Kors black suit with a lavender dress shirt, silk tie and diamond studded cufflinks. *Is he still selling dope?* Yolanda knew his family had some money from businesses and he was a growing entrepreneur in his own right, but she had never seen a convicted felon go from the pen to the penthouse. Michael cleared his throat, giving Yolanda the evil eye. Yolanda immediately focused elsewhere, like on his sister, Rocky.

"Good afternoon everyone," Terrence sensed the tension. "Sable, you look as good as an Ebony Fashion Fair model. You haven't aged a bit." He smiled.

Sable smiled demurely. "Thank you. So kind of you to say it." Sable paused and checked him out from head to toe. "You look like you went from felon to fashion model yourself."

Yolanda groaned and took her seat. She should have known better than to believe Sable wouldn't throw a jab. Terrence took it well. He nodded. "God has been good to me. Some felons come out hopeless but I came out with the hope of glory." He said it with such conviction and joy, even Sable was stunned, albeit momentarily.

"Well, He is a way maker." She paused as she pulled her chair closer to the table. "Why couldn't you have been like this out the gate? If you wouldn't have took my daughter's drawers, this could be a different situation. No offense, Michael."

Michael's vein throbbed in his neck, as it often did when he was ready to set it off. He squeezed Yolanda's knee so hard under the table she let out a yelp. Everyone was taken aback, so she played it off. "Sorry, I have been having a little...uh...leg cramps." To divert the attention, she spoke to Rocky. "Hello, Rocky. I didn't know you were coming."

Rocky rolled her eyes and sucked her teeth. "I bet you didn't. This is my brother. What he deals with, I deal with. I was there getting things ready

149

when he was locked up so he could come out and get legit." To Yolanda's surprise, Rocky looked ready to weep. She didn't think Rocky was capable of feeling much less crying. She quickly composed herself. "I promised I would help him get his life back, including his daughter."

For a moment, everyone was silent, quiet in their own thoughts. The waitress came over. "Hey, Mr. Terrence." She seemed to know him well. "You have a beautiful family." She was a tall, leggy redhead who looked more like a ballerina than a waitress. "Terrence and his team are here like every week. He's my best tipper." Terrence laughed heartedly with the waitress. She glanced at Michael and cocked her head to the side. Yolanda's hair on her neck stood up.

Michael suddenly became consumed with reading the menu. He wouldn't look up for anything. Yolanda glared at him.

"I'm...I'm going to wash my hands first." Michael got up from the table. "Baby, go ahead and order. You know what I like." He bent down and kissed her on the cheek. She smiled with her lips but her eyes were clear.

Why she looking at you all sideways and why you nervous?

"Hmm hmmm. All right." Yolanda smiled at the waitress and said, "If everyone else is ready, I'll order for me and my *husband*."

The waitress caught on and smirked. "Most certainly. If you know what your *husband* really wants," she said cattily.

If Yolanda didn't need to take care of the Noel situation, she would have gone out of preacher style into "I'm-about- ready-to-take-this-chick-and-pop-her-upside-her head" mode. Yolanda prayed she could make it through the dinner without choking Michael or the minimum wage

150

waitress. Terrence discerned the situation and said, "Clarice, I need to talk to Roy. If he's working, why don't you have him serve us?" He pulled out a fifty-dollar bill. "I still got you." She looked a little confused but Terrence explained, "I need to see Roy's customer skills before I bring him on as an intern. I'll let your boss know." Clarice shrugged and stuck the money in her shirt pocket. "Sure thing." She cut her eyes at Yolanda and then sauntered off to the kitchen.

"I don't know why you did that," Sable folded her arms. "Shoot, now we got to wait to order. Skip it. I'll do the buffet brunch." She swiftly got up and headed for the buffet as Michael came back to the table.

"I'm gonna keep it one hundred, T. I know Yolanda is tired of living a lie. I love Noel myself like she's my own, but I know you have a right to know your daughter."

"And she should know the truth," Yolanda agreed. For the moment, she forgot about the waitress fiasco. "I think the longer we delay it, the worse the outcome."

Terrence and Rocky nodded in agreement. "Well, let's go on and do it. In fact, I'd even be willing to get with Noel today," he said.

Yolanda choked on her water, going into a major coughing spell. Michael thumped her on the back. "Today? I was at least hoping I could pray and fast for maybe twenty-four hours on this." She looked to Michael for help but he was fidgeting with his phone. Yolanda tried to give him the benefit of the doubt about why he was nervous, but in the back of her mind that waitress' reaction kept popping up. "Baby, what is on your phone that's got you so twisted you can't say anything?" Michael straightened up and put his phone down. "Sorry..." he stammered. "I just got a bit distracted with some office emails."

Sable remained quiet after making her way back from the brunch

151

buffet. Suddenly, she perked up. "Aw, Lord," she muttered under her breath at what she saw across the room. She was in shock at the display of affection she saw taking place before her eyes. Apparently, Terrence took note as well.

"I can't believe that! I know I haven't been the perfect father, but if she was my daughter, I'd have her head for behaving like that." He pursed his lips together and shook his head. "I mean, no decency whatsoever."

"What?" Yolanda was puzzled.

"Well," Sable began, "You said if it was your daughter you'd get her. Get on up. That's her over there."

Yolanda spun around. Her mouth agape not just at what she saw, but "who" she saw. Her seventeen-year-old daughter was practically sitting in Minister Boyd's lap. While they kissed, Noel had the audacity to rub her tongue ring on his bottom lip. Yolanda's heart beat so fast she thought it was going to explode. Michael stood, took off his jacket and made a beeline for the table. Before Yolanda knew it, Michael snatched Noel off Minister Boyd's lap and grabbed him by his collar. Patrons gasped in horror. Someone yelled, "Call the police!"

Terrence calmly went to the manager and whispered something, causing him and his staff to retreat. He pulled Michael off. "Don't do that here, man. Calm down. We can work it out."

"Aw, brotha, please." Michael said sharply and snatched his arm away from Terrence's reach. "Don't tell me nothing. This is my daughter up here acting like a public slut with her tongue down this supposed-to-be-youth pastor's mouth." Michael fumed. Minister Boyd was frozen. Noel was crying, covering her face from the embarrassment of being caught in the situation.

152

"So, Minister Boyd," Yolanda began softly, as she finally made her way to the table. "I trusted you with my daughter and this is what you do? How could you?"

"Minster Howard, I am so sorry. But… I'm in love with your daughter." Michael pulled his arm back, about to punch him. Noel screamed, "No, Daddy!" She tried to hold him back, but Michael was over a hundred pounds heavier than her. Michael's fist was about to hit his face when Minister Boyd popped up and threw a straight jab with such force Michael spilled backwards. He toppled over a table, sending all of the plates and silverware crashing to the floor. Other customers scrambled to get out of the way. They lingered far enough away to be safe, yet not miss out on the action. When Michael managed to stand up, blood trickled from his bottom lip. For a moment, Yolanda's feet were cemented to the ground. Rocky stepped in between the two men, as Michael was ready to redeem himself. Much to Yolanda's surprise, Minister Boyd also looked ready to pounce.

"Hey, you two," Rocky warned. "This is not the place, okay? Let's get our stuff and just head over to Terrence's so we can handle our business." She turned to Minster Boyd, who was now putting on his jacket.

All of a sudden, Noel noticed the two other people all up in her business. "Well, no disrespect, ma'am. But why would we go to…you?" She looked at Terrence, who nodded in response. "So why would we go to Terrence's house to discuss anything? I don't know this man and who are you?" Face filled with disdain at the hot-ghetto-mess she saw before her eyes, Noel noticed she had on some expensive gear - black Louboutin heels, a Tracey Reese sleeveless dress, but her accessories were gaudy and her yaki weave multi-colored.

"Look, heffa," Rocky spat at Noel, "I'm trying to help keep your man from getting his a--"

Before she could finish the sentence, Terrence stepped in. "Hello, Noel," He extended his hand. As he stood next to Noel, Yolanda held her breath. Looking at the two together, she saw their matching jawlines, almond shaped eyes, and dimple in the same left cheek. Though his skin was the color of dark chocolate, it was easy to see the two had a familial connection. Noel, not one to miss a detail, seemed to sink in Terrence's face. Her eyes locked on him, not even shaking the hand he offered. She looked slowly at Michael, back to Terrence and dropped her head. "Hi," she said softly, finally shaking his hand. Her eyes filled with questions.

"Aw, Lawd I can't take it." Sable fanned herself. "Shoot, I'm tired of this. This girl is a light-skinned-ed version of this man and I can't sit here and wait for y'all to go on and come clean, so I will."

"No, Mama!" Yolanda hollered. Everyone around her jumped.

"Girl, you done got me caught up in your mess, and I am not going to hell for none of y'all. If I wanted to dance with the devil, I would have stayed in the world and went to hell VIP style. Noel, baby, meet your real daddy. He took ya mama's cookie. Michael felt guilty cuz it was his fault and since he a punk as you can see," Sable gave Michael a disgusted sideways glance, "Almost got his tail kicked by a youth minister. If I cussed, I'd have some names for him. But back to you, ya daddy a jailbird gone God because everybody finds Jesus in jail and so now he wants to do right by ya." She stopped and looked at everyone. "Did I get it all out?"

As everyone sat in stunned silence, Terrence reached to hug Noel but she pushed him back. "My whole life has been a lie?" Tears streamed down her face.

Yolanda stepped toward her, tears beginning to fall. Observers turned back to their plates. It was awkward to have such a private matter aired in a public setting. "Baby, I'm so sorry. I should have told you, but Michael has always loved you so much. I never thought I'd see Terrence again." Yolanda's voice trailed off. The pain on Noel's face made her speechless.

"I knew it." Noel fell back into the booth. Her head flung back as she gazed up at the ceiling. "I always knew. I just wanted to see if you loved me enough to tell me the truth." She paused and looked directly in Yolanda's eyes, now seated in front of her. "I heard a conversation when I was eight. You were drunk, arguing with Mama Sable. You told her 'I'd just send her with her daddy but he locked up.'" Noel paused. By this time, the whole family had sat down, pulling up chairs around the booth, prepared to interject in the moment. "And I hated you...hated you...hated you." Though Noel whispered, her voice was filled with fury and pain.

Yolanda's heart sunk. She and Noel had always had a tumultuous relationship but she never knew she didn't have her daughter's love, and it hurt. It hurt worse than Terrence taking her body in exchange for a drug deal gone bad.

"I have tried to love you, Mama. And I think I do. I just...don't feel it sometimes. I can't respect such a hypocrite who preaches on doing the right thing and you have had seventeen years to get things right and you never have."

"Baby, your mother did what she thought was best," Michael interjected. "And I have loved you like I fathered you myself."

"I know. And I love you for it. I always will. But you, woman of God," Noel laughed. Her voice gritty, as she choked back tears.

155

"Now hold up," Sable snapped. "She is a different woman than when this happened. I won't let you disrespect her nor the assignment God has given her."

Everyone was shocked at Sable sticking up for her daughter. The two had always been at odds over Noel.

"I know your mama was a drunk floozy, but God redeemed her from hoe-ism and now she is holy."

Yolanda and Michael knew it was too good to be true. Sable always managed to say something inappropriate and ruin the moment.

"Noel," Terrence said, "I understand if you don't want to get to know me right now. This is a lot to take in. I want you to know, I want to do right by you while still respecting the father-daughter relationship you and Michael have."

Noel nodded. "I guess. I'll get back to you." She stood and grabbed her purse. "Ready, baby?" she said to Minister Boyd. He nodded and got up.

"I'm sorry for how things went today. I didn't mean to bust your mouth. I always respect my elders but you took things to a whole other level." Minister Boyd offered his hand to Michael. Michael slapped it away.

"Little boy, get out my face and leave my daughter here." Michael's voice boomed with bass.

"No, Daddy," Noel said, before looking at Terrence. "Sorry, dude. I just met you so I can't call you daddy. Daddy, I need to process this. I just wanted some salmon and garlic mashed potatoes and I got a scene from a reality show and Maury combined."

156

"You looked like you was giving Minister a lap dance or about to get pregnant," Sable quipped and shook her head.

"If so, she got it from her daddy. The one she knows."

Yolanda spun around to see the waitress from earlier. She made her slick comment and then headed to another table in her section. Yolanda got ready to go check her when sharp pains in the left side of her chest made her sit back down.

"You okay, baby?" Michael looked concerned.

"No, I'm not okay." Yolanda snapped. "My daughter struggled with hating me. She's fornicating with our youth minister and then that trick..." Yolanda was loud enough for the waitress to look in her direction. "She all up in our family business, been giving us mess since we arrived. I want to know what her problem is. Or is her problem somebody she knows who's with us?"

"Clarice?" Terrence inquired. "I can call her over here and get it straight."

"No!" Michael responded so quickly his voice was shaky from nervousness. "I mean, she's just young. Trying to do her job. We don't know her so let's just ignore her." His voice trailed off. He avoided looking at Yolanda whose eyes narrowed suspiciously.

"Naw," Sable said. "Terrence, call her over here. I need to see what she got to say."

"Do that," Noel pulled Minster Boyd up by the hand. "We're out. Sorry for lying to you about Daryl and for acting this way in public. But I'm not sorry I can't trust you, Mama." Noel paused. "I love you but I hate your deceit, hypocrisy and your weakness which made you wait to face the

157

truth. You always said you can't conquer what you won't confront." Noel turned and walked away without even glancing back.

"I ought to go grab her behind and make her sit down right now." Sable was beside herself.

"No," Terrence responded. "It's best to leave it alone. This wasn't the way I wanted to tell her," he added pointedly, looking at Sable.

"What?" Sable looked innocent, as if she couldn't believe anyone would blame her for the fiasco. "Y'all was taking way too long and we needed this over with."

"Give her time. When she's ready, I'll be here." Terrence stood up. Rocky followed suit. "If you all need anything at all, please call."

Minister Boyd was still gathering himself together when he touched Yolanda on the shoulder. "I am so sorry, Minster Howard, for all you've faced and even what you had to deal with today." He stopped. "I have always loved and respected you. I see so much of you in Noel and that's why...I do love her. If you want me to let her go, I will." He looked sad, as he fidgeted with his hands nervously.

"I...I..." Yolanda stammered. "I don't have the energy right now to deal with this. Excuse me." Yolanda got up and went to the restroom. She thought a walk away from the scene of the drama would do her well.

Yolanda went in the stall, buried her face in her hands and cried. She decided all she could do was surrender the situation to God. After all, that was the problem. She stuck to her own methods of living life and dealing with deceit instead of doing it God's way. All Yolanda could do is hope the Lord would move on her behalf.

Yolanda exited the stall and went to splash water on her face. She heard the door creak open. There was Clarice, the woman who seemed to know her husband.

"Excuse me? You're Clarice, right?"

Clarice rolled her eyes up and cocked her neck to the side. She sucked her lip and looked at Yolanda from head to toe. If Yolanda weren't so emotionally spent, she probably would have slapped her overbite into the back of her throat.

Apparently Yolanda's thoughts were unveiled through her eyes. Clarice's disposition changed. She cleared her throat. "Yes, I am," she politely answered.

"I noticed today you seemed to be observing my husband. Then you made that snide comment in the middle of family trauma. It was rude. And unnecessary. So...I'm going to ask you one time. How do you know my husband?" Yolanda tapped her foot impatiently and put her hands on her hips. This time, she cocked her head to the side and waited for an answer.

"I don't know your husband. He knows me."

"How?"

"He knows me from a girl I worked with. That's all. She used to...wait on him." Clarice's demeanor changed. When she realized Yolanda wasn't going to hit her, she became a little more confident and cocky. "He was her favorite client to wait on." Now, Clarice smirked.

Yolanda reached up and grabbed the girl's hair. She yelped in pain. "You're not acting very pastoral." Yolanda dropped her hair, remaining within an inch of her. "All I can tell you is your husband is a *great* tipper.

159

Now, unless you want me to file an assault charge, get out of my way and stay out of my face. Some of us got real work to do." She brushed past Yolanda and went into the stall.

Yolanda was confident the type of customer Michael was to her "friend" certainly wasn't a family-filled atmosphere. She thought about bum-rushing the stall and forcing it out of her, but God's still small voice spoke.

What's done in the dark, will come to light. I will reveal what you need to know in due season.

Yolanda wasn't ready for the answer. She decided not to confront Michael. Yolanda couldn't tolerate another lie today. She recalled 1 Peter 5 which told her to cast her cares on God so she would. It was too painstaking to carry them alone.

Chapter Fifteen

Kennedy could barely contain herself at the idea that she was going to be a mother. For many years, she actually loathed the idea of getting pregnant. Now that she and Eddie were closer, she was ready to increase their family.

As Kennedy went into the kitchen to prepare lunch, she wanted to call someone to share her good news. Kennedy longed to share the news with Yolanda, but didn't think she'd be too receptive to rekindling their relationship at this time. *Boy, I miss my best friend. I feel like a part of me is missing.*

Kennedy sobbed. She had Eddie but still felt alone. Yolanda was her rock. She was the only woman she could share with. She sat at her counter, put her head into her arms and prayed. She sniffed and wiped her eyes with a nearby napkin. "I cannot make it through this pregnancy without a friend. You know my situation and the lack of support I have." Kennedy felt better after her prayer. She believed she and Yolanda would reconcile.

Little did she know the circumstances that would reunite them.

✝✝✝

After preparing dinner, Kennedy set the table and waited for Eddie to arrive. She knew he often stayed after church to help count the offering, but today he was later than usual. She picked up the phone to dial his cell when the garage door opened. Eddie burst in looking flustered. He rushed inside and immediately plopped into a chair. Kennedy went over to her husband and sat on his lap. "Hey baby!" She kissed him tenderly on his lips and massaged his balding scalp. "Why you come in here like your pants were on fire?"

"Girl," Eddie shook his head in disbelief. "This day was crazy. First, Pastor's niece joined the church. She pregnant by a married man. And why Mother Stone was the one to meet her at the altar?"

"Uh oh!" Kennedy knew his judgmental old hag of a mama probably went to town on the poor girl.

"You right! I love Mama but when she tried to rebuke a demon of marital destruction from the girl, even I was like you doin' too much."

Kennedy shook her head. "Poor thing. How did she react?"

"She was scared to death until Minister Howard took her to the side to counsel her. You should have seen her. It was awesome how she spoke forgiveness and peace. She loved on this young pregnant sister."

"I know you two haven't been talking," Eddie stated hesitantly, "I just really wish I could help you with that or at least know why you all fell out. Y'all been thick as thieves since parachute pants were in."

The two shared a laugh before Kennedy sighed. "I can't even say why we haven't been hanging, but we will. I'm sure of it."

"Good, because I know you miss her and I am sure Minister misses you." He grabbed Kennedy and kissed her passionately, leaving her breathless.

"Okay, Deacon. Don't start nothing you can't finish."

162

"Oh, I am ready! Got it smelling good in here. Don't know if I should eat first or work up an appetite."

"Let's eat in reverse then," Kennedy said seductively. "Start with dessert and then we can reheat the main course." Eddie stood and scooped Kennedy in his arms. "You ain't said nothing but a word." He turned and headed toward their master suite.

After their afternoon session of love making, they lay in bed snuggled enjoying the rhythm of their hearts beating. Kennedy loved that the spark was back in their sex life. She was certain if it had been like this before, her affair with Marcus would have been non-existent. Kennedy would always regret cheating but knew it was over for good. Since she and Eddie were about to be parents, she was ready to press past the past and propel into the future.

"What's on your mind?" Eddie asked softly rubbing her hair.

Kennedy didn't prepare for how she was going to tell him she was pregnant. She was tempted to just say it but decided to ease it into their conversation.

"I know we have a nice life. Just the two of us."

"That we do, baby. We can afford what we want. Do what we want. We're truly blessed." Eddie kissed Kennedy on her sweaty cheek.

"I agree," Kennedy stated. "Do you think when we get older we'll regret not having kids?"

Eddie stiffened. "I mean, you...you changed your mind about having children which was fine with me. You don't remember? We can't regret nothin' we decided years ago."

Kennedy noticed the tone in his voice was no longer soft and loving. If she wasn't mistaken, it was defensive. She wasn't sure why. Then it dawned on her. He had lost a kid so maybe he was scared to try again.

"I know. But I've been thinking, Eddie. I'd love to give you the chance to father a child. I mean, you are a father who lost his child. You have so much to offer-- I think you'd be a great father."

Eddie didn't respond. He rolled over onto his side. His back faced Kennedy. "Thank you," he whispered. "Maybe we can adopt because at my age, I'm scared either I can't get you pregnant or... isn't there some study that said old dads make your babies come out wrong?"

"Well, there is always a chance when you parent late that your child could have challenges. But isn't that what having faith in God is all about?" She pushed her breasts into his back and ran her fingers softly over his arm. "Even if something were wrong, we would love the child and do our best. I'm believing God for a healthy normal child."

Eddie pushed her arm off and sat up. "You know my son was stillborn. How I look trying to replace him?"

Kennedy was scared. What if he really didn't want this baby inside of her?

"I think if you want a kid, let's rent a foster baby." Eddie smiled, though it appeared disingenuous.

"Rent a kid?" She could not believe her ears. "You don't rent kids, Eddie. You keep foster kids and if possible, adopt them. I want a kid from infancy."

"Ok...we'll get one from the hospital. Maybe even the girl at church who is pregnant by the married man. We could buy her baby."

Is he crazy? Kennedy was confused by Eddie's reaction. "Eddie, you can't just ask someone to let you buy their baby. It's a human, not a used car! Why do that when we can have our own?"

Eddie looked down. *Lord, I have to say it. I just don't know how.* "Kennedy," his voice was soft and filled with regret. "I hate to tell you but--"

Kennedy interrupted him. "Wait! Let me say this--"

"Kennedy, this is something you need to know. It affects you having a baby."

"I already am though!"

"Am what?" Eddie jumped out the bed.

"Eddie, I'm...I'm pregnant." Kennedy smiled as she sat up and rubbed her belly.

"What? You lying!" Eddie appeared to be excited.

Or confused?

Kennedy couldn't register what he was feeling but it wasn't the joy she was hoping for. "No, I missed my period and I took a test. Two pink lines means positive!"

Eddie put his boxers on and looked at Kennedy, his eyes cold. Kennedy got nervous, he didn't want to have a kid after losing his son. She wasn't ready for his next response.

"Who's the father?"

"What the he..."

"Who's the father." This time it was a demand, not a question. Kennedy was puzzled. Yes, she had cheated with Marcus but had been careful. Besides, Eddie had no idea she stepped out.

Or did he?

"Eddie, you are my *husband*!" Kennedy shouted, now on her feet facing Eddie. "You are my husband and the father of my child. I know you lost your son, but don't go accusing me of something out of fear." She tried to hug Eddie to comfort him. He pushed her back so hard she fell on her bottom.

"I tell you I'm pregnant and you physically assault me. Are you out your mind?"

"Yes, I'm your husband but I can't be your child's father. I can't have kids."

"What? You had a kid so what are you talking about?"

"I had a son who was born dead. After..." his voice trailed off.

"After what?"

"After he was stillborn, I got fixed. I felt guilty about what happened. I blamed myself and said I never wanted to chance that pain again. So I can't be your child's father."

Kennedy thought she was in a nightmare. What she dreaded was

166

coming back full circle. Somehow she had to be carrying Marcus' baby. As she thought about how to respond, suddenly a sharp pain shot across her forehead. Hot liquid ran down her face then she fell into blackness.

Eddie had knocked his wife unconscious.

Kennedy opened her eyes. Her head throbbed. She tried to recall what had occurred. She wanted to sit up, but was light-headed. She noticed her shirt was covered in blood. She steadied herself and leaned her back against the bed. Then she remembered.

Her husband had hit her.

Her body crumpled as she cried. Not a soft, tender cry but gut wrenching sobs that came from the depth of her being. She knew Eddie was hurt at the possibility of her carrying another man's baby. That alone was enough to hurt Kennedy. But then he actually put his hands on her. Eddie could be stuffy, possessive and demanding but never disrespected her body. To knock her out knowing she was pregnant was the vilest thing he could do. Kennedy considered calling the police to file a report, but didn't want to face the repercussions of why he hit her in the first place. Kennedy had no family she could call. She hadn't worked in the past two years, so she really had no social circle. The women at church were gossips. She barely knew her neighbors. Sitting there in the midst of her physical and emotional pain, Kennedy had an epiphany.

All these years of serving the Lord, reading her Bible and attempting to deal with her personal issues, she never developed real relationships with *people*. Sure, she had Yolanda. Even their relationship had crumbled. "I have no one," Kennedy whispered. In her mind, Hebrews 13:5 sprang up, *I will never leave you or forsake you.*

167

All she could do now was own up to her sin and move on. She prayed Eddie could somehow forgive her. She knew abortion was out of the question, yet knowing Marcus was married to Monica...

Monica!

Now Kennedy feared for her life. Never did she imagine Minster Caine – former gangbanger who could still scrap if she needed to – was Marcus' wife. Of all the men in a newspaper, how did *that* happen? She knew Romans 8 talked about all things working together for good but there was no way Kennedy saw anything "good" about dealing with Minister Caine. She didn't understand why Monica didn't have her own husband's last name. So how would she know? Still, Kennedy knew her sexual vice one day would be her downfall. She'd managed to dodge STD's. Never got pregnant. Her reputation, spotless. Her hidden sin stayed secret.

Until now.

Kennedy sat there wondering what to do next. She heard the bedroom door creak open and jumped. She feared Eddie was coming back to finish her off. But when she saw his face, there was no anger. Yet, she couldn't quite read what was going on in his mind. The usually dapper deacon looked rough. His hair, what was left of it, wasn't slicked down but all over the place. His shirt was untucked, eyes red, as if he'd shed tears over his wife's indiscretion. Kennedy was heartbroken for putting her husband through this. He just stared at Kennedy in silence. Kennedy couldn't say anything. She was still in shock over his punch. She was angry. Still, she almost accepted it as her fate even though she knew a man should never hit a woman. Her heart beat fast with anticipation as to what would happen next. Eddie surprised her by sitting down on the floor by her side.

"I'm sorry I put my hands on you," he said tenderly. When he spoke, Kennedy knew why he was so disheveled. His breath reeked of alcohol. This again shocked Kennedy. He often gave her a speech about drinking "devil juice" as he called liquor. With what she'd told him, she couldn't even blame him for tossing back a drink, or a few, to numb the pain.

"I never should have touched you, but I can't believe my wife is having another man's baby. Something I can't even give you." He choked on his words and held back tears. "Do you know how a man feels when something he holds as his most prized possession is violated? How can you do something so slutty, especially as a woman of God?"

No he didn't call me a slut. Kennedy was ready to curse him out. She took a deep breath. She wasn't going to defend herself, but explain what led to her cheating without being demonized by her husband. She wondered if he always thought of her as used. Unclean. Unvirtuous. After all, it came up on more than one occasion. Since she was the one who broke their marital vows, her argument was meaningless. "I'm...I'm...so...sorry. I felt so alone. I just needed someone to hold me. For so long, it seemed like the church was your wife."

Eddie cut her off. "Now look here," his voice sounded more like the "deacon" instead of the broken man she had started to feel sorry for only moments before. "You know I put God's work first. That ain't gave you no right to go get ya rocks off with some type of Samson. You played the role of a harlot and I rebuke that spirit of lust in the name of Jesus." Suddenly Kennedy felt herself tip over backwards, as he had poked her so hard in the head during his mini-exorcism. Even in a time of despair and what she thought would be healing for them both, he'd turned it into a holy roller moment. When she sat back up, Eddie straddled her. He put his face within an inch of hers. Kennedy wondered if he kept a secret stash of booze. "I ain't through with you yet. I'm calling Mama to come over. Once and for all, we both will get you free

169

from this demon of sex that has you all caught up." He huffed and puffed hard. His eyes bulged from his head, as if he was in a deep spiritual battle with a demon – her. If she weren't so emotionally distraught, she would have laughed. She almost wished her camera phone was taping this mess.

"Eddie," Kennedy said softly. "You are hurting my stomach. There is a life inside of it regardless of the father."

"Speaking of which," Eddie drawled drunkenly, suddenly laying his head on her belly. "This life I couldn't give you. The life giving sperm of another man in the throes of my wife's belly. How you expect the deacon to deal with that?" Eddie became eerily still. It made Kennedy nervous. She was glad he seemed to calm down, but it felt like the eye of a hurricane – the calm before the storm's resurgence.

She was right.

Quickly, Eddie jumped up and grabbed the chair in front of her mirror and struck her with it, aiming for her abdomen. Kennedy rolled over, screaming from fear of losing her baby. Yes, it was conceived in sin but she believed this child was meant to be here. The wooden chair splintered against her back. Its sharp pieces jarred her skin through her clothing. She was unsure if she should fight back or run and lock herself in the bathroom.

Be still. Kennedy heard the familiar still small voice that had been with her since her teen years. Though she was afraid of her fate for lying there, her feet seemed to obey the voice of the Holy Spirit. She couldn't pull herself up. *Be still. I have you in the palm of My hand.* Kennedy silently prayed for the baby within her. *I have covered you with My hand – all of you.* At that moment, Kennedy braced herself. With one final blow, Eddie struck her in the back of her head. When he saw her limp, still body, he managed to pull her down the stairs.

He stopped momentarily. In his drunken state of mind, he wondered what he should do next. Sure, he could call his mama but he wasn't quite ready to hear her "I told you, you can't make no 'ho into a housewife" speech. He'd always defended Kennedy. Telling his mother she wasn't a whore. The last thing he wanted was for her to be right. Eddie moved Kennedy to the bottom of the step. He couldn't believe how he had assaulted his wife. He hadn't hit a woman in years. Once he had gotten saved, he thought all his anger was behind him. Sitting there, Eddie knew.

His religion was a Band-Aid for emotional scars that needed surgery.

Eddie rubbed his wife's back, sorry he'd done this to her. He wanted to take her to a hospital but knew he'd be arrested for assault. Then not only would he lose his credibility as the head deacon, he'd also lose his employment. Pastor Griffin made it clear if your personal life was out of sorts, he'd have no problem letting you go. Beyond the life and reputation Eddie had worked so hard to build after his sinful past, he also wanted to protect Kennedy. Though he was hurt and unsure if he could ever truly forgive her, he didn't want anyone else to judge or attack her due to her mistake. A mistake, if Eddie were honest, was his fault. He knew for years he was trying to "work" his way into God's grace instead of believing by faith that he had it. By ignoring his wife's needs, she'd found in another man what he wasn't providing.

Eddie took the small bottle of Crown out of his back pocket. He took a long swig. He hadn't had a drink since the day his first love died after giving birth. After hitting Kennedy the first time, he was so scared and shocked at what he had done, he couldn't help but head to the liquor store to toss a few back. Now as he looked at her battered body, he knew he had to do something. He thought about what she told him, how he was "married to the church" and for some reason, her comment

171

hurt almost as much as her being pregnant by another man. *That's because you know you are in church but not in Me. You wear religion as a badge and do everything in My name but don't really know* **Me** *beyond My name.*

Eddie jumped at the inaudible yet loud inner voice that whispered to him. He had never really heard God speak but at that moment, he knew he had what he had been working so hard for. He'd heard the voice of the Lord speak to him. Eddie remembered reading about the Pharisees and Jesus warning them that in the end, they'd be told to go away because the Lord never knew them, no matter how much they did in His name. Eddie was convicted he was a Pharisee. He had verbally given his life to Christ out of desperation and then worked his way into godliness. So he thought. In the end, it hurt his real relationship with Christ and affected his wife.

Eddie put his face in his hands and wept. He knew how he got to where he was, but he didn't know how to get out. "Lord," he slurred aloud. "I been faking with You. I believe in You but have never given myself to You. If You will have me, I will give You all of me." Eddie sobbed so hard his whole body shook. He was a mess on the outside. Inside, he felt something he had never experienced in all his life.

Peace. Real peace.

Eddie sighed and looked at his wife as she slowly sat up. He looked at her swollen eye and realized he was just as responsible for her straying. No, he would not be able to trust her for a long time but he could manage to work this out. Besides, who would ever know the kid wasn't his? Eddie pondered if he could really love a child knowing it was conceived outside of their union. *Lord, I can't.*

No, you can't, but I can help you. Again, he felt as though the Holy Spirit spoke directly to his heart. Then Hosea came to mind.

He remembered in the Bible where Hosea was told to marry Gomer, a prostitute who was an adulterer and had bastard kids. God used the marriage as a parallel to His people not being faithful to Him though he was always faithful to them. No, Eddie was not crazy about it but he knew what the Lord commanded. He wrestled with Kennedy's revelation but recalled what Yolanda had spoken to him at the Faith Festival.

"When God reveals what you need to see, be attentive. Do not take anything He shows you for granted. Though it may appear to throw you off track, please know that nothing surprises God. No matter what happens, He can work it for good if you let Him. Be prepared to disclose what has been secret. And be willing to do what He would have you to do."

Eddie believed deep down the Lord wanted him to stay. He wanted to put Kennedy and her baby out but above all, he wanted to obey God. He wasn't happy about it nor did he think he could stay. *Lord, your strength is made perfect in weakness. I need a double dose of strength to deal with this.*

"Eddie…" Kennedy's voice was barely above a whisper. "I'm…sorry. I wish it never would have happened." She reached over and touched Eddie's calf.

Eddie's anger subsided. "I'm sorry I hurt you and…and…our…baby."

Kennedy jolted up and looked incredulously at Eddie. "What? Even after…"

"Yeah," Eddie said nodding. "I think the Crown wore off long enough for God to check me. Kennedy, I am so hurt for what you did. I can't trust

173

you right now and I can't promise there won't be days where I almost hate you." He paused. "But I'm willing to see if we can raise this child as our own and leave it at that."

Kennedy cried tears of joy. She knew she should be calling 911 to get Eddie hemmed up for what he had done. While she hoped the baby was all right, she was relieved at Eddie's change of heart and grateful God had intervened. She knew the Lord was always faithful even in the midst of their unfaithfulness. Then it dawned on her.

Would Eddie still want to know who she had been with?

As if they were thinking on one accord, Eddie said, "So...do I want to know who the father is or what?"

"I...I don't know," Kennedy stammered. "There was only one man. Just know I never plan on seeing him again."

Eddie exhaled and wiped the sweat off his forehead. "Let me ask you, did you love him?" His eyes welled with tears, surprising Kennedy. She'd never seen Eddie shed a tear since she met him. In spite of the bruises on her body, her heart filled with love for her husband. Was he wrong to abuse her? Absolutely. Should he go to jail? Without question. However, Kennedy was willing to cover her bruises in exchange for uncovering her infidelity.

"Did you love him?" Eddie asked again. His voice rattled with nervousness.

"No. Never. Not even close." Kennedy said firmly.

"So, are you okay never to tell him about the baby?"

174

Kennedy was scared if they hid this from the child's real father they might regret it later. Right now, she was willing to go along with Eddie's plan if it meant she could keep her marriage and motherhood.

"Yes." Kennedy knew God always revealed what was done in the dark. At the moment, she was willing to take that chance. After all, Eddie could have put her out and she would have been forced to come clean with Marcus. She didn't really want to raise a child with him. And then, to top it off, his wife...Monica. Kennedy couldn't imagine what Monica would do if she found out she had slept with her husband.

Eddie picked her up and held her in his arms as if she were a tender child. He kissed her cheek and said, "I am so sorry I lost it and hit you. I will never hurt you again. I will repent everyday if I have to. That's not who I am. I know who I am now. A man who has God's grace and extends it to you. My Gomer." He kissed her again.

Kennedy's heart melted at his tenderness until his last comment. He referred to her as Gomer, the prostitute Hosea married. She knew he meant well, but did he always have to put his foot in his mouth? Kennedy got ready to fuss him out and then remembered.

She was unfaithful. So was Gomer.

Hosea was forgiving. So was Eddie.

God was in that story and theirs.

Chapter Sixteen

Michael sighed, shifted onto his side, and turned his back to Yolanda. "Hey baby..."

"Yes?" Yolanda answered coldly.

"What's your problem?" Michael sat up, facing her dead on. "I'm up here about to ask you did you want me to look for your daughter and now you wanna get all funky?"

Yolanda jerked her head back as if she had been slapped. "What you mean *my* daughter? All of a sudden when the stuff hits the fan, you want to put all this on me?"

"You seemed so quick to want yo' boy all up in the daddy mix. So you right, I said *your* daughter. I love her but you want to be pushing me out the way so the man who bought you can come back like he all on the up and up and you falling for it." Michael didn't mean to be so harsh, however he knew a fight would be one way to distract her so he could get out. He wanted to confront Chantal about her homegirl, the waitress. And to be honest, he missed her.

With Chantal, he always felt good enough. There was no obligatory need to stick around. No guilt trip to force his hand. He wasn't sure if he was in love with Chantal but he knew one thing was certain.

He loved Yolanda. He always would. He simply wasn't in love. He wondered if he ever was. Michael believed he could never measure up to being a "preacher's husband" or being everything Yolanda wanted him to be. When she turned her life around, she seemed to spring up with sudden success. She found purpose in ministry. Yes, he married her out of guilt and then stayed out of need. Michael was educated and had business sense. Still, he had to credit her for his own success. It was her inheritance from her father's insurance policy that launched their business. Then it was her marketing savvy that made it grow. After building their clientele, Yolanda still kept grinding in the corporate world until she was certain they'd be more than okay. So while he loved her, there were other benefits for being her man. Now, that was changing.

He got up and put on his pants. "I'm going to catch a breath of fresh air." He grabbed his cell phone and his wallet. Snatched his keys off the chest and said, "Sorry for all the yelling. I'll just holler at you later." He slipped on his top siders and hurried from the room.

Pain shot through Yolanda's chest. She knew stress was the culprit. She managed to get out of bed to pray. Yolanda laid it all on the altar before getting up.

✟✟✟

Michael went over to Chantal's ready to confront her again about being so chummy with his wife at the party a couple of weeks ago. He also wanted to check her about Clarice being so blatantly obvious in the midst of the dinner fiasco with his family.

However, the intended confrontation led to consummation. Again, they were in bed. Michael loved the way Chantal treated him in and outside the bedroom. He knew she wouldn't strip forever. She was in nursing school. At least with her, he didn't have to be such a holy roller.

"You know your wife is probably blowing up your phone," Chantal

178

whispered seductively. She licked his neck as she grasped his shoulder while they spooned.

"And?" Michael sighed. "I came over here pissed off you had buddied up with her. I was ready to end it for good too."

Chantal laughed. "Yeah, right. You always say that." She kissed him on his back and snuggled up even closer. "Honestly, I didn't put two and two together until you walked up. She's pretty though. Uncle never told me she was such a cutie."

"Yeah, I bet." Michael grunted. "Your uncle so worried about my house, he need to make sure his own is in order. With a niece like you..."

"What!" Chantal popped him playfully on the back. "Real talk. I was venting because I do love you. Had no idea it was her. Maybe God let us meet."

"What?" Michael asked with surprise and irritation in his voice. "God didn't have nothing to do with my side-girl meeting up with my wife. Then you had to sit by her in prayer service, making her think you all are besties. Don't you feel bad?"

"No," Chantal answered quickly. "I know what I want and it's you. She doesn't even appreciate you. She downplays your contribution to the house. She expects you to be all goody-goody and perfect." She paused. "Plus, there are things she won't give you like I would."

"And what would that be other than mind boggling sex on a regular?"

"You always complain her life is all about ministry first and foremost." Chantal carefully constructed her approach in her mind. She didn't want to scare Michael off, or set him off. "You've been with her all these years. She doesn't want any more kids?"

"First, it was her getting saved so we waited to have sex again until marriage. By then, she was finishing college. She went into marketing. Then, it was seminary. Now, it's "my ministry". He mimicked Yolanda with disgust, resentment in his voice. "Finally, I gave up. Let her keep the shot every three months and just took care of Noel."

Chantal knew that was her in. "Well, you deserve to be a father. A biological-no faking-the-funk or covering-up-sin father. And we can have our own family. Don't stay obligated to something you're not feeling anymore."

"So you want me to just knock you up and leave my wife?"

"All you need to do is leave. I'm already pregnant and it's yours."

Michael felt like the air had been sucked out of him. He sat up, detangling himself from their spooning position and looked her in the eye. "What? You can't be! You don't look it!"

"I'm only four months. And because I'm so fit it may be hard to notice at first. You couldn't tell at *all*?"

He thought Chantal was bloated but blamed it on PMS. Her breasts were fuller than usual. Her nipples were even darker than before. As he thought about it some more, Michael realized her supple bottom did seem rounder and bigger. "But, we always used protection." Michael was never that careless. Except...

"Except when Yolanda was away at a conference and we spent the weekend together." They said together. Michael remembered they were so hot and bothered they made out on the elevator. By the time they reached the rented condo, they immediately began a long, steamy

180

sex session with no condom. Michael pushed it out of his mind. He assumed Chantal was on the pill.

He'd thought wrong.

He knew he couldn't just be angry at Chantal. It was his fault as well for being so careless. He almost felt relieved. He could be a father to his own child. And maybe have an out from a life he didn't sign up for.

"Look, I'm not asking you to leave your wife. I'd love for you, our son and me to have a life together. I'm almost out of school. I'm about to be done at the club."

"A son?" Michael wanted to cry. He wanted to be free from a marriage by guilt. Free to live his life outside the whole church bubble. And more than anything he wanted a child of his own. He knew it was a risk, but realized he'd made enough business contacts so he'd no longer need Yolanda. While he wasn't sure he wanted to marry Chantal, he knew he loved being with her and would love to be with their son even more.

As though she were reading his mind, Chantal said, "I'm not saying marry me today. I'm saying give us a true shot to see where we can go."

Michael lay back down and put his hands behind his head. He sighed as Chantal snuggled against his chest. She playfully stroked his abdomen. "So what are you thinking about?" She asked softly, almost terrified of the answer.

"How to make our family work."

Chantal squealed with delight and hugged and kissed Michael. He laughed and squeezed her close. He rubbed her belly and bent down and kissed it. "Hey, little man, your daddy is waiting for you." For the first time in a while, Michael felt elated. He wasn't sure what made him happier, the fact he'd finally be a biological daddy or the fact he was having a son.

Or that he was getting his life back. At least, one not caught up in his past or in his wife. Though Michael didn't want to hurt Yolanda and had no plans to abandon Noel, he made up his mind. It seemed absurd to leave his wife for a jump-off stripper, but Michael knew Chantal was smart and the pole was a temporary means to an end. He would make her vow to hurry and finish her degree before their son turned one.

Michael didn't know how to tell Yolanda his decision. First, there were other issues he needed to handle to make sure he was able to make this way of escape.

"Lord, forgive me... I'm leaving."

Chapter Seventeen

It was the fourth Monday of the month, which meant the prayer meeting for the church board, ministers and ministry leaders. Usually Eddie was the one who prayed. This time around, he thought he might need intercession himself.

He was still processing the fact his wife had stepped out with another man. Though he'd made a choice to forgive and let God heal their relationship, there were still moments when he wanted to strangle her. He knew he wouldn't, especially after how he'd already roughed her up. He was truly repentant and grateful. Not only were Kennedy and the baby okay, she had chosen not to press charges. Eddie knew he'd snapped.

He also couldn't fathom the idea of some random man up in his wife. He kept having perverse imaginations of her in all sorts of sexual positions. With man after man after man, too. He knew the devil was messing with his head, but he didn't know how long he could handle it. He had cast down the imaginations as the Bible said but every time he touched Kennedy, he envisioned a young Denzel type of brother getting it on with his wife.

Eddie snapped back to reality when Kennedy squeezed his hand. The one good thing that came out of their recent blow up was the intimacy they seemed to share. They no longer prayed solo prayers. Now, they prayed together every morning. Kennedy was more compliant in assisting him in his ministerial duties. He thought the guilt of being pregnant by another man may have been a contributing factor. Regardless, she was the epitome of what he had wanted in a wife.

If only she hadn't slept with someone else.

Kennedy was so tired she could barely hold her eyes open but knew how important it was to Eddie that she be by his side. They hadn't told anyone, not even his nosy mama that the two were expecting. While Eddie agreed to play along as if this was his child, the two weren't quite comfortable with the revelation of this news just yet. Even though this was supposed to be a prayer meeting, Kennedy noted no one had prayed yet.

"Well," Pastor Griffin began, "I am liking our fellowship today, but we doing more shipping than praying." Everyone laughed with him. Then Kennedy's heart sank to her feet when the door burst open.

It was Yolanda.

How she longed to hug her best friend and reveal to her what was going on. She missed her dearly, but somehow she just couldn't get the courage to call her and set things straight. She had been praying since their fight at the spa for the right time to approach her. Kennedy silently prayed today would be the day of reconciliation.

Yolanda caught her eye and offered a gentle smile. Kennedy's heart jumped. Though her mouth was smiling, her eyes looked puffy, as if she had been shedding many tears and hadn't slept in days. Kennedy pushed back the empty seat next to her and tilted her head toward it. Yolanda took a deep breath and walked around the table to sit next to Kennedy.

Before Kennedy could at least say hello, the jovial mood in the room shifted when Pastor Griffin loudly cleared his throat. "Minister Howard, how nice of you to grace us with your presence, even though you are close to an hour late. I pay my ministers nicely to attend **on time** to church business when called."

The room was silent. Yolanda dropped her head. "I'm so sorry everyone. I started an early prayer meeting at my house. My...my daughter is not well."

Hushed murmuring went throughout the room. Kennedy stood. "Pastor Griffin, if you don't mind, I'd like to go pray with Minister Howard privately."

"Uh, no!" Monica Caine stood, looking ready to throw down. "If we prayin', we prayin' together. There's no secret prayer chains up in this house. Y'all ain't even been talking so how *you* gonna take her aside like there's something going on that we don't need to know."

"You know what? I am sick of you being a holy rollin' bully! You of all people talking about secrets and you can't keep your house in order." Kennedy didn't mean to go there and knew she had opened a can of worms.

"What you mean I can't handle my house?" Monica's chest heaved like she was ready to fight.

"Ladies, this is not the place nor the time for this! While I agree with you, Minister Caine, this is the place for openness. It's not a place for strife and personal attack." He stared pointedly at Monica. Without taking her eyes off Kennedy, she slowly took her seat. *That's why your man can't bear to sleep with you. Probably got a brother so scared he can't even perform.*

Pastor Griffin continued, "I must say, Minister Howard, you come in late. Looking a hot mess, saying your daughter isn't well. I am a little concerned about your household."

185

"It's that old trifling husband of hers," Elder Whitmore lamented. "I ain't one for divorce but if I were, that fella sho' nuff would have his single card back. No offense, sister, but you got yo'self a doozy when you chose him."

"She said it was her daughter, knucklehead." Minister Leems retorted, much to everyone's surprise.

"Knucklehead? Let me take my teeth out and take off my hair," Elder Whitmore said angrily, "I will show you a knucklehead." He picked up his cane to wave in the air, lost his balance and fell over backward.

It was dead silent in the room. Eddie ran over to help him back up, while everyone else tried to contain their laughter. When he got back to his seat, Elder Whitmore lowered his head and said no more. After he regrouped, Pastor Griffin continued. "I want us to act like we love each other with the love of the Lord. We fighting a spiritual warfare, not each other." He looked at Kennedy, Yolanda and turned his hardest glance to Monica.

"Why you eyeballing me? It was all good till ya girl showed up all late." Monica ranted.

Pastor Griffin then turned to Yolanda. "She's right, Minister. You mentioned prayer for your daughter. Let's talk and have some transparency."

Yolanda sighed and Kennedy reached out to hold her hand. Yolanda looked at her and smiled though her eyes were filled with tears. "As you know, my daughter was raised by her grandmother. And...and...there's some tension. She's wanting to...date and all...just been some conflict."

186

Everyone knew there was more to the story, seeing how upset she was. However, no one pressed her for details. Even Monica felt sorry for her. She didn't have a child of her own but could imagine the pain of not raising your child and then the guilt it could carry.

Eddie spoke up. "Minister Howard, you have been a blessing to me and my family in so many ways," his voice heavy with sympathy. "There's nothing like having family. And we will pray for restoration and peace."

"Thank you," Yolanda said softly.

To everyone's shock, Monica burst into tears. No one had ever seen the woman sad much less cry. Kennedy secretly called her the Tin Man because she didn't think she had a heart to even feel. Normally, Kennedy would enjoy seeing her in pain, but something about this hard harsh cry, made her heart melt.

"What's wrong with you?" Pastor Griffin said with astonishment in his voice. "I mean...that didn't come out right."

"I know." Monica sniffled, reached for the Kleenex and then dabbed her eyes. "I know I come across rough like nothing ever bothers me. And I give folks a hard time but...hearing Minister Howard talk about her daughter just...just...really got to me." Monica sobbed hard again.

"You don't even like kids. In fact, I didn't even think you liked your husband." Pastor Griffin's wife, Candace, spoke up. Everyone turned to look at her. She was a woman of quiet strength who wasn't seen except on Sunday. For her to make this remark quieted everyone down, even Monica.

"I don't like my husband because...he can't give me kids."

Kennedy thought she would pass out. She had to pregnant by Marcus.

187

Eddie confessed to a vasectomy so how could Monica's husband not be the father of her unborn child? Kennedy tried to maintain her composure but she was reeling on the inside as she prayed for an answer.

The answer came next.

"For years, I struggled with being able to get pregnant. We always assumed it was me due to scar tissue from previous issues."

"You mean those abortions?"

Everyone jerked their heads toward the first lady. She had an edge to her voice that was unlike her usually sweet demeanor. Even Monica was taken aback. Pastor Griffin looked uncomfortable. But for some reason, he didn't correct his wife. Eddie, Yolanda and Kennedy found the whole scene odd. They knew there was a back story.

"Excuse me?" Monica tears suddenly dried up. The gangster-girl attitude returned.

"You heard me. You walk around here attacking people for their home lives and let's be clear, you have some skeletons, too." Candace stood up, her five-foot frame looking unintimidated by Monica's or her street reputation.

"I am so sick of these women who lash out at others while they are guilty of some of the same things." Candace glared at Monica, as her husband touched her arm. She shot a look to Pastor Griffin that caused him to let go and sit down. "While I feel for you, I don't feel you. You are so disrespectful to other women and their issues. Yet now, because you finally start to confess, you want us to help dry your tears. Now, dear, I apologize for putting you out there, but I refuse to let you draw us into

188

feeling sorry for you when you aren't sorry for things you've done to people in this room." Candace sat back down.

It was so quiet you could hear a pin drop.

"And another thing, you all give Minister Howard such a hard time. But at least she *owns* her past and presses through it. Whatever her husband does don't got nothing to do with any of you." She abruptly turned to Yolanda. "Honey, whatever you need, God has got your answer. It may not be what or how you think it should have been, but He's got you." She turned back to Monica. "Now, what's your story?"

"Well, after your little showdown, I'm not in the mood to tell it." Monica snapped.

"Sister," Eddie began, "you can't keep holding it in. Just spit it out. Candace, I mean, First Lady has already put you out there."

Monica rolled her eyes. "You know, I had a moment I should've kept to myself. In case you actually care, I can't have kids. Wish I could, but I can't and yes it makes me miserable." She looked pointedly at their first lady. "I made some mistakes in the past and had two abortions. Now excuse me." Monica pushed back from the table and stormed from the room.

Kennedy didn't know what to feel. On one hand, she thought Monica may have been reaping what she had sown. On the other, she knew she had something Monica wanted – a child.

A child by Monica's husband.

Before she could process what to do, Eddie jumped up. "You know the devil is always busy." Everyone murmured in agreement. "Minister Howard needs prayer for her family. Sister Caine needs prayer to deal with her pain of not having kids. In the midst of the need for prayer, can I give a praise report?" Kennedy thought to herself, *Oh no! He's about to tell it.*

"I am about to be a daddy."

Everyone applauded. Kennedy managed to smile, although she felt as if she were going to faint. Even Yolanda reached over to hug her, the first she had given her in months. As her friend embraced her, she whispered, "We need to talk." Yolanda pulled back and nodded, a sad look on her face.

Kennedy wanted to know what was going on with her best friend, but she had another concern. She wondered how long she and Eddie could proclaim to have a child who was not his.

✟✟✟

When Kennedy went to the restroom, Yolanda followed. It had been so long since they had talked to one another. Kennedy missed her. The two found the minister's bathroom near the pastor's office, and locked the door. When the door clicked shut, they immediately hugged one another.

Yolanda pulled herself back and said, "Girl, I already look a hot mess as pastor said. Now, I'm snotty and blubbering like a little girl." She wiped her arm with her sleeve. "I'm so sorry I didn't reach out to you, Ken Doll."

Kennedy smiled. "Ken Doll? You haven't called me that since college and back then it was usually when you were drunk and needed a ride or bail money." They both laughed, hugging each other again. "I've really missed you, Yo. I needed you so bad. And I'm so sorry when you called

190

me out on the carpet for my sin, I didn't want to receive anything you had to say."

Yolanda leaned back against the wall. "Yeah, but we actually threw blows. I never thought we'd fight each other." She paused. "I didn't think we'd ever talk again. It scared me. I was too mad and stubborn to make amends."

Kennedy sat on the marble counter and leaned her back on the mirror. "True, but so much has happened, I don't know where to begin." Kennedy pondered coming clean about her pregnancy but decided to wait and deflect the attention. "What's going on with my play daughter now?"

"Girl, you can have that heifer." Yolanda rolled her eyes in exasperation.

Yolanda hopped up beside Kennedy. "We met with Terrence. He's actually a changed man. God has done a work in him. He is in his Word, working for his family business, has a good home. This man is...incredible."

Kennedy's mouth dropped. "You mean *that* Terrence? Hold up!" Kennedy hopped off the counter and moved directly in front of Yolanda. "Okay, so dude who pretty much was like...I won't say rape...but...bought you, then goes to jail on a racketeering and drug charge is suddenly 'incredible'? Girl, please!"

"Trust me, I know it sounds crazy. But honestly, he repented. Wanted to meet Noel and stop lying." Yolanda told Kennedy everything from the first letter to the incident at the restaurant up until just hours ago. By the time she finished, she was back crying over Noel cutting her off.

"Yolanda, I know she said she doesn't want him to be her father. She's hurt you and Michael lied. I just think you need to give her time."

191

"Well, I get that. But I come home and find a letter telling me what a liar and hypocrite I am. And then she says she is going to stay with this church youth pastor or whatever he calls himself and his family." Yolanda stopped to wipe her eyes. "She said she wants me to sign over parental rights to my mama or let her live with Daryl and his family."

"Do you even know his family? They live in Detroit, don't they?"

"No, I thought they were all here." Yolanda's heart beat so fast she thought she was going to pass out.

Kennedy didn't want to get Yolanda worried, but she knew she needed to tell her who Daryl really was. She had no idea Noel had become involved with him. If she had, she definitely would have intervened. Although Kennedy had her own issues to worry about, she knew Yolanda deserved to know her daughter could be in possible danger.

"I'm not trying to scare you," she said slowly and carefully. "Minister Daryl wasn't always a minister."

"I know. Neither was I." Yolanda tried to laugh to cover her nervousness and the fear creeping through her insides.

"No listen," Kennedy said firmly. "I only know this because of Eddie's position on the board. I know God can change anybody. And I pray Daryl is one. But he...his family--"

"What? Just spit it out!" Yolanda's voice rose in volume and anxiety.

"They had one of the largest underground prostitution rings in Detroit. Though Sister Boyd seems very well put together, there are rumors Daryl's uncle is still in the business."

Yolanda's heart dropped to her feet. "You don't think he would...try to exploit my daughter do you?"

Kennedy sighed. "I hope not. If I were you, I'd get her home or to Sable's to be safe." While she was happy they were talking, she feared for Noel and hurt for Yolanda. Though she avoided explaining her own plight, this didn't lift her mood or make her feel better. She could see Yolanda crumble on the inside. She immediately grabbed her and pulled her close and prayed.

"Amen." Yolanda was glad she had the person who knew her best, besides God himself, back in her life. She clung to Kennedy tightly and then remembered. "Oh yes! I'm so happy I'm going to be an auntie! Took y'all long enough." Yolanda burst out laughing until she saw a look in Kennedy's eyes. She could not describe it, but it was not one of cheer as most expectant mothers have. "What's wrong, Ken?"

Now it was Kennedy's turn to come clean. "Girl. This baby is mine."

"Duh! It's in you. You the mother."

"Yes, I am the mother. But Eddie...can't be the father. Remember his first child was stillborn and the mother died from HIV complications?"

"Yes, but what's that have to do with anything? Eddie was cleared of HIV."

"He had a vasectomy."

Now Yolanda was confused and shocked. Her best friend was pregnant. Her husband had a vasectomy. That only meant one thing. "It's from your affair?"

193

Kennedy nodded slowly, a single tear rolled down her cheek. "I did step out on Eddie with this...this guy Marcus." She took a deep breath. "It's his baby."

"Does he know?"

"No."

Yolanda grabbed both of her hands and held them while Kennedy allowed her bottled up emotions to flow freely through her tears.

"Eddie acted so happy. He had to forgive you. That's good."

"Eddie and I are going to raise the baby as our own."

"Don't get caught up in deceit," Yolanda warned. "You see what's going on in my life? Shoot, my lies are how I got in this mess."

"It's not that easy," Kennedy said defiantly. "You know Eddie's pride and not wanting to be embarrassed."

"True. But what's worse, his ego being hurt or a child not knowing the truth about their bloodline? Look at my life, Kennedy. I beg you, don't do this to your child."

Yolanda paused. "Does Eddie know it is Marcus' baby?"

"Girl, he hasn't even asked what his name is, okay?" Kennedy snorted.

"My husband's ego is so big he doesn't want to know nothing about nothing. He just playing along."

"Yeah, that's all good for now, but what's going to happen down the

line? And is it fair for Marcus to not know he has a child?"
"Yes when the stepmother would be Monica."

Yolanda knew she couldn't have possibly heard right. Her eyes widened with surprise and horror at the thought of Kennedy carrying the baby Monica always wanted but could not have.

"Let me make sure I got this straight. Marcus belongs to Monica?" Kennedy nodded. "Of all the men you could have found, why in the world did you choose her man?" Yolanda asked incredulously. "She is liable to bust a cap in your behind over this if she finds out!"

"You think I don't know?" Kennedy asked with irritation in her voice. "I had no idea he was her husband or I would have gone home, popped out my triple A's and used BOB."

"Bob? Another brother?"

"No, dimwit. Battery Operated Boyfriend. A 'marital aid' to put it nicely." She paused. "He used a different last name. I'd never met Monica's husband. *No* one ever saw him! I got myself in a pickle."

"So, out of curiosity, how did you feel when she cried about not being able to have kids?"

"I felt...guilty. I have something she wants by her man." Kennedy wiped her eyes "It's the most awful feeling ever. She's evil but even she doesn't deserve this."

"Well, you prayed for me so I need to pray for you."

After she prayed, Kennedy kissed Yolanda on the cheek. "Thanks for praying for me." They embraced again. Both were scared for what their futures held, but they were glad to be pressing past their past and into freedom from it.

They washed their faces and headed out of the bathroom. They made sure they had all of their belongings together before leaving.

If only they had checked the shower stall before they started talking. They would have known they weren't sharing between the two of them. A third party with a stake in it all had heard everything they'd shared.

Chapter Eighteen

Noel leaned back on the passenger side, as Daryl headed on I-70. They were going to Springfield to pick up one of his college buddies. She noticed the gas hand was getting pretty low. "Babe," she said over the loud music. "You may wanna pull over at Quick Trip before you run out of gas."

Daryl looked at the gas hand and noticed he had just under a quarter of a tank. "Oh snap!" he exclaimed then looked at her and said, "See that's why I need my sweet baby girl with me. You always got my back." He rubbed her knee, making a chill go up her spine.

It wasn't that she intended to become intimate with Daryl. Noel couldn't resist him. Pretty soon, kissing led to heavy touching. Then marathon make out sessions. Until one day, they took it all the way. He'd been a little hesitant, but once their relationship went in that direction, there was no turning back. Sex with Daryl was totally different than her first encounter at fourteen. He made her body feel things she didn't know she was capable of experiencing. He did things to her she had only read about and thought of as "nasty", until he performed them on her. Even though they were a few years apart, she believed they were made for one another. When she told him she didn't want to go back home, he offered her a place to stay. But she hadn't seen it yet.

In fact, they never went to his house. They usually went to a hotel or to one of his homeboy's spots. She didn't think much of it until now.

"Did your aunt say it was okay for me to stay for a while? We talked about it, but I still need to take my stuff over there."

197

Daryl suddenly seemed agitated. "Don't worry about it. I'll talk to her. She's been in and out of town. We'll go over there when we get back."

"Maybe I should call my mother. I left her a letter and told her my plans. I'm pissed off at her, but I don't want her to worry."

Daryl rolled his eyes and grunted. "She'll be all right. We'll talk to her when we talk to her. Besides, she hasn't been worried about you. How she gonna lie about your pops and expect you just to be all happy?"

Noel got nervous. She'd never seen this side of Daryl before. Ever since she packed her Pink bag with clothes and left, he seemed to have a mean edge. Easily irritated. Bossy. Talking sharply at her. It was nothing like the loving, tender, soft-spoken Daryl she'd seen before.

Noel's discernment antenna peaked. Thinking back over the last couple of months, there were times he was distant, even secretive. Now when he got a call or a text, he'd walk off instead of responding in front of her. She thought back to a Saturday when they were supposed to go to dinner and he stood her up. He didn't call her back, and offered a half-hearted apology when he saw her at church the next day. In fact, he'd been absent from the past few Wednesdays when the youth ministry had mid-week study. Noel wasn't sure what was going on but was uneasy for the first time in his presence. Something seemed off-kilter. She hoped everything was okay between them.

"Are you mad at me?" She asked meekly. "You seem like you been irritated with me since we left."

"Naw, I ain't mad," he snarled. "I just want you to shut up and sit back. We got work to do and I just don't want to play black Dr. Phil talking out your problems." He turned and glanced at her. "Lay back and nap."

198

Then he pushed her back into the seat.

Noel stiffened in fear. As mad as she was at her mother, she'd rather be home than where she was right now. *But, Daryl loves me. Maybe he's just tired.*

They pulled into the parking lot of the gas station. He shut off the car. "I'm going to pay for the gas and grab us some sodas. Just chill till I get back." He didn't look at her as he slammed the door and headed inside.

Noel sneezed and realized she didn't have tissue in her purse. She opened the glove compartment to get something to wipe her nose. Inside was a small handgun in there, along with a small bag of marijuana and his license.

It seems Daryl was more than a twenty-year-old youth minister.

He was actually twenty-three.

Noel always liked older boys. And it was only three years, but the fact that he lied made her wonder what else he could be hiding. Before he returned, she closed the glove compartment and prayed for God to see her home safely. She wanted to run but didn't know where she could go.

A Bible verse popped into her spirit, *if I go to the heavens you are there; if I make my bed in hell you are there; even if I go to the uttermost parts of the sea, even then your hand shall guide me.*

Noel knew for the first time in her life, she needed God to get her out of the mess she'd created.

She tried to gain her composure as Daryl sauntered back to the car. He slammed the door and tossed a 16-ounce bottle of soda at her. "All right, let's get back on the road." He started the car and abruptly squealed out of the lot. When they headed back on the highway, Noel's fear escalated.

"Hey...do...do you think we'll make it back for church tomorrow?"

He looked at her as if she'd lost her mind. He chuckled then threw a sideways glance her way. "I doubt it. Pastor Griffin knows I am outie tomorrow. We'll take care of business then get back when we get back."

"Business?" Noel said with a little more force in her voice than she intended. "I thought we were going to a college party, pick up your friend and head back."

"Hold up! Don't get all buck with me. Who you talkin' to? I know what I *said* and we will do what I *say*. You better sit yo' fast tail back and relax. Here..." he dug around in his console and pulled out a joint. "Smoke this and sit back."

Noel's fear turned into anger. She wasn't a perfect church girl but she didn't like being lied to either. All her life people lied to her. Now someone she thought had her back and her best interest at heart was taking advantage of her. She couldn't take it.

"No. I don't do drugs. I know what drugs did to my mother and that's the one thing I say no to."

"Please. Now, I dig your mama. She's from the streets but now a saint. When I wife somebody up, that's what I need. Don't get it twisted, though. Your mama used to be a straight up 'ho. She used to get turned up but look at her now." Daryl rolled his eyes and took a lighter out of his pocket to light up the joint. He took a long drag. "You actin' like some weed is gonna have you in rehab tomorrow." He laughed at his

200

own joke.

Noel was not amused. "I don't care what my mama used to be. At least she is living her life for real. That's more than I can say for you Mr. Pretend youth pastor wanna be gangster who has to lie about how old he is." Noel didn't mean to let all that out but once he disrespected her mother, he'd crossed the line.

Noel felt a stinging pain across her mouth. It took her by surprise. She froze as blood oozed from her bottom lip. "Did you just hit me?" Noel cried. She hit him on the shoulder. The car swerved and barely missed a guardrail. She pulled on the door handle, willing to roll out of the car onto the highway, but Daryl pushed the lock button down to block her escape. He managed to get the car back into the lane, and then veered off the next exit ramp.

When they came to the end of the ramp, he grabbed Noel by her shoulders and held her so tight she yelped in pain. Daryl leaned in and whispered, "I didn't mean to hit you. You made me snap."

"You made me snap disrespecting my mother like that. And why did you lie to me about your age?" His grip remained tight around her shoulders, but he didn't respond. Noel went on, "How could you be a youth pastor and live a total lie? Take me home."

He pulled back and stared at her before a slow wicked grin came across his face. "You know, you right. I should have told you my real age. I figured it was better to shave off a few years. That's all. I'll take you home. After we get done."

"Get done? With what?"

"Look, I got to take care of some business. Sorry I lied about my age. What can I say? I don't mind a younger woman. Besides, what's an extra three, three and a half years?"

Noel's fear gave way to anger about being lied to. "When we get back home, just leave me alone." She sat back and held her mouth, which was now swelling up.

"Okay…have it your way. I was going to give you a life you never had." He had the audacity to shake his head, as if he couldn't believe she was turning away an opportunity of a lifetime.

"Oh please," Noel responded, as he got back on the highway. "I have a good life. I just didn't know it until now. How will the pastor feel when he finds out you're a liar?"

Daryl laughed. "He knows everything about me, just like I know about him. Did you forget? We blood. That's my fam. There's nothing you can tell him that'll shock him. He got enough to worry about, between his old mess coming back to haunt him and a stripper for a niece that's pregnant by a minister's… Just know this is the least of his concerns. Besides, it's your word against mine."

"So you think he'll be okay with the fact that you've been screwing a teen who happens the daughter of one of his employee's?" Noel snapped at him.

Daryl laughed. "Like I said, it's your word against mine. Do you know how many teen girls be crushin' on me?" He laughed even harder. "He'll think you're just lying because I have taken you out as a *mentor and minister* but rejected your advances." He thought about something. "I know we got caught making out at that restaurant but I can say you came on to me. You can't outthink me, baby girl."

Turning her body away from him, Noel stared out the window.

Soon, they arrived at a small bungalow. This was not the college dorm Noel expected.

"I thought we were going to a college party and pick up your homeboy." Her heart thumped faster, hoping the party wasn't here.

"We're at the party. I need to make some quick money before we head back. Although, I'd make more if your lip wasn't busted. Get out the car." Noel sat there, frozen. She heard loud music coming from the small house. Red lights glared out the window. There were a few houses on the block, apparently oblivious to the "party" taking place.

"You got a few seconds to get out that car or you gon' be sorry." Daryl had a loud rough edge to his voice that shocked her even after learning he was not who he said he was. Noel knew she was screwed either way. If she tried to resist, there was no telling what he would do. If she went in the house, there was no telling what would happen.

She recalled her earlier prayer and trusted God to get her out her mess. She didn't want to repeat the sins of her mother. Her heavenly Father had to come in.

And if He didn't, Noel was ready to walk away. From it all.

Pressing Past the Past

Chapter Nineteen

Kennedy was resting when her phone interrupted her thoughts.

She got out of the tub and looked at the caller ID.

It was Marcus. How did he get her home number? Kennedy panicked and debated whether or not she should answer but finally did.

"Hello?" Kennedy said with agitation in her voice.

"Kennedy...I hadn't planned on calling you again," Marcus began without even so much as a hello. I need to see you. For real."

"It's over. I confessed to my husband. He forgave me. We're moving on. So there's no need for us to talk."

"Yes, there is. We have some unfinished business to handle."

"No, we do not."

"No, Kennedy...I think we do. I need to know if you are carrying my child."

Kennedy froze. She almost dropped the phone. Even though Yolanda was the only one who knew she was pregnant by Marcus, for him to even question it caused her to reel over.

"Kennedy, is it even a chance you could be pregnant by me?"

Kennedy gulped. "No, actually it isn't. My husband and I reconciled, re-consummated our marriage and bam, I got pregnant." She tried to force a cheerful laugh but Marcus wasn't fooled.

"So if I legally obtained a DNA test, it would come back with no probability I'd be the father?"

"Marcus, where is this coming from?" Kennedy tried to mask her fear with anger.

"Let's just say the next time you decide to confess something, make sure no one else is around. My source tells me you had my name all up in your mouth recently. A couple of months ago I was all up in you so I have reason to believe you're pregnant with my child."

Kennedy was scared she was going to faint. She thought back to her conversation with Yolanda but couldn't figure out who the culprit could be. It couldn't have been Monica because she would have promptly called her out and beat her tail.

As if he'd read her mind, "And no, it wasn't Monica who heard. Things would've gone a whole different direction, trust."

"Well, your source must have been confused. Maybe they're just starting stuff because I didn't say that."

"But you did." An all too familiar female voice chimed in.

Her own mother-in-law.

"I always knew you was a ho. When I first had you tailed, I couldn't figure out who you were creepin' with," Mother Stone snarled. "Then when Eddie told me you were pregnant, I had my doubts. Oh, but God is able! Hallelujah! When you took your little tail to the bathroom after the prayer meeting, I stayed in my shower stall just to hear what was happening and I done caught ya!"

"Look here, you old wench. How about your *son, my husband* knows it's not his because he had a vasectomy years ago? How about that?"

"How about I ain't accepting no bastard grandbaby?"

"Hold up, Mother Stone," Marcus said. "Now you going too far."

"And why do you care about Marcus? In fact, why are we even having this three-way call like we in junior high? It's not like you know each other."

They were silent. "What? You all can't say nothing?"

"Kennedy...she set you up."

"I met you through an ad in a newspaper. How could she set me up?"

"I hadn't planned to hook up with you again. It was to be a one-time hit it and quit it. She was hoping Eddie would catch us and divorce you." He paused. "She followed me after one of our hook ups and...well. Now you know. She made me a deal I couldn't resist. I dig you, but I also dig some dividends."

Kennedy was crushed. She thought of how low it was for Eddie's mother to take measures that far.

"Oh, my son gets whipped so easily. Got it from his pappy, I guess."

207

Mother Stone sighed. "I'm down but I'm not out. This ain't over so don't get too comfy you hear me?"

"What type of woman of God sets up her son's wife for failure?" Kennedy retorted with venom in her voice. "You are a spawn from hell. I'd beat your a--"

"Oh, wait a second now!" Mother Stone hollered into the phone. "You questioning my godliness? I will do anything to protect my sons. Just like Jacob's mama in the Bible, if it means pulling a trick, oh well. I hate y'all pretty women who think just because you don't look like me you better than me." She stopped, her voice breaking. "You steal people's husbands. You break up happy homes. You use your feminine wiles to destroy lives. You killed my marriage. I'll be doggone if I'm gonna stand by and watch you kill my son by breaking his heart."

Kennedy was in shock. This woman had truly lost her mind. Yes, Eddie's father was a rolling stone but why was she blaming her – her son's wife? "Mother Stone, I hate what Eddie's father did to you. But why are you referring to me?"

"Because he left me for a woman just like you." she spat out with fury in her voice. "The ultra-sexy pretty Jezebel chick. I knew Eddie's daddy was unpleased with me. So when the double D bandit came along, my marriage was over. Do you hear me? And when Eddie brought you home...you just like *her*."

"I am not her! You hate me because I remind you of what you're not and why your husband left? When you spouting all these Bible verses at folk you need to repent and read them yourself!"

"Ladies," Marcus tried to intervene, "Let's not do this, okay? Kennedy, you are beautiful and I did have feelings for you. Yes, it was wrong for me to receive payment to set you up. However, it's just as wrong if you keep my baby from me."

"So you plan to tell your gangster wife and then what?"

"Whatever happens happens. I want my child."

"I would never let your crazy wife near any baby that comes from me."

"Too bad. If it's mine, I will fight for custody. Monica will have to deal with it."

Kennedy could not believe what she was hearing. And would Eddie believe his own mother set her up? These thoughts raced through her mind when she heard a click. She thought they'd hung up. She pressed "End Call" and slipped back in the tub, her head spinning on what to do next. She was devastated- both Marcus and Mother Stone betrayed her. But Kennedy was convicted. She couldn't blame them solely for she had betrayed her God. She actually felt sorry for Mother Stone. She was so bitter over lost love that she'd turned into a vile, miserable person.

Kennedy heard the garage door. Eddie was home. She figured she'd tell him what happened. After all, surely his mother would if she didn't. She silently prayed for courage and recalled Christ saying how the truth would make one free. Yes, He was truth and Kennedy knew the only way to resolve this was to go forward in truth. No more lies.

Eddie came into the bathroom, looking refreshed as he often did after a golf outing. "Hey, sexy pregnant lady." He came to the edge of the Jacuzzi tub and sat down. He noticed Kennedy had been crying. "Baby, what's wrong?"

She sighed and tearfully told him the conversation she had with Marcus and his mother. Throughout it, his face showed no emotion. In fact, he barely blinked. Kennedy was in full fledge sobs by the time she finished.

Eddie was silent. Then he stood up. "I can't live like this anymore."

Kennedy's heart sank. She was about to be a divorcee.

"Let's just take the DNA test to shut him up, then go forward. I can't live in deceit. Nor will I be blackmailed by him or my own mama. For years, she made me feel guilty for my daddy's recklessness. She has tried to run my life, disrespected you and even caused you to further sin." Eddie shook his head. "My mama needs prayer. And to get out of our business." He paced back and forth. "I am committed to God and my marriage. That's it. After this is straightened out, I don't know how we'll handle it, but it won't be this foolishness." He walked over to Kennedy, bent down and kissed her on her forehead. "Get out of the tub so we can eat."

He turned and walked out the room.

Kennedy was elated. She knew God had done a work in her and her husband. He was going to stand by her. Stick up for her. And finally choose her.

Even over his mother.

Kennedy prayed a prayer of gratitude and asked God to give them more miracles in their marriage. She believed with Him all things were possible.

Chapter Twenty

Yolanda headed to the bank before going home. It had been two days since she heard from Noel. She filed a police report for her being a runaway and had been fasting and praying for her to safely return home. In the meantime, she was even more confused about Michael.

He too had been missing.

His cell phone was off and when Yolanda tried to go online to check the records, the password to his account had been changed. To make matters worse, most of his clothing was gone. When she went on the work sites, none of his workers had seen him or so they said. She knew he was upset over her reconciliation with Terrence but she didn't think he'd just vanish.

Yolanda pulled up at the bank ATM machine and put in her pin. What she saw made her head spin.

Zero balance.

She knew there had to be a minimum of six thousand dollars in their main checking account. Her heart beat fast and hard, as Yolanda feared what happened to their bank account. She found a parking spot and went in to the teller she knew well.

"Hey there, Minister Howard." Janice spoke cheerfully. "How can I help you this Saturday morning?"

"Janice, there must be a mistake. I tried to withdraw some money but it said zero. You know we keep our main account pretty full."

"Yeah, I know," Janice said looking concerned. "Let's see. Oh." She paused. "You had three accounts with your husband – business, personal and then your money market?"

"Yes, Janice. What do you see?"

"When did you decide to sign a signature card and take your name off the personal account?"

"I didn't." Yolanda felt dizzy. Her body broke out in a cold sweat.

"Somehow, it looks like Michael took your name off of the accounts. Then, he made a ten- thousand-dollar withdrawal from your personal one, and your money market has...two hundred dollars."

Michael had withdrawn two hundred, fifty thousand dollars?
"Minister Howard, if you believe you are the victim of fraud, legally you have a right to pursue action. Even if he is your husband. He is still your husband...right?"

"I don't know, Janice. I don't know."

"It happened on Wednesday when I wasn't here. I am going to have our manager look over the tape to see when he did this transaction and get the signature cards to see how he got your name off." Janice reached over to touch Yolanda's hand. "Have a seat. I want to help you, woman of God." Yolanda smiled weakly and made her way to the sofa.

Her phone vibrated. She looked to see Terrence's name on the caller ID.

212

"Hello?"

"Hey, I just got a call from the police station. Noel is there. Thank God she's ok." Terrence said excitedly. "You want me to come get you?"

"I'm at the bank right now. Why don't you grab Sable and I'll meet you?" She was grateful her daughter was okay but was so confused at what was happening.

"What's wrong? I can hear it in your voice."

"Michael managed to take my name off our bank account and took over two hundred thousand dollars. His phone is off. No one has seen him at the work sites. I don't know what's going on." Like Job, what Yolanda always feared had come upon her.

Her husband had robbed and left her.

"Yolanda, I'm sorry to hear that. If I can help in anyway, please let me know. You handle your business and we'll get to the bottom of what happened with Noel. I got some words for Minister Daryl anyway. I'm 'bout to lay hands on that fool."

Yolanda forced a laugh. "Thanks, Terrence. I'll meet you at the police station as soon as I can." She hung up the phone and said a prayer of thanks that her daughter was back. Now she needed to see if her husband was coming back.

Janice and the manager walked over to her. "Minister Howard, this is Cary Brown, our branch manager. Can you come with us?" The manager had a grim look on his face. His brows furrowed in concern. Yolanda detected nervousness.

They went into a back office and sat at a round table. "First of all, let me apologize," Cary solemnly stated. "A new girl was working and failed to follow proper procedure to verify identification. Looking at this video, obviously this woman is not you."

Woman? Yolanda's heart felt as if it dropped to her feet. They replayed the video from earlier in the week of Michael coming in and indeed a woman was with him. Yolanda looked closer and what she saw almost made her faint. He was with a pregnant woman, someone who looked eerily familiar.

"Can you zoom in closer to her face?" Yolanda asked.

Carey complied. Yolanda gasped aloud, causing Janice and Cary to sit up straighter. "Do you recognize who was with him?"

"Yes. A young woman I ministered to recently. So, did she sign my name?" Janice looked pointedly at Cary. He sighed and said, "We do apologize and will comply with every pursuit to make sure the parties involved are prosecuted and our employee promptly dismissed for carelessness."

"Thank you. Now, my other account..."

Janice smiled widely. "It's all good." For years, Yolanda kept a personal account. She didn't intentionally hide it from Michael; she simply thought it would be wise to keep it to herself. Now she was relieved she made that decision.

But her heart was broken. The same woman she ministered to at Eddie's party was apparently in cahoots with her husband. She should have known by how uncomfortable he was when she introduced them. Then it dawned on her.

214

Could he be the man she spoke of – the married father of her child?

"Mrs. Howard, how do you want to proceed?" Janice asked again, her voice filled with concern. It seemed Yolanda had checked out.

"I'll be in touch. Do what you can on your end. I have an emergency to attend to."

Cary and Janice nodded. "Once again, I do apologize for the negligence of our employee." Cary reached out to shake Yolanda's hand before she turned and headed toward her car.

As she walked back to her car, a sharp pain exploded across her chest. Yolanda felt nauseous and assumed it was her nerves. She stood still until the pain eased up some. Then she hopped in her car and headed to the police station to meet Terrence.

Instead, she found herself headed to Michael's office. She'd done drive-bys for days and had yet to see his car. Finally, his black Lexus was there. Yolanda saw Michael step out of the office with files in tow and Chantal by his side.

She floored the gas. Michael saw the SUV coming, shoved Chantal back inside and jumped back, his eyes wide in fear. When Yolanda did a U-turn in the lot, she heard the Holy Spirit whisper Ephesians 4:26, *be ye angry and sin not.* She slammed on her brakes and put her head on the steering wheel, sobbing. So many emotions: anger, hurt, sadness and even relief.

Though she didn't want to face the repercussions of a very public divorce, she knew from the time she accepted her call, Michael was not

215

the one. She always believed he married her out of guilt and would never love her the way she needed. He could never be her spiritual covering and he didn't want to be. Still, the way their marriage was ending was not what she wanted.

Yolanda was startled out of her thoughts as Chantal actually beat on her window and dropped some "f" bombs, calling her every name but a woman of God. Yolanda was relieved she was pregnant because she would have laid down her anointing to beat the mess out that little girl.

"Don't you see I'm pregnant?" Chantal screamed hysterically. Michael was still too dumbstruck to move. "You better hope I don't file attempted murder charges against you. Aren't you supposed to be a preacher, you fake prophetess?"

That was it. One way to hit a nerve with Yolanda was to question her call. She opened her door. It slammed into Chantal's protruding belly. Though Yolanda didn't want to hurt an innocent baby, she found her hands around Chantal's neck. She didn't choke her, but grabbed her hard enough around that her eyes widened in fear. Chantal realized Yolanda was not playing with her.

"You can try and claim attempted murder," Yolanda whispered with pure fury and venom in her voice. "But I got you on tape forging my signature. So if you're pressing charges, both of us will be in a cell. Although me trying to hit *my husband* with a car is your word against mine."

"He…it…was…his idea." Chantal whispered. She was barely able to breathe due to Yolanda's grip around her neck. Yolanda, convicted, released her hold.

"If it was his idea to steal my money, whose idea was it to get

216

pregnant?" She didn't even want to look at Michael. He was too much of a punk to even say anything to her. It reminded her of the night she was traded. He wasn't a man then and even less of one now. Though Yolanda wanted to confront him, she felt a surge of power come over her. She could have said so much. She wanted to punch him. Tell him how he hurt her. Still, it wouldn't change a thing.

"So, Michael, you're going to be a daddy for real, huh?"

"Look, Yo..." Michael's voice quivered. "I never meant for this to happen. I just couldn't take being your husband. I married you out of guilt. Truth is...I love you but I was never in love with you. And yes...Chantal is the mother of my son."

"I'm sorry I emptied the accounts and all. I was trippin'. I didn't know how to come to you and just settle this." He started to walk over to her and Chantal. Chantal smiled smugly as he draped his arm around her shoulder. "I'm happy. I'll finally be a real father."

"You may be a real father but you still aren't a real man. And congrats on the baby...if it's yours."

"What you mean "if"? Chantal snapped. "Just because I'm a dancer don't mean I sleep with every Tom, Dick and Harry."

Yolanda laughed bitterly and looked at Michael. "So the church folk were right. A stripper? You didn't even cheat up."

"You betta be glad I'm pregnant." Chantal said with a ghetto twang now in her tone. "Them fighting words."

"Sweetheart, you better be glad you pregnant and I'm saved." Yolanda looked at both of them with pity. She toyed with the fact that Chantal could be lying to Michael about him being her child's father. She pondered if he ever really gave his life to Christ. But all that was not her problem anymore. Though her heart was crushed, she was glad his deeds done in the dark were now coming to light. She turned to get back into her SUV. Before opening the door, she turned around. "Get my money back or catch a case."

"Wait a minute," Michael said with an attitude in his voice. "Some of that is my money too."

"According to the records, only $45,569.97 is yours. The fact is, you committed forgery which is punishable by imprisonment if I file charges against you and your baby mama." She felt another pang in her chest but attributed it to the stress of this situation. "I will have my attorney send a letter to you since your phone is off. Let's wrap up our divorce quickly. I need to move forward."

"Wait!" Suddenly Michael's smug look turned to one of concern. "What about Noel? I do love her."

Yolanda smiled. "Don't worry. You have a *real* baby on the way. She's with her *real father* as we speak."

"How are you letting some cat that caused all this back in your life?"

"The same way God came into my life. By His grace, I forgave Terrence. God has changed him. He has been a rock while you been playing hide and seek with your baby mama."

"You know my name! Stop calling me baby mama!"

"Ok. Tramp. Whoremonger. Paid and laid for dollars. Is that better?"

"And you call yourself a preacher?"

Yolanda was convicted...again. Sometimes she wished she wasn't so sensitive to the Spirit. "You know, I am. Which means I need to be an example. You disrespected my marriage but you reap what you sow. I will be praying for you because unless you repent, God's wrath is coming. He has the last say. God can do more to both of you than my actions ever can. I'll pray for His mercy because if I don't, it's no telling what will happen." Yolanda closed her car door. She was done with this conversation. Michael could have all the lap dances he wanted now. Finally, he was free.

And so was she. She just didn't know what to do with her freedom.

When she pulled off, Yolanda realized she wasn't even angry anymore. It was like a black cloud lifted from her shoulders. Out of nowhere, the dream of the black cloud came to her remembrance. Maybe this was what God had been telling her all along. As she pondered this, her phone vibrated. She saw a text from Terrence saying he convinced Noel to let him take her back to Yolanda's house. Yolanda was grateful God's providence brought him into Noel's life. She would know her father and Yolanda could stop running from her past. No longer did she have to live a lie. Though her history with Terrence was tarnished, perhaps God would let their reconnection turn into a relationship of sorts, she mused to herself. Though she was fearful about her future, at least she was righting the wrongs of the past.

Chapter
Twenty-One

Noel sat on the passenger's side of the tricked out black Tahoe in complete silence. Though she was glad Terrence came to her rescue, she was having a hard time dealing with the fact that this man was actually her father.

She studied him closely, taking in every feature comparing them to her own. He had deep smooth chocolate skin that was vastly different from her caramel complexion. *Obviously, my grandmama's high yellow genes run strong. This cat looks more like Djimon Hounsou.* Noel noticed his deep dimples, small ears and full lips, which were a replica of her face. She even took note of his long thick lashes, much like the ones framing her almond shaped eyes. She took in how clean cut he was. His Jordan's were paired with a button down Burberry shirt and well starched jeans. He looked like he could be on the pages of Complex Magazine. His hair was cut close. With the preppy glasses he wore, it was hard to believe at one time he violated her mother.

And yet, her mother actually sent him to her rescue.

It was all very confusing for Noel to wrap her brain around. She was still in shock from the earlier part of her evening. Once she and Daryl arrived at the house, it was filled with smoke, darkness and scantily clad women. It looked like a meat market as girls would approach a man and soon they would disappear into a back room or go downstairs.

"Why do you have me here?" Noel had asked.

"Why you think?" Daryl had given an evil chuckle, and took a sip out of a plastic cup. "Look, all you have to do is use them pretty full lips on a couple of brothers here like you do me. That's it. Then we'll bounce."

"What I do with you is just for you. I give myself to you because I thought we had a relationship." Noel was genuinely hurt. She gave her body to a man with whom she thought there was a spiritual connection only to find out he was not the man he portrayed.

"Don't get all sensitive. I'm putting you on. You pretty. This could lead to a modeling gig. Maybe some music videos. Just savor the moment. Nobody will hurt you. I'll protect you." He pulled her close and forced his tongue in her mouth.

When she tried to push him away, he grabbed her by the back of her head and forced her down the hall. He opened a door to a bedroom where red lamps caused the white walls to look like an inferno. There was one couple on the bed; another on the floor; a man standing against a wall holding a joint as a young girl about thirteen serviced him. Noel was not innocent but she had never seen anything like this.

Daryl pushed her on the bed, next to the couple getting busy. The man appeared to be high and out of it. It was hard to tell if he was asleep or enjoying what was happening as another young girl straddled him. When Noel looked closely at the girl, she noticed she had on a school letterman jacket with a cheer skirt and nothing else. Her blond ponytail had a blue ribbon around it, as if she had just come from a football game. She paused in her gyrating movements to grab a pipe next to her. She took a long hit and threw her head back, laughing maniacally.

Noel was scared for her life. She noticed Daryl standing in the door. He glanced back at her and then turned to someone who was outside the door. She had no idea what was going to happen but determined she would not end up like the other females in this house. She knew she couldn't run out the door without him catching her. She saw a bathroom in her peripheral and then noticed a better option. There was an open window being used to circulate air and rid the room of the smell of drugs and sex. It had no screen on it. Noel figured she could squeeze through it. As Noel pondered her next move, Daryl came over to her.

"Baby," he whispered, "You are so pretty. I got a cat out there willing to pay double just for you to take off your clothes and rub on a brotha a lil' bit." He nuzzled her neck, knowing that was her soft spot. "You hot. I knew you would add to the business the moment I saw you. Can't you do this for me? For us?"

Noel sighed. She pulled him close and kissed him deeply. "If you don't leave me here alone, I can. But, I really need to clean up. Let me use the bathroom first. Can you get me some rum and coke to loosen me up?"

Daryl hesitated. Noel silently prayed he'd fall for her act. He nodded and turned out the room. Noel jumped up and headed to the bathroom, pulling the door closed behind her. She locked it and stood on the edge of the tub, trying to determine if she should go feet or head first out the window. A loud banging on the door interrupted her thoughts.

"Why is this door locked?" Daryl bellowed. "Get out here, Noel. We ready!"

"I'm on the toilet. My stomach is upset," she cried out as she shoved her feet out the window. When she felt them hit the mud, she ran and ran. She ran for two blocks until she felt safe enough to ask for help. An old woman with white hair opened the door. Noel forced her way inside. She broke down crying on the lady's floor. The woman called the police on her behalf and the rest...

Got her here.

"You know, I'm telling the pastor about your boy, right?" Terrence interrupted her thoughts. Coincidentally, when the police picked her up and took her report, Terrence was at the station waiting for her.

"Although with you pressing charges and the police charging him with attempted sex trafficking, drug possession, and sodomy with a minor, I probably won't have to."

Terrence turned to look at her to see how she'd respond. "Look," Terrence tried to talk to her again. "I know this is awkward for you. You may not even want a relationship with me. At least show a brother some gratitude for saving you."

Noel sighed and rolled her eyes. She was appreciative for what he did, but how could he expect her to be more ecstatic than confused? "Thank you, okay? Now, you happy?"

Instead of responding, Terrence pulled the car over. The last time Noel was pulled over in a car, things didn't end so well. Her body tensed up. She grabbed the door, prepared to run again in case he went crazy. Her heart beat so intensely she thought it would explode in her chest, fear ran through her mind. When her eyes widened, Terrence laughed.

"Stop trippin'. I would never hurt you. Let me be clear. From the conversations I've had with your moms, you've played on her guilt for years and disrespected her to the utmost. I sho' nuff won't put up with that mess. I know you don't know me. Trust me, I have repented. I

224

made a decision to right all my wrongs. Just give me a chance, baby girl." He looked in her face. Noel refused to look him in the eye. "Can you look at me? Please."

She didn't want to, but Noel was curious about this man who was her father. She wanted to know why he did what he did. How did he live with himself? What did he want now? But she also wanted to know more about herself. Noel thought that if – a big *if* – she did get to know him she may heal from her past hurt. She took a deep breath then chuckled, opening her eyes extremely wide sticking her face within an inch of his. "I'm looking at you. Is this what you wanted?"

He was taken aback by her sudden change and laughed himself. It was easy to see her sarcasm was an inherited trait from her aunt Rocky. He wrapped his arms around her neck and pulled her close, smelling her hair tainted with the odor of weed and cigarette smoke. "If I have to spend the rest of my life making everything up to you, I will," he vowed.

Miraculously, Noel found herself embracing him back. No, she didn't know him and what she did know, she hated. But something about Terrence made her feel loved. Wanted. Appreciated. That black hole she felt most of her life seemed to close.

Chapter
Twenty-Two

Michael sat at a table with Reggie at the Black Onyx. Even though Michael had Chantal, he still liked to unwind in the strip club. He hated to admit it was the one place where he believed he had control and power over women.

A freckled faced man with glasses sat at the table next to them. Michael thought it was odd he brought in an envelope. Michael wondered how much cash he had. Apparently, the man noticed Michael looking at him and smiled. Michael was taken aback. *What dude comes into a strip club smiling at another man?* Unexpectedly, he walked over to Michael's table.

"Hey man! Can we help you?" Reggie asked, looking at the man from head to toe. His mouth set in an angry scowl.

"I was wondering which one of you is Michael Howard." The man started smiling that goofy smile again.

"He is. What you need, partner?"

Michael cut his eyes at Reggie. "My bad, bro. Blame it on the al-al-al-alcohol." Reggie sang to the Jamie Foxx song which blared throughout the club.

"Are you Michael Montez Howard?" the man asked, this time with a serious look on his face.

"Yeah, why?"

"Michael Howard, you've just been served." He shoved the envelope at Michael and abruptly walked away.

"Served?" When Michael opened the envelope, he saw a Dissolution of Marriage agreement.

Yolanda had filed for divorce.

"What is it, bruh?" Reggie leaned over and snatched the papers from Michael. "Dawg, you free, man! No more holy rollin', no more trippin'. You back to you! Congratulations!" Reggie signaled for one of the girls to come give Michael a celebratory lap dance.

Michael shook his head. "Reggie, man, it's been real. I'm out." He laid some cash on the table to cover his drinks.

"What?" Reggie looked angry. "Man, you need this. This is like therapy."

Disgusted with Michael for leaving, he took another Patron shot. "Man, raise on up. I'm gettin' a few more dances." He motioned for another dancer to come his way and turned his back on Michael.

Michael shrugged it off, and turned to leave. As he got in his Lexus, his phone vibrated. It was Chantal. "Going to mom's for the night. Call you tomorrow. Love you." Ever since her mother found out she was having her first grandson, she and Chantal spent more time together. Though there had been tension between them for years, Chantal was beginning

228

to enjoy reconciling with her mother. Everyone around him was reconnecting with their past. Yolanda and Terrence. Terrence and Noel. He sighed. Here he was walking away from his past but unsure of what the future held. Initially, he thought he was about to be living the dream with his new boo and son on the way. Now, he pondered if this was the beginning of a nightmare. Something was shifting in the atmosphere. He just wished he could figure out what.

He thought about calling Yolanda just to make sure this divorce was what she wanted. He knew she wouldn't be willing to talk on the phone so he decided to head over there. As he got on the freeway, he pondered what he would say. He knew he'd plead forgiveness for forging her name and taking the money. Michael couldn't believe what he did. When she served him with the divorce papers, it confirmed what he always knew.

She didn't really need him. He was an option not a necessity.

That's why he loved – or thought he did anyway – Chantal. He knew he was needed and wanted. He took care of her financially and she took care of him emotionally and mentally. She couldn't hold a candle to Yolanda as far as being business savvy or spiritually firm. But she was fun and she let him be the man. Deep down, Michael knew he needed more than "fun" for a real relationship.

Michael eventually made his way into his former subdivision. He prepared to turn down their cul-de-sac, but stopped in the middle of the street. There was Terrence, holding Noel's hand talking with a police officer. Yolanda's petite frame was huddled on Terrence's opposite side, her head buried in his chest. Michael pondered running up on him like Yolanda had days before. But with the cops there and the whole money thing, he just decided to slowly put the car in reverse, hoping they didn't see him.

229

He couldn't believe what he saw. The man who made him feel like less of a man one night years ago, hugged up on his wife. To make it worse, Terrence was holding Noel's hand as if he hadn't violated her mother, which resulted in her birth. What hurt more than anything was Terrence looked like he was something Michael never was.

A protector.

Chapter
Twenty-Three

At five months pregnant, Kennedy's voluptuous curves were turning into mounds of fat. Though Eddie loved her newly formed double chin and her now E cups, she still felt overly pregnant. Which is why she started hitting up the gym.

Kennedy watched the news while doing her dreaded treadmill walk for the day. Walking put her mind at ease.

After finishing, Kennedy headed to the locker room. She thought she'd listen to one of her favorite pastors, Paul Sheppard in California while sitting in the pool. Kennedy took off her workout clothes and transitioned into her swimsuit.

"Well hello, Sunshine! I heard pregnant women had a glow, though I've never known from experience."

Kennedy snatched her head around. There stood her worst nightmare smirking at her, while anxiously tapping her left foot.

Monica.

"Hey, there." Kennedy tried not to show her nervousness but inside she trembled with fear. *Do not fear, for the Lord Your God will fight for you,* she heard in that still small familiar voice. She prayed God would order this conversation and not let Monica go straight thug on her.

"Congratulations on the baby," Monica snarled sarcastically, starting to undress. Kennedy didn't mean to stare but Monica was a total brick house. Kennedy thought being so bloated with pregnancy was the reason her eyes were drawn to Monica's twenty-six-inch waist, washboard abs and perfectly rounded thirty-eight inch hips. Kennedy was trying to enjoy her pregnancy, despite the drama, but she often missed her old body.

Monica knew Kennedy was taking her in and made it worse by actually striking a pose. She placed her hands on her hips and tilted her head to the left. Her shoulder length bob swung in the same direction.

"Wonder how I hid this bodacious body under those frumpy church suits, I suppose?" Monica laughed at her own attempt at humor. "Or maybe you wonder how a man could leave all this for a desperate side piece."

Kennedy sighed. "Look, Monica, say what you got to say. I know you know."

"Know what?" She continued to put on her sports bra and yoga pants, like Kennedy wasn't there.

"About...about the baby," Kennedy wanted this confrontation to come to a head so it would be over.

"Oh, your illegitimate bastard baby?" Monica laughed hysterically. "Girl, please. I'm not trippin' off that. By the time this is over with, everything will be going my way anyway."

"First of all, my baby is no bastard. He has a daddy. My *husband.* So you

232

can cut the bs with that."

"Are we sure?" Monica's voice dripped with sarcasm. "From what I understand, your bastard baby may be my husband's." She shook her head. "Of all the brothers for you to get with, how in the world did you pick him?" She sat down on the bench and looked at Kennedy.

"What do you mean?" Kennedy slowly realized Monica might not know the full story.

"My husband has had a sex problem for years. I mean, with my fine a-- I mean body – most men wouldn't feel the need to stray." She paused. "But, if Eric Benet can creep on Halle, anything is possible."

"You not Halle," Kennedy burst out.

"Hold on, whore. Neither are you." Monica rolled her eyes. "My husband was a sex, porn, prostitute, call girl type of dude." She looked down to avoid Kennedy seeing her eyes brim with tears. "I thought it was over but, he backslid after..." she trailed off and stared into space.

"After what?" Kennedy mistook the hurt in Monica's eyes for a soft spot. Thinking she and her nemesis could speak sensibly about the indiscretion between them.

Monica wiped her eyes and looked angrily at Kennedy. "I don't care how you met. All I know is my *husband* came crying to me talking about he wants 'his baby'. How you think I felt? If it was some random chick I could get over it. But you supposed to be all holy, my sister in the Lord and this is how you do me?" With rage in her eyes, she exploded. "I even suspect if we had our own child, I could more easily get over it but...you took what was mine!" She slammed her locker so hard Kennedy felt the momentum in her feet.

"Monica," Kennedy stammered. "I had no idea Marcus was your husband. I didn't even find out until we had broken things off. I'm not that...that type of woman to knowingly mess with someone's man who I know."

"No? You just mess around with someone else's husband, as long as you don't know the wife?"

"No. I fell into this affair. There were some things that were not cool in my house. Maybe you have never been ignored or lonesome or just...craved something you couldn't get from your own husband."

"Let me stop you right there," Monica said firmly. "No. In fact, I dare say my husband paid way too much attention to me. I have never missed anything in my relationship."

"Then how did Marcus end up with me?"

Kennedy knew those words could cause Monica to flip out. She jumped to her feet and shoved Kennedy in the shoulder, before looking at her swollen belly. "Girl, you better be glad you pregnant. Don't you dare disrespect me again – ever! He ended up with you because he is a former *sex addict.* When you don't commit your fleshly issues under the obedience of Christ, you revert to what you were before salvation. You cannot conquer what you don't confront."

Monica's statements pierced her heart with conviction because she often used sex herself to cope with problems. Yes, she repented from sin through confession but she never *gave* her issues to God for Him to heal her totally. No matter whom she married, how many Bible studies she led or church stuff she did, she never confronted her childhood issues. And because she didn't, her sin continued to reign in her body.

"Before we got married – not that I owe you any explanation, you trick whore – my life was a mess. I met the Lord doin' a lil' time and when I got out, a friend invited me to bible study. There was a guy there I met and we started to hang out. To make a long story short we fell in love." Monica stared into space, as if she was reliving the past. "We couldn't be together for various reasons so I went ahead and married Marcus. I tried my best to fall in love with him." She paused. "I love him, I do. I just struggled with my feelings for the other man. It was hard to let him go.

"When I committed my life to Christ and accepted His call. I got totally engaged in my work, leaving my past indiscretions behind. Then Marcus discovered what was going on and couldn't accept my affair. He knew the guy loved me. Marcus also resented me going into vocational ministry. That's when he confessed his past addiction."

"I hate all this happened to you," Kennedy said, really feeling for Monica. "I'm confused. What does this have to do with this baby situation?"

"You know, you pretty but dumb as a box of rocks." Monica shook her head. "You slow and you just don't get it. I do not want your baby. I want my own baby. I can't have one. So if it is Marcus' baby you have, we will fight for custody." Monica got ready to walk off, but this time Kennedy grabbed her.

"Wait a minute!" she slammed Monica's body into the wall, near the hand dryer. "If you don't want my baby, why would you fight for custody?"

"Girl, if you don't back up off me... I will toss you to the ground. Pregnant and all!" Kennedy moved back. She feared Monica would snap.

"A baby may cause Marcus to forgive me totally. I promised God I would make this work despite not getting my first love. This can be my way of making Marcus see that I do love him." Monica's tone softened, catching Kennedy off guard.

"It's not fair to take my baby from me."

"Maybe not," she agreed. "That's between you and God. I can't tell you what God wants for your household but we need something to hold us together. If you were happy with Eddie, you wouldn't have ended up with my husband."

"Minister Caine, you need to pray on what God wants for this baby. Don't use him as a tool to keep something together that may not need to be." She shook her head. "Our attorney will contact you for a DNA test prior to the baby's birth. Then, we can handle visitation. Know there's no way in heaven or hell you will have *this* baby." She turned and left the locker room, headed to the pool.

"You got what I need to keep my house right." Monica yelled hysterically as Kennedy left the room, causing other gym goers to whisper and wonder aloud what was going on. "Home wrecking ho!" Her voice trailed into the wet area as Kennedy rushed out amid the stares.

She vowed to fight for her baby. There was going to be glory in her story.

And God would reveal it.

Chapter Twenty-Four

The morning sun poured through the curtains, making Yolanda cover her head. She had finally fallen asleep around 4:30 a.m. She pondered lying under her comforter the entire day but was interrupted by the chime of the doorbell. She wasn't expecting anyone and couldn't imagine who it would be. She glanced at the clock. It read 8:00 a.m. Now Yolanda was enraged. She didn't like unexpected guests as it was, but early ones were a definite no-no.

Whoever it was kept ringing the bell. Yolanda yelled, "I'm coming." She managed to run down the steps and looked through the small peephole. Her heart raced with nervousness when she saw the visitor.

It was Sister Boyd, Daryl's aunt.

"Look, wench," Sister Boyd snarled. "I know you see me out here. You better open this door before you make me lay down my salvation."

Yolanda thought about grabbing the bat from the hall closet but the last thing she wanted to do was assault a senior citizen. She prayed in her head she was doing the right thing and opened the door.

"Morning, Minister. Sorry to wake you. But if I can't sleep, why should you?"

"Excuse me?" All nervousness immediately vanished. One thing Yolanda didn't like was someone confronting her when they were in the wrong.

"You can at least let me in. I mean, my nephew got locked up because of your fast tail daughter," she spat.

"Are you serious?" Yolanda asked incredulously. "Your nephew lied about his age, took my daughter out of town, smoked drugs in front of her, took her to a whorehouse to work for him and you think I care he was arrested?" Yolanda rolled her eyes. She was fuming now. "Girl, please. You and your criminal family better stay off my property and away from my family."

Sister Boyd clutched her chest. "No, you didn't!" She straightened her tilted wig and stepped within an inch of Yolanda's face. "Look, we all know about your past and apparently your daughter got her lil' wild streak from you." She stepped back a bit. "I know Daryl was wrong. But you trying to take my boy away from me. He's my baby. Lost my youngest son in the streets." Sister Boyd cried out. "I was hoping you would suggest leniency for Daryl's sentencing."

Yolanda was flabbergasted. This man almost had her daughter raped and she wanted leniency.

"Sister Boyd," Yolanda said calmly. "I'm going to ask you to get off my porch. You do realize your "baby" was helping run a prostitution ring. I guess it doesn't matter he almost had my daughter caught up, right?" A sharp pain jolted her shoulder. Yolanda figured her anger was causing her body to react. "Even the Bible says you reap what you sow. He did it. He will sow it and now I demand you get off my property before I..."

A strong pain struck her left eye. She fell back into her foyer. Her head hit the marble floor.

Sister Boyd had punched her. The old lady had knocked her to the floor.

"Listen," she heard Sister Boyd hiss in her ear, "You have no idea who you messin' with. I didn't mean to hit you, but the devil made me do it. Him and your nasty attitude. You either speak up for my nephew or my *other* son gonna make you lose all you got."

"Other son?" She wanted to get up and give Sister Boyd a beat down. But her head was really hurting and she felt a little disoriented.

"Yes. Pastor Griffin."

Yolanda's heart sank. Now she knew why he'd been so unsympathetic when she and Noel met with him for counseling. In fact, he'd been reluctant to fire Daryl, only doing so because the board demanded it. Yolanda wondered if anyone knew Sister Boyd was his mother.

Sister Boyd seemed to read her mind. She said, "No...no one but family knows he's my son. Had him when I was young, back when you didn't have babies out of wedlock like they do now. His daddy had another family and didn't want anything to do with us once I was pregnant. My older sister took him as her own. She passed and I took in her son – Daryl. His daddy serving a life sentence."

Much to her surprise, Sister Boyd helped her up. "Sorry I had to knock you out, but I know how to hold my own. Don't let my church outfits fool ya."

"I would whoop your tail now. But I know I need to respect my elders. I don't care what you do. I will not suggest leniency for a criminal. Maybe now you can get a two for one."

Sister Boyd looked confused. "A two for one?"

"Visit two prisoners in one trip."

Sister Boyd pulled her right arm back to hit Yolanda again. This time, Yolanda caught her by the wrist and twisted her arm behind her back. Sister Boyd yelped in pain. "You better be glad I'm saved. Castle doctrine is much alive in our state," Yolanda's voice was filled with fury. "In fact, you assaulted me in my home. I could pull out my Magnum and pop you, but I am not a murderer."

Sister Boyd was visibly shaken. Yolanda let her go with a shove toward the door.

"I have a restraining order against your *baby*." Yolanda said, sarcastically emphasizing "baby". "Please don't make me go to the station and get one on you. I'm gonna act like this never happened. So go."

Yolanda shut the door behind her and immediately crumpled to the floor. She cried not only for what happened just now, but for the nastiness of her church and the ministry that should have been the focus. Yolanda didn't see how so much deceit, willingness to cover evil and even violence could co-exist in the body of Christ. She knew at that moment she would have to find out if the Lord would even want her to stay in this group of believers. While she enjoyed the work she did, she didn't know if it should be there.

Pain shot through Yolanda's shoulder again, this time going around to her back. She knew it was stress. Though she was expected to be at the church today for an event, Yolanda knew she needed to lie down and rest. She was physically and mentally tired. Emotionally, she was drained. Yolanda heard her phone rang and remained in the hallway. She sat on the floor as tears streamed down her cheeks.

The machine came on. She heard a familiar voice that was oddly comforting. Too comforting.

Terrence.

"Hey, Yo. It's T. Calling to check on you. One of your neighbors sent me a text and said some old chick dressed like an Easter basket was trying to act a fool with you. Wanted to make sure you're okay. Call me back. If I don't hear from you soon, I'm headed over. Peace."

Now Yolanda was confused. How did a neighbor know to contact *him*? And why was he so worried about her? Many questions ran through her mind, but one thing was certain.

Yolanda knew she was cared for and protected. It seemed she was safer than she ever was with Michael. While it scared her, she now had a sense of comfort and peace. She believed with Terrence on her side, she could overcome anything. The question was: to what degree was he trying to be in her life?

"God," Yolanda said aloud. "This makes no sense. How does the man who got me in this mess make me feel so...so...good?"

Isaiah 55:8 popped in her spirit.

My ways aren't your ways and my thoughts are not your thoughts.

And apparently, this was something God was doing that definitely was not in her line of thinking.

Chapter Twenty-Five

Michael was having a better day then he had in weeks. He'd just gotten a development deal for a new commercial property that could definitely put him at multi-millionaire status. He had managed to find a new luxury villa and even treated himself to a wardrobe makeover. Guilt about taking money from Yolanda still lingered. At first, Michael considered giving the money back. He knew the God in Yolanda would be more forgiving than her anger. Yet, he also didn't want to risk catching a case if he ticked her off.

Michael couldn't believe his good fortune. "Who says God can't bless mess?" he chuckled to himself as he sat back in his leather office chair. He pondered going to the golf course when the office phone rang.

"Yes, Cassandra?" He didn't mean to sound irritated. He liked his receptionist. But in his mind, work was over for today.

"I hate to interrupt you, Mr. Howard. I just have a concern over a cancelled check."

"Okay. What's up?"

"Well, I know we have a few vendors we use, but I don't have any information or payment orders for Hills Realty."

Michael sat up straight so quickly that his body sent papers falling to the floor. "Hills Realty?" He thought back over the past few weeks. Nothing sounded familiar. "What date is on the check and when was it cashed?"

"It's dated for June fourth. It was cashed just yesterday. The day before the 90 day no cash rule set in," Cassandra's voice was filled with worry. "Mr. Howard, it says *your* name but...I'm afraid it's been forged."

Michael began to sweat. He was nervous, thinking somehow what he and Chantal did to Yolanda was coming back to haunt him. "Cassandra, calm down," Michael faked surety in his voice. He tried to remember anything about June fourth that stood out. His mind couldn't recall anything unusual, as he was still in the house with Yolanda, and he had found out he was...

Becoming a father.

No, no! Michael thought. He couldn't have been got by Chantal. Michael tried to convince himself he was paranoid. That he was just tripping off nothing. Deep down something was not adding up. "Cassandra," he said, almost not wanting to know how much the check was for, "How much is the check written for?"

"Well, let me say this, I don't even know how our accounting didn't catch this. Oh! I know. I forgot. You made a large deposit that covered it."

Michael's stomach dropped to his feet. "Let me guess. The check was for $250,000?"

Cassandra uttered with surprise, "Yes. How did you know?"

"I did it," Michael admitted. "What made you think the signature was fake?"

"Well, the way the I was written. You don't make a loop on the bottom of your 'I'; this one has a loop. I mean, I guess if it were fake, the bank would have caught the signature. Sorry, sir, for the worry."

"No problem, Cassandra," Michael said with assurance in his voice. "Glad to know you lookin' out for a brotha that close." He hung up the phone.

Yes, there was a problem. Cassandra was looking out for him while someone else was looking out to get him.

"Michael, baby, what's wrong?" Chantal cooed, rubbing her big belly against his back.

"Nothing," he murmured, as he stood at the island in the kitchen, preparing a salad. "Just a lot on my mind."

"Wanna share? They say sharing is caring and I am all about both." She managed to turn Michael toward her, putting his hands on her DDD pregnant breasts. She leaned in to kiss him. He turned his head.

"So now you rejecting me?" Chantal pouted. "What's going on with you?"

Michael didn't want to upset her. But, he couldn't get it out of his head that she possibly took his money and used it to pay a realtor. He couldn't fathom how she would have accessed his business checks. Michael could count only two times Chantal had been to the office. The day Yolanda showed up and the day after to take him to lunch. He never

245

brought his checks home. It really puzzled Michael.

Maybe he did need to investigate before he accused her. After all, she knew all she had to do was ask him for what she wanted and it was done. Michael made up his mind to tell the bank he hadn't signed the check and if need be he'd ask everybody – from Cassandra to the cleaning people what was up.

"I'm sorry, sweetie. Come here." He pulled Chantal into his arms and squeezed her tight. "I had a rough day."

"So have I." Chantal whined. "My feet are swollen. My nose is spreading. And my neck is darker. All this to carry your big head baby."

Michael hoisted her onto the counter. "Say it again."

"What? Your big head?"

"No. The last words…"

"Ohhhh…" Chantal smirked. "Your baby?"

"That's right. My baby." He went in for a deep passionate kiss and found himself getting worked up, forgetting about the whole check incident. What got her pregnant in the first place was about to go down right there in the kitchen.

"Baby," she whispered seductively, "You know we need to get prepared for our shower."

"Yeah. First, let's get dirty so we *need* a shower." He picked her up, her belly creating space between them. Michael wobbled to get her to the sofa. She squealed with laughter and delight at him carrying her at close seven months. He finally made his way to the soft, reclining leather sofa, out of breath. She kissed him on the cheek after he laid her on her favorite side – the left. "I love you," she purred at him softly. He undressed her.

He smiled. "Love you, too."

Michael believed he would love their new life together. He still couldn't erase the image of a $250,000 check from his imagination. For now, duty was calling. And as usual, his body was ready to answer, as his brain tuned out all other concerns.

A trait he acquired and would always bite him in the end.

Chapter
Twenty-Six

Sitting in the waiting room, Kennedy was nauseous. Not the morning sickness type of nausea, but the type of feeling where her nerves were getting the best of her. The ride over to the doctor's office had been eerily silent. Kennedy's silence was due to embarrassment. Having to get a DNA test for a baby she knew couldn't be her husband's to appease her former side guy was too much.

Eddie assured her no matter what, they would get through it and he would stand by her side. She still had doubts. He wasn't the type to renege on a promise to God, yet Kennedy feared the reality of the outcome would cause him to stray or to stay with resentment. She sighed loudly, not even realizing she did.

Eddie glanced at her with a little smile on his face. His demeanor and attitude had been very pleasant and surprisingly calm. Kennedy knew this had to be just as difficult for him.

"Baby," Eddie reached over to squeeze her knee, reassuringly. "God's got this. No matter what happens. So stop worrying. Turn your worries into prayers."

"I know. It's not that I don't believe that; a part of me just wonders..." her voice trailed off as her eyes filled with tears. She choked up.

"Stop it!" Eddie said sternly, with a hint of anger in his voice. "We have talked about it. Prayed about it. And we agree with what God said about it. So if I'm all right, why you still trippin'?"

"I know," Kennedy said, trying to force some surety in her voice. She cleared her throat. "And I am very grateful. I just need to know one more time that you will love me and this child as if what happened didn't."

Eddie took a deep breath. "I promised God first, then I promised you I would love you and the child. It's not the baby's fault."

"I just hope when he gets here there is peace." Kennedy wanted to enjoy her pregnancy but between Monica's crazy shenanigans and Marcus trying this whole paternity mess, it was too much. He'd really started badgering them after Kennedy found out she was having a boy. He even had the audacity to send her a list of suggested names. Luckily, they discovered her own doctor could do a DNA test prior to the birth. Though there would be risk of miscarriage utilizing the amniocentesis, Kennedy knew the anxiety of not knowing who the father was until after the baby was born could also cause her stress to the point of miscarriage.

Eddie pulled into the facility slowly. After he turned the car off, he sighed deeply and took Kennedy by the hand. He looked her squarely in the eyes and prayed for her.

Kennedy kissed his hand. She closed her eyes. Warm tears fell onto Eddie's hand. She kept her lips rested on his thumb knuckle.

Kennedy said amen and dabbed her eyes with her sleeve and smoothed her hair back. "Ready?"

"More than you know."

✞✞✞

When they got to the waiting room, they were nervous. Marcus and Monica hadn't arrived. Kennedy and Eddie filled out their paperwork and waited for their turn. Kennedy continued to gulp down water as the doctor had ordered prior to collecting the baby's fluid. In addition to that, Kennedy, Marcus and Eddie would give blood for paternity testing. Kennedy, though embarrassed, explained Eddie's situation to the doctor. Her OB-GYN, Dr. Marion Steward, was convinced she should test Eddie as well. She had agreed to use the amniotic paternity test to speed up the process for visitation and custody. She also told Kennedy she would be praying for peripety.

Kennedy looked at the clock. She noted Monica and Marcus were twenty minutes late. In the back of Kennedy's mind, she hoped they had changed their minds and given up. When the door to the waiting room loudly burst open, her dream dissolved into the harsh reality of what was about to transpire.

Marcus muttered a hello to Eddie. Eddie grunted in return and kept reading the sports page. Monica hadn't even so much as looked at Kennedy since their confrontation in the gym. Today though, her demeanor was calm. Eerily calm.

"Sorry we're late," she happily chirped as if they were at a party and not a doctor's office. "Let's get this paperwork together and get this party started." She clapped her hands together, a little too happy for Kennedy's liking.

Irritated, Marcus chided her. "Calm down. We don't need all that. This is nothing to be so chipper about." He grabbed the clipboard from the receptionist, as he checked in. "It's enough you made us late and now you just running your mouth. Shut up for once."

Everyone looked stunned. Eddie and Kennedy glanced at one another, waiting for Monica to snap into her usual ghetto gangster self. Much to everyone's surprise, she simply shrugged her shoulders and sat down. "Okay." She looked at her watch. "Sorry we held everyone up but we had to get Mama. Her crown fell off so we killed two birds with one stone. She's on the second floor."

Now Kennedy was agitated. This wasn't a family reunion. Why in the world did she bring her mother? "No offense, but why would you bring your mother to *my baby's* DNA testing?"

Monica snapped her head to look at Kennedy with a menacing glare. She scowled and then suddenly smiled. "Why wouldn't I bring Mother? You all *do* plan on having Mother Stone be the child's grandmother don't you?"

Eddie threw his USA Today on the floor and stood up. His chest heaved. Other than their physical altercation months ago, she had never seen Eddie look so menacing toward a female.

"Look, here," Eddie exclaimed. "This ain't a game. We talking about the life and well-being of a child, Monica. You wouldn't know that I guess from how many of your own you killed."

Even Kennedy knew that was a low blow. The story of Monica and her alleged abortions was brought up in a minster's meeting but never talked about again, due to a mandate from Pastor Griffin. It was set by the board that all personal issues revealed on the floor were not to make it outside the room. Failure to comply could lead to dismissal from the ministry without pay until further notice. For the first time ever, Kennedy needed Eddie to stay employed.

Monica looked stunned. She didn't respond. She simply stared at Eddie, like she was confused. Marcus popped up and pushed Eddie in the chest. "Hey man. You not about to step to my wife. You didn't even have to go there, partner." He took off his jacket. Kennedy thought they were about to fight.

"Let me tell you something, youngin'," Eddie snarled back. He walked within an inch of Marcus' face. "I'm from the old school. Don't let my suits fool you. I'm from the block. I'm not no tryin' to-be-hard young cat whose wife's got bigger balls than him." Marcus backed up.

"Hey, who you trying to punk, you wanna-be-pastor?" Monica hollered as she jumped up next to Marcus. "You best get out my husband's face before I report you to Pastor for breach of personal information."

"I can't believe any of you go to church, let alone are Christians acting like this!" They all quickly turned around to see Dr. Steward. She was incensed at the outburst in her office. Though no one else was in the waiting room at the time, it was still embarrassing to be caught acting so unclassy in front of a woman Kennedy admired. Dr. Steward swept her salt and pepper bob behind her ears and grimaced at all of them. "My place is a place of business. I appreciate you treating it as such. I actually hope for the child the Lord has ordained to come into this world all of you get it together." She hit her clipboard for emphasis. "A bunch of foolishness. We have a real situation to straighten out and I have to--"

"Tell 'em, Doc." Everyone turned around to see Mother Stone nodding in agreement. She walked over and put her arm around Dr. Steward. She had slipped in unnoticed in the midst of the fracas. "Doctor, you and I are the only ones acting like we got some sense and the conviction of the Holy Spirit. Hey!" She gave her church yell and jumped up and down in place, as if she were getting the Spirit.

Dr. Steward rolled her eyes. "Who are you and why are jumping in my

253

office like a fool?"

Mother Stone immediately stopped. "Say what now? I was getting my Holy Ghost on till you came at me like that. Ever been beat by another saint? It ain't pretty, chile."

Dr. Steward put her hands on her hips and looked Mother Stone up and down. "Sit down or remove yourself from my office. I have security I pay really well. Don't make me call them. God did not give you a spirit of unholy mess but of self-control. Have a seat and do so quickly."

Much to everyone's surprise, Mother Stone went and sat down. Kennedy wanted to high-five the doctor but she didn't want to get served next. Dr. Steward cleared her throat. "Now, if we are ready to handle what we came here for, let's do this. Kennedy, we will do your CVS and amniotic fluid drawing right after we take your blood. At that point, Mr. Stone, we will draw your blood and then you, Mr. Roberts. Results may take a week. Are we clear?"

Everyone nodded then Mother Stone raised her hand. Dr. Steward rolled her eyes to the ceiling and breathed deeply. She looked at Mother Stone with a blank stare and said, "Yes?"

"My son's fish line got cut years ago. Why you testing him?"

"I'm glad you asked, Mama. I wondered the same thing." Monica exclaimed, sitting down next to Mother Stone.

"Not that I have to tell you," Dr. Steward curtly replied. "It is standard practice I test all parties involved, no matter what we *think* the results may be." She turned her back on them and said, "Kennedy, are you and Mr. Stone ready?"

254

Kennedy looked at Eddie. He pulled her close and gently kissed her on the lips. "Yes."

Mother Stone smirked. "Better be careful kissing her. You don't know where her mouth been. Isn't that why we here?"

Pressing Past the Past

Chapter Twenty-Seven

Terrence and Yolanda sat in silence for a few moments, watching the sun set before them. The wind gently blew on their faces as they took in the beautiful scenery around them.

"You know, I'm scared to go to church Sunday," Yolanda confessed. She stared straight ahead to avoid eye contact with Terrence. He had a way of making her think he could peer inside her soul. It made her nervous for two reasons: his gift of discernment and his eyes turned her on. His long thick lashes framed honey brown eyes. His lids slightly drooped, giving him a bedroom look. Yolanda wanted to avoid looking at him as much as possible. It had been months since she'd had a sexual release.

"God has not given you a spirit of fear. I know your pastor's behavior toward you has thrown you for a loop. Remember, no matter what, God got you."

She turned to look at him. As suspected, he was peering deep into her eyes. Her heart beat wildly in her chest. His succulent lips wrapped around his glass, as he finished off his drink. "I will be at service on Sunday, you can bet on that." He paused and leaned in close to her. Yolanda prayed he couldn't feel her shudder when she smelled his Burberry cologne. "If any foolishness goes down, I'll be there."

"Thank you. You know, it's messed up what happened between us years ago, but I realize I played a part. You didn't rape me per se. I agreed to the terms of that night. I'm sorry I allowed myself to believe otherwise all these years."

Yolanda realized for the first time that she needed to take responsibility for her role in what happened.

She had allowed Michael to plant the language of "rape" in her head to describe what happened and for years, she grasped at the notion. In reality, she'd played the role of a prostitute. Collateral for what he didn't have. She sacrificed not only her body, but also her self-esteem.

"I receive your apology and your acknowledgement. I know Michael manipulated that into your head. I also knew one day you'd really accept the truth. Both of us are new people. New creatures in Christ. The truth has set us free."

He was right. After really doing some soul-searching, Yolanda concluded her relationship with Terrence could be good for her. After all, he wasn't guilty of what she falsely believed about him all those years. Still, she was confused.

"If you thought it was consensual, why didn't you defend yourself?" Yolanda almost didn't want to know the answer but if they were going to co-parent and get closer, she wanted to make sure he had no ill will whatsoever toward her.

"Because I knew you needed that to cope. I wanted to lash out, fight back, and clear it up. But when I got locked up on those trafficking charges, I figured I deserved whatever was said to further tarnish my name."

"Do you forgive me?" She looked at Terrence closely. After all, this was the first time she'd verbalized the truth of that night. She explained it

258

somewhat to Noel but never wholeheartedly acknowledged the truth about her part.

Terrence sighed and moved in even closer, his lips inches from hers. "Yeah, Babe," he whispered sultrily. "I forgave you seventeen years ago."

When Terrence reached out to Yolanda, he never imagined he would develop feelings for her. The moment he laid eyes on her in his home, it was like he saw her for the first time. She was not only physically beautiful but her spiritual strength outweighed her looks. The more they talked, he realized they had a connection. The connection went beyond sharing a daughter. They both had carried the weight of an ugly truth for many years. Now, they were being set free. Together. As parents. Born again believers. And Terrence hoped perhaps they would bond even closer. He hadn't intended to fall for her but he'd be lying if he denied it. It seemed too soon and too fast but he couldn't help what had been building up over the months. Terrence believed they were brought together by God's sovereign plan. He just hoped she felt the same way.

All of a sudden, his hand grabbed Yolanda by the back of her head and pulled her lips onto his. Yolanda thought she would faint from the lust rising up within her, and the throbbing between her legs. They kissed deeply. Terrence pulled her onto his lap. She straddled him, held his face, then moved her hands across his back. He rubbed her hips, moved his hands around to her bottom and squeezed her tightly.

When Yolanda got ready to remove her tunic, Terrence abruptly stopped. He leaned back and placed his hands behind his head. "Man, I got a little turned up. I can't go down that road."

Yolanda was shocked. Yes, he was a man of God but the operative word in her mind was *man*. She knew sexual sin was wrong but she didn't want to be right.

"You are beautiful. Super sexy, even more than you were as a young firecracker. But I will not sin against God. I want Him to bless our relationship."

Yolanda climbed off his lap and pondered what he was saying. "You're right. But what are you hoping God will do in our relationship?"

He smiled. "He's doing it now. Be still and wait."

Yolanda nodded and took a long swig of water. "Do you want to stay over? You can sleep on the couch."

"No!" he exclaimed between belly busting laughter. "After what just happened? You know I wouldn't stay on the couch. Nice try though."

Even Yolanda had to laugh at him figuring out her scheme. She knew he was right, which is why she suggested it. "Okay. You got me. Go on and leave now."

"Oh, it's like that?" Terrence said, expressing fake shock. "Yeah, flee from temptation so I'm about to Olympic sprint out of here. You get me weak."

The conversation ceased. An awkward quietness fell over them. Yolanda thought how ironic it was that he was holding back and she wanted to press forward.

Terrence stood up and stretched. He wanted to at least hug Yolanda good night but now was not the time. He knew his flesh well enough to know a hug right now would end up totally wrong.

260

"I'll take you to breakfast tomorrow. We'll prep and pray for whatever goes down Sunday, okay?"

"Sure," Yolanda said nonchalantly. She tried to ignore the sexual frustration bottled up within her. "You know tomorrow my ex is having his baby shower?"

"Really? Wanna stop by and drop off our gift?" Terrence tried to hold back his laughter. He was glad the conversation shifted in another direction.

"Fool." Yolanda yelled, to which Terrence responded with laughter. "I ought to drop off a 'thank you' note. She can have all that."

And Yolanda finally meant it.

Pressing Past the Past

Chapter Twenty-Eight

"Thank you, mama!" Chantal exclaimed, opening a three-foot-tall gift basket with diapers, toys, baby lotions, shampoos and other items. It was perfect for a first-time mother.

"You welcome, baby. Nothing but the best for my daughter." Chantal's mother was a replica of her daughter, down to the dimple in the left cheek and the same sassy attitude.

"I'm so happy to have a grandbaby on the way and a future son-in-law, too." The whole family cheered loudly, as Michael forced a smile.

"You don't seem too engaged with your guests." A voice came from behind Michael.

He turned around and his stomach sank to his feet.

Chantal's uncle. Pastor Griffin.

Michael had to admit for such a clean cut and proper man, he was surprised that he was a member of this crazy family. Since he and Yolanda weren't together anymore, he hoped maybe the tension that had always existed between the two would now cease.

"Oh, you not greetin' me? After all, you are the father of my soon to be nephew. Don't you think we need to get to know one another?" Michael didn't like the sarcastic undertone and wanted to ask him what his problem was.

Sensing Michael's anger, Pastor Griffin softened his tone. He knew when to leave well enough alone. "Look, man, I'm not trying to start nothing. You have to know this is uncomfortable. It's enough my family's not the cleanest crew on the block." He paused and looked down at his feet, trying to compose himself. "I'm a pastor with a large congregation; got some family dirt. A niece who strips and gets pregnant by one of my employees' husbands. This is straight out of a Tyler Perry play, man."

Michael chuckled. "Pastor, you right. Trust me when I say, being married to a female minister just wasn't for me. I'm not saying what I did was right. But..."

"First of all, stop all this 'pastor' stuff. Right now, I am simply Gary Griffin from the block. I know it's not easy being married to anyone in vocational ministry. But you made it hard for your wife. Her credibility was shot because her home life was out of order."

Michael got defensive. Although she was no longer his wife, he didn't appreciate her credibility questioned. He knew her relationship with God was real and her desire to serve was one hundred percent committed. "Hold on. Don't discredit her because of me. Her walk with God is *very* real. I can't let you say that, Gary."

Pastor Griffin held his hands up, signaling he didn't want any trouble. "I didn't say it wasn't. People often view you looking at your whole life – relationships included. It's par for the course."

"Okay, then let's talk about you. Your youth minister was arrested for trying to pimp off my...her...daughter. Your family rep is not Cosby clean. Then, you always have money issues in your church that randomly coincide with you getting a new crib or a new car." Michael shook his head in disbelief. "So how can you say *anything* about family?"

Pastor Griffin frowned, angered by Michael's words, no matter how real they were. "Let me tell you something," he hissed. All fear of a beat down left. He had to defend the religious dynasty he was trying to build. "When you have done effective ministry like me. There's often some grace that you receive. Because of the impact my church has had on the community, you could say I get a pass. I never said me nor my family is perfect. Now, your wife – well ex – is not at my level. And she's a woman. That makes her under a worse microscope with more scrutiny. You caused her to be criticized even more."

Michael knew Pastor Griffin, Gary – whoever he wanted to be called – was right. He felt bad for falsely supporting Yolanda's dream, one that he didn't want to be a part of.

As if Pastor Griffin knew what Michael was thinking, he placed his hand on his shoulder. "Look, you don't have to apologize for not having the same vision as her. We aren't supposed to morph into our spouses nor be what we're not. She is who she is and if you couldn't roll with it...well...it is what it is." He paused then took his hand off Michael's shoulder. "All I ask is you do right by my niece. And, don't worry. I doubt you got to worry about her preaching." They both burst out into laughter at the thought when Chantal walked up beside them.

"What y'all laughing about?" Chantal looked irritated. "Baby, we still got a gang of gifts to open and you're not even over here to see how we getting hooked up."

"Alright, I'm coming. Let's open the last ones together." Michael kissed her lips and Chantal smiled as she pulled away.

"Let me go sit with my woman." He nodded at Pastor Griffin, and then offered his hand. Michael never liked him but knew he'd still be a part of his new life with this new woman. Pastor Griffin shook his hand firmly and turned to walk to the buffet.

"What's up, people?" The already loud room got louder when Michael's best friend Reggie made his entrance. His baby mama, Vera, was lagging behind him. He ran over to Michael and embraced him in a man hug.

"Whass up, boy?" Reggie exclaimed, grinning all goofy, which told Michael one thing.

He was lit.

His eyes were a little bloodshot and when he hugged Michael, he smelled like he'd downed a bottle of Crown Royal. Michael prayed he didn't meet with a potential client in his condition. Michael had strict rules about any extracurricular activities when dealing with any of their clientele.

"You good, man?" Michael asked. He tried to keep his voice under control. "I hope you did all that extra after you met with ol' boy about expanding his crib."

Reggie laughed. "Of course. When it's about the money, I'm always on my game. I just needed some extra to get me through all this."

"Here," Reggie said as he shoved a small blue box at Michael. "For lil' man."

"Thanks, partner." Michael laid the box on the table with the other gifts and sat down next to Chantal.

Chantal rolled her eyes at Reggie, as she proceeded to open more gifts They "ooed" and "awed" as Michael leaned in to take a picture.

"I really want to thank you all for what you have given us today. We are – as my holy rollin' uncle would say – blessed and highly favored." Everyone applauded and cheered.

"Hey!" Reggie exclaimed in a loud and drunken drawl. "You forgot my gift, Chan."

Chantal sucked her teeth and reached over to the table and grabbed the tiny box. "Wow. Wonder what this could be. I mean, I hope it's some money. Can't be no baby gift this doggone little." The guests chuckled, as she unwrapped the box. When she opened the lid, she gasped.

"What is it, baby?" He prayed she wasn't about to act a fool.

"It's...it's...a Tiffany baby booty pendant," she said with surprise on her face and awe in her voice. She held up the platinum piece for all to admire. She jumped up and went to hug Reggie, lightly embracing him. For some reason, Michael sensed she wasn't crazy about Reggie. In fact, he was surprised Reggie went out of his way to give her such a luxurious gift, as stinginess was at the helm of he and Vera's issues.

Vera.

Michael prayed she was too distracted to see what was going on, but no- she was standing right in front. Her arms folded across her chest. Her head leaned to the side, like she was trying to figure out what was going on.

"That's real nice, baby," she remarked. "I can't believe you would be so generous to a baby mama other than your own."

Reggie pulled back from Chantal and went over to Vera. "Aw girl," he kissed her on the neck. "I did all this for my boy. Me and Mike like fam. You know dat. Besides, you and I are on a break, so why you care? He my ace from way back when so I got to get in good with his baby mama." He winked at Chantal, to which she rolled her eyes.

"You ungrateful, wench." Vera yelled, shaking Reggie off of her. She took out her earrings and actually pulled a tube of Vaseline from her pocket and smeared it on her face. "Pregnant or not, I need to know why my man gifting you. I won't hit your stomach but I will dot that eye good." She charged at Chantal. Reggie and some other guests held her back.

Pastor Griffin rushed in between her and Chantal. "Sister, no type of woman should ever hit a pregnant woman. Think about it. You are putting her at risk of losing her child, over what?" She acknowledged him, but was still furious with Reggie's gesture. "So your man gave her a nice gift. He did it because he is trying to...maybe make amends with his childhood friend's mother-to-be. That's all. So calm down or I *will* have you escorted out."

"First of all, he's not my man right now, just my tired baby daddy. Second, you ain't got to go-cart me anywhere. Because you a man of God, I won't cuss you. And no, I don't want to hurt the baby. I just..." Vera's voice trembled. "I ...I'm sorry."

Michael couldn't believe what had happened. He knew Vera was jealous, with reason. Still, he couldn't fathom why she'd been ready to fight Chantal over a gift. Michael reasoned maybe it was because they had some financial issues due to Reggie's child support increase. He knew she couldn't possibly have thought Chantal and Reggie had something going on.

268

"You coming?" Vera asked Reggie pointedly.

"No. They got an *open bar.* You can come back and pick me up around four." He turned to Michael. "Can you walk her out?"

"Sure," Michael said. "Vera, don't you think you owe my girl an apology?"

"I guess," she said, rolling her eyes. "Sorry, I was about to go Southside Chicago on you. I don't want my man buying nothing for nobody but me. Nothing personal."

Chantal curled her lip up and waved her away.

"Oh, okay. It's like that? It's your day so I'll let you slide. This was real nice. You a classy stripper. I give it to you." She turned to Michael. "I'm ready. I'm leaving to get my toes done. I'll pick your boy up after." Michael followed her out to the parking lot.

"Vera, I know you and I aren't on the best of terms. What was up with you goin' in on my lady? I mean you ready to throw blows with a pregnant woman."

"Michael, I was wrong. You know when I get liquored up, I lose it. This fool didn't even acknowledge my birthday last week. Then he gets her some platinum. *You* should wonder about that."

She turned to unlock her door and hopped in her ride. "I know my Reggie better than *anybody.* He don't ever do anything nice unless it's to cover up for something."

"What would he have to cover up that would make him buy her something expensive? You don't make a lick of sense."

"Really?" she asked with shock in her voice. "Let me tell you what I know. His motive wasn't generosity. Trust. He may be your boy, but he also wishes he were you."

Michael was stunned. He never saw Reggie as a wanna-be type of brother. "Vera, I think you a little off. Or still drunk. You need me to call a cab?"

"Naw, my Cîroc wore off. But I'm not off."

"This don't make any sense at all."

"I know you all see me as ghetto and I am." She stated matter-of-factly.

"Mama didn't raise no fool. I watch what people do and really listen to what people say."

"Your point?"

She hit her hand with her fist for emphasis. "You always came out on top first. You may have brought him with you but he has *never* had his own first at anything. He is the leftover type of guy."

"Vera, that's cold. That's my main man. My brother from another mother. I can't let you disrespect him."

"I didn't. Reggie has a lot of great qualities but can't see them because he wants to be like you. Did he tell you when Yolanda started preaching he suggested I go to theology school?" Her eyes widened incredulously. "When your business started booming – although you hired him as your right hand man – he thought we could move into your subdivision too. There's other examples. Please remember this, there's a fine line

270

between admiration with gratitude and a simmering resentment because you never feel good enough."

Michael was floored. While he didn't want to take Vera seriously, for the first time in his life, he questioned whether or not Reggie was jealous. He always applauded Michael's success. He worked hard at everything for Michael. Michael entrusted Reggie with his struggles.

But Reggie also celebrated with him *after* failures. Not like he was happy at the failure itself but pushing Michael toward the opposite of where he needed to go. *No, that's my man...100 grand.* He wasn't going to let her make him paranoid about the real Reggie he trusted all his life.

"Vera, I think you tripping. I've known Reggie decades before you. He's never wronged me. I think your insecurity is overtaking you."

"On that note, I'm out." Vera shrieked. "I may not be the hot chick like your girl, but I am loyal, honest and know when I'm right. So when it all falls down and you need some help, holla at ya girl." She rolled up the window and backed out, not giving Michael another glance.

Michael shook his head and headed back into the ballroom. He noticed they had tables full of gifts that needed to be put in the truck. He decided to go ahead and pack the car. He needed to keep his mind busy.

Michael sorted out the gifts from big to small and got all the cards together and realized one was on the floor. It was in a blue envelope – just like the box Reggie had given Chantal. He picked it up, realizing Reggie dropped it and forgot to give it to them with the gift. The gift was enough so Michael wasn't worried about the card. He started to pitch it, when something on the envelope caught his attention.

"To Michael and Chantal" the card read. Though that wasn't what caught his eye. In the office, field employees rarely wrote anything.

Much of their work was processed on tablets and laptops. In fact, Michael had never focused on Reggie's penmanship. Until now.

The "l's" had loops at the bottom. Just like the forged check.

Chapter
Twenty-Nine

Yolanda heard the door creak and popped up in bed. She hadn't been the heaviest sleeper but as of late, any little noise woke her up. "Who is it?"

"Mama, it's me. Can I lay with you?" It was Noel. Ever since the incident with Daryl, she was rarely in the house. She would sleep over at Sable's and often stayed with Rocky for days at a time. When she was home, she'd sleep on Yolanda's chaise, which Yolanda didn't mind.

"Yeah, baby," Yolanda answered, yawning. "Grab the throw. It's by the chaise."

"No. I want to lay *with* you."

Yolanda's ears perked up. While she and Noel's relationship was slowly getting better, Noel still withheld affection. Every now and then, she would lightly hug her mother but lay up and cuddle? Out of the question. So Yolanda welcomed the childlike tenderness from her almost grown daughter. She pulled back the comforter and motioned for Noel to lie down.

Noel hopped in the bed, pulling the covers around her neck and nuzzled over to her mother. Yolanda was touched, grateful the moment she longed for was coming into fruition.

"You still having trouble sleeping?" Yolanda asked. Though Noel didn't want to talk about the situation with Daryl after his arrest, she knew Noel was still shaken by it. Yolanda understood, which is why she allowed her to attend church with Rocky and Terrence. Yolanda felt guilty staying there after that went down but tried to explain it away. Noel shouldn't have got involved with him, which was true. But it didn't change the uneasiness of working in a ministry where her daughter was put in harm's way.

"Not as bad," Noel admitted. She put her arm around her mother's waist. "I mean, he's on house arrest until his court date. I heard he'll be headed back to Chicago after he does his time." Noel paused. "This was someone I trusted and really cared about."

Yolanda clasped her hand. "I know. I have to admit. I have had some thoughts about leaving the church. This person was supposed to be trustworthy and come to find out he was someone totally different."

"I was mad at you at first. I understand you needed a job and if I wouldn't have been so shady in the first place, it wouldn't have happened." Noel's voice was cracking. She still got emotional thinking what could have happened if she didn't escape.

"I figured you were mad. Terrence and I discussed it." She rubbed her left shoulder as that stress pain flared up again. "He said I should just be still and let God's divine providence take place."

"Figures." Noel chuckled. "He's a walking Bible. But I like him. I kind of love him even."

Yolanda was shocked. She knew Noel was becoming less guarded around Terrence but had no idea she'd so quickly allow love to develop

274

for a man she had known for only a small fraction of her life. "Really? Do you think about Michael anymore?"

"I miss him in some ways. He was the only man I knew as my daddy so I still love him." Her face grimaced. "I don't like him though. Choosing to knock up a stripper young enough to be his daughter."

Yolanda didn't mean to laugh out loud but she did. "Honey, people make mistakes. The baby is meant to be here, so just pray for him. How you go from a preacher to a stripper is unlikeable, but at least respect him for being a father to you."

Noel was silent for a moment. "So now what do we do?"

"What do you mean?"

"It's only us. It's never been just us together."

It was true. They never had a chance to bond on their own. A wall always existed between them. A tear slowly rolled down her cheek. "Are you okay with it being just me and you?"

Noel's silence scared Yolanda. Finally, she said, "Yeah, I guess I am. It kinda feels weird. I know you, but I don't really know you well. I'd like to try, though."

Yolanda rolled over and embraced her daughter. Both of them shed a few silent tears. Noel stroked her mother's hair. "I know in a year or two, I'll be away at college and...and...I don't want you to be alone."

Yolanda's heart beat rapidly. She anticipated what Noel would say next.

"It's okay, Mama. You can forgive him. He's a good dude."

Yolanda couldn't believe what she was hearing. Her own daughter was okay with her reconnecting with the man who played a big part of their past pain and deceit.

"Mama? Helloooo? You sleep?" Noel sounded slightly irritated.

"No. I was just thinking about what you said."

"And?" Noel looked directly into her eyes. She tried to read how her mother was feeling.

"I have forgiven him. I am as much to blame as him. I am sorry that I put all of it on him instead of accepting responsibility for my role."

"Good. Jesus says forgive others if you want forgiveness. That's Bible 101, Mama."

Yolanda rolled her eyes. Her daughter had a smart mouth.

"Hush, girl! I don't know what you want me to say."

"Okay, let me spell it out because I know this is an act. If you want to be with Terrence, I would be okay with that."

Yolanda smiled softly. "Thank you. I don't know if that will happen or not."

"Do you like him?"

"Yes."

"You love him?"

276

Yolanda pondered that question. They had been reunited a little less than a year, but were so in sync it was like they'd been together for the past seventeen years. She thought about how he always came to her side and made her feel safe. He knew her whole story; he was a major part of it. He witnessed the ugliness she didn't like to think about. Yet, he was someone who wholeheartedly believed she was a different person because he was too.

"Mama, it's two a.m. I need my beauty sleep. At your age, you do too. So, please answer."

Yolanda playfully swatted her daughter's behind. "I guess I do." Yolanda was shocked to hear what she said but even more surprised it came from her heart.

"If you love him and I am sure he loves you, then do something about it."

"I have a question for you now. Will you ever refer to him as your father?"

"I know he is." Noel said matter-of-factly. "I'll call him Dad or Pops one day. I've got to get used to it because Michael was Daddy for so long." She sighed. "I'll make a pinky promise with you," Noel said as she extended her pinky. Yolanda wrapped her pinky around hers, as the moonlight shone through the picture window.

"I will call him Dad by the time you marry."

Yolanda was taken aback. "Who said anything about marriage? If we never marry, you can't keep calling him Terrence."

"I know. Okay, I pinky promise to start calling him something fatherly. And I also promise I've forgiven you and I'm thankful for all you have done."

Pinkies locked, Yolanda kissed her daughter on the cheek. They both fell into a blissful rest. For the first time in their lives as mother and daughter, they were at peace with one another. If Yolanda didn't live another day, this was the best way to live her last.

✞✞✞

Yolanda was more refreshed than she'd been in ages. Noel decided to go to church the next morning with her mother. She was glad Terrence picked them up. He refused to let Yolanda go into a den of vipers without covering from a man of God.

As they walked in, Yolanda felt the stares. She knew the hushed whispers were about her coming to church with someone other than Michael. Their divorce had been finalized fairly quickly. Since it was evident he had moved on, Yolanda was angry people appeared to be judging her. That always disappointed her about church folk, ready to judge without taking the log out of their own eye.

"Minister Howard, you don't miss a beat!" One of the ushers came up and loudly exclaimed, embracing her in a perfumed hug. "Honey, your ex was okay but your next is fine. Baby, you related to Idris Elba?" She smiled widely displaying her two gold buck teeth, while she salivated over Terrence.

"Nice to meet you, my sister in Christ." Terrence extended his hand.

"Sister Pamela don't do hands. I only do hugs." She eagerly embraced Terrence and actually rubbed his back, stopping at his belt. "Hmmm...yes. God is able," she hollered out, practically grinding on him. Noel gawked, in total shock at what was displayed before her.

Yolanda stood frozen. She didn't know if she should snatch him and leave or grab her by that awful cheap synthetic burgundy lace front.

Terrence wrangled himself loose. "Sister, I appreciate the welcome but I can do without the R. Kelly bump and grind. It's nice to meet you though," he said pointedly then took Yolanda by the hand, leading her away.

Yolanda spotted Pastor Griffin. She headed toward him to introduce Terrence and inquire about where her new office was. She'd been locked out of her old office on Friday, but hadn't received a pink slip or a demotion, so obviously he was doing some movement among the offices – nothing new for his staff.

Before she could get to him, Sister Boyd stepped directly in front of her and Terrence. "Well, Minister Howard," she sounded cheerful, although Yolanda knew there was no love lost between them. "You are looking well. You certainly are a Romans 8 woman."

Yolanda was puzzled. "Excuse me?"

"You're a minister. You know Romans 8:37. You are more than a conqueror." She clapped her hands together. "You overcame a wayward teen past. Then, a husband who didn't want you. And now you come in with a chocolate Adonis." She reached out to shake Terrence's hand. "I am Sister Boyd, auntie of the illustrious Pastor Griffin. And you are?"

Terrence shook her hand and responded, "I am Yolanda's mate, Noel's biological father." Terrence cocked his head to the side, seeming to read her from the inside out.

Apparently, it made Sister Boyd uncomfortable which was evident in the way she shifted her eyes from his gridlocked stare. She slowly pulled her hand back. "Well," she said, clearing her throat, "God is certainly amazing. Enjoy the service." She glanced at Noel. Yolanda noticed it was actually more of a glare. "Noel, dear," she sneered. "So wonderful to see you've recovered. I do apologize for what happened but when we live in rebellion, it often--"

"Hold up!" Terrence barked, interrupting her sentence. Pastor Griffin was nearby and looked up. He narrowed his eyes, aware something was going on. He looked like he was about to rush over until one of the elders pulled him to the side.

"Here's what you're not gonna do," Terrence said with his former thug edge in his voice. He had caught her off guard, because the normally cocky Sister Boyd moved back in fear. "You're not gonna put blame on my daughter for what your so-called nephew tried to do. Be grateful, because if it wasn't for the Lord, you best believe we may be here for his funeral today." Her jaw dropped at his answer. She looked him up and down like he had lost his mind. "But," Terrence smiled at her, "I will hold on to the Lord's unchanging hand. Amen?" He hugged her, while her arms remained stiffly at her side. "I like that hat. Reminds me of the one we buried my mother in back in '82. Enjoy service and may you be blessed today." Terrence walked away to get them seats. Noel beamed wildly, trailing close behind him. Yolanda wanted to high-five him and slap Sister Boyd. She was so overjoyed that for once the lady was speechless.

"I admit, he more of a man than that last one you had. He still in my life since he knocked up my sister's fast tail grandchild." Sister Boyd shook her head. "Your real baby daddy, he got some brass ones. Kind of turned me on."

This time Yolanda's jaw dropped. She couldn't believe Sister Boyd went there. Before she could respond, Sister Boyd hugged her and whispered in her ear, "I might actually miss you after today. You do add a little spice to my church life." She pulled back, held Yolanda at arms' length, and glanced at her in admiration. "I like your preaching. Your sass. Back in my day you would have been in my crew." She sighed. "But all good things must come to an end. I often wonder why you didn't make your move sooner."

Yolanda was startled. "What move? Am I getting moved to a sister church or what?" Yolanda was relieved. She wouldn't mind a change. Yolanda pondered quitting after the whole incident with Daryl but believed God was telling her to be still and wait for the time to be released.

Sister Boyd smiled widely. "I don't want to ruin the surprise." With that said, she turned on her heel to be escorted to her front row seat.

Yolanda's stomach was in knots. She thought back to the front porch slap down they had not too long ago. Sister Boyd didn't seem to be the type to let go of a grudge so easily. Yolanda didn't want to be naïve but didn't want any surprises either. She had been so stressed with headaches and pain she feared one more surprise or problem could take a toll on her. She decided to ask Pastor Griffin about her office before worship started.

Yolanda headed over to the meeting room where they met for prayer. Luckily, no one was in there except Pastor Griffin. He sat with his back toward Yolanda. She lightly tapped him on the shoulder.

When he turned around, his expression went from calm to one of disdain or subtle anger. Whichever one, he didn't seem too pleased to see her.

Pastor Griffin realized his feelings were on his face and immediately forced a smile. "Hello there, Minister Howard. We're not ready for prayer yet so if you want, have a seat or better yet, take one in the sanctuary."

Yolanda was taken aback but not deterred to force him to answer what was going on. "I am fine here," she said firmly, not wanting to show that she was nervous. "Pastor, are you moving me or changing my office? My key hasn't worked since Friday."

He folded his arms across his chest. "Oh? I can't recall having the locks changed."

Now Yolanda was getting hot. She didn't like his passive aggressive pretending instead of just being upfront with her. She thought about just grabbing Terrence and Noel to leave, but Yolanda was too stubborn – and curious – to let him off that easy. "That's funny," she coyly responded. "I sure think your *auntie* seemed to know why." Yolanda smirked, knowing he was playing games with her.

He rolled his eyes. "Really? Well, if she does know something, I guess we'll both find out. But I have a message I need to pray for and announcements to make. This little office issue can wait." Suddenly his mood lightened. "I know we're doing some moving around. I guess they hit up your space a little soon. During service, we'll see if we can't get that announced."

Yolanda wasn't sure if she trusted him. Something inside her was screaming, "Leave." She knew the church had its issues. She hoped her comfort and familiarity wouldn't be fatal to her. Yolanda wanted to give him the benefit of the doubt but discerned something was off kilter.

Pastor Griffin detected she was trying to sort everything out. He touched her shoulder. "I see you are moving on since the divorce. Affairs are hard to get over but when a man wants what he wants, you got to let him go. But I am glad to see you reconcile with your child's

282

real father. You didn't miss a beat. Is the ink dry on your divorce papers?" He chuckled. Yolanda was disgusted by his poor attempt at humor.

The other ministers filed in, including Monica. Monica looked smug, her nose in the air. She sauntered across the room in a new, profound confidence. Monica always thought she was all that but today, it was extra. She had on a curve fitting red dress, four-inch strappy heels, emphasizing her toned calves. Her makeup was flawless, looking like she just stepped away from a MAC counter. Her chestnut waves cascaded around her face. Monica was a beautiful woman. Yolanda had to admit she couldn't understand how a man could step out on her. When Monica opened her mouth though, Yolanda knew exactly why a man could get fed up.

"You all, I am so excited about this day. I am believing God for the miraculous, do you hear me? My husband and I are going to have a child – even though it's his side baby, I'm claiming it as my own." She looked demurely at Yolanda and continued. "You know as fearfully and wonderfully made as I am, a man would be a fool to step out on me. But all have fallen short of the glory of God." She jumped up and down, her bodacious booty bouncing. It was obvious she was Spanx free today. The male ministers followed the junk in her trunk with their eyes, watching her behind go up and down. Yolanda pondered how many squats she did to get all that. She noticed Pastor Griffin taking a peek. He smiled, looking like he was in deep thought.

He straightened his face when Candace walked in. She looked with disgust at Monica, who was still doing her holy dance with the booty bounce. "Stop it!" She rolled her eyes. "This ain't Magic Horse or Strokers. Why isn't your robe on anyways?"

"Pastor said since we have some announcements and it's a special Sunday, we don't need robes today," Monica faked meekness, shyly

283

gazing at the ground.

"So, of course the day there's no robes you come in with your whoremonger red dress on, looking like you just left the club." Candace snapped. "I know one thing- you better not have one of your falling in the floor moments in *that* dress."

Uncomfortable with tension between the two, Minister Leems stepped in. "Why don't we go ahead and pray so we can let all our issues fall by the side, bringing them captive under the Lord's authority?"

As they exited the room. Monica paused in front of Yolanda. "You know what? I've never had anything against you."

She hesitated. "Sometimes there's not room for everyone at the top so you have to...figure out ways to get around it. I just thought I'd let you know. Besides, you have good bounce back power." She abruptly turned and hurried out the room before Yolanda could question her further.

✟✟✟

Pastor Griffin came to the podium. He stood, eyes closed, appearing to meditate in the Spirit. He lifted up his hands and shouts of praise rang out in the sanctuary. All six thousand seats were full and everyone was moved. After a few moments, Pastor opened his eyes and adjusted his headpiece so his microphone was in the right place. He motioned to the cameramen, who frantically ran to the control room. Pastor cleared his throat. The noise slowly died down, as the congregation anticipated that the sermon was about to start.

"Saints, we have had a good time in the Lord today. Amen? But even in the midst of the good, we have to deal with things that don't feel good at the time. I consider us a family. A family within the family of Christ.

284

And every family needs to have a "come to Jesus" meeting." He smiled and the crowd laughed softly. "When there is change needing to take place; correction which is necessary; and situations not yet handled – at those times, we must come to Jesus to do the right thing. Even if it feels bad at the time."

He walked across the pulpit, as he often did when he was getting amped up. "You see the Bible says, speak the truth in love. When we continue to operate "as is" so we won't hurt someone's feelings or rock the boat, we are hindering the growth of our brother or sister in the Lord." He looked right at Yolanda. Immediately, she knew something was about to go down. "Like they say, 'the truth hurts'."

He took an envelope out of his pocket. He stopped and glanced at Yolanda. "Part of the truth is owning your past mistakes, no matter how ugly. When you hide secrets for so long, you begin to think some things never happened."

He walked down the stairs to the front row and grabbed Monica by the hand. He stood her up and motioned for her to follow him up into the pulpit. Her curvaceous hips swayed sexily back and forth. Yolanda didn't know what was going on.

When Pastor Griffin and Monica got to the center of the stage, he grabbed a microphone and handed it to Monica. He turned back to the congregation. "I asked the cameramen to stop filming. We have a family situation and it is between family only, amen? In your own family, you know dynamics change. Kids grow up. People marry. Babies are born. People move." He looked at Monica and smiled. "People move on. Others move up."

"Saints," he continued, once again glancing at Yolanda. "We need more women in leadership. My beautiful wife is my ministry partner but she has no desire to work here." Everyone laughed. "We have Minister

285

Howard, who has gone through her own changes this season. God is blessing her with reconciliation of old relationships even in the midst of one ending."

There was an uncomfortable silence. Michael had stopped coming to church months ago, but no one had spoken directly about their split.

"But, I applaud her faith. She keeps serving. Keeps praying. Keeps forgiving. Keeps ministering. And for that we salute her." He motioned for the congregation to stand and applaud her, as her face was shown up close on the jumbo screens. Terrence pulled her to her feet and she waved at everyone, mouthing "Thank you". Though she smiled, she waited for the other shoe to drop.

"Minister Howard, can you come up here please?" Pastor Griffin beamed at her. Monica motioned for her to hurry to the stage.

Yolanda walked to the center of the stage. The envelope Pastor Griffin had pulled out of his pocket was thrust her way. She grasped it in her hand while he leaned in to hug her. He had moved his microphone to whisper in her ear, "You tried to humiliate me and my family. Now it's your turn." Yolanda wanted to leave but couldn't move. Her knees were weak. Her heart plummeted into her stomach, more stress pains shot through her shoulder area.

"As Minister Howard opens her notice from the church, I want to go ahead and let you know the new direction we are taking. As I said, we need new female leadership and while Minister Howard has been a blessing to us and deserves this honor, she is not going to get it."

It became eerily silent. Yolanda sensed the congregants could hear her now shallow breathing. *Lord, what's happening?*

286

Trust me. This will not be the end, Yolanda heard in her spirit.

"Instead the co-pastor of New Life Christian Center is none other than Minister Monica Caine." Monica waved to the church, like she'd just won a beauty pageant. No one responded at all. Most of the congregants' mouths were wide open in shock.

"I know you are thinking why? Why her? What will happen to Minister Howard? It makes sense on paper that Minister Howard would be the easy choice. We have appreciated her and acknowledge what she has contributed to our church. That's why we know with the seed we have given her, she will be fine when she moves into another ministry."

Murmurs filled the building. Yolanda's face flushed. She saw Terrence leave his seat and storm to the front. The Armor Bearers blocked him from coming into the pulpit, which caused a momentary disruption. Yolanda couldn't move. She knew she should leave but honestly, she was in shock. She waited to hear perhaps he was moving her to one of their sister churches but what came next changed the course of her life.

"Minister Howard, may God bless and keep you. We are so happy you have reconciled with your child's real father. We believe now maybe your own daughter won't fall prey to the things that led you astray. We know wherever God takes you, you are a survivor. The fact is," he continued, each word stabbing deeper into her heart. "You are so devoted to the title and task of ministry your own house is in shambles. For years, your own daughter disowned you and you led her to believe her father was a man who was simply a small time dope dealer turned boyfriend who was too much of a punk to defend your own honor."

"Hold up, Pastor." Sable stood up and hollered out. "You not about to put down my daughter while making the wanna be pastor's wife the co-pastor. If I wasn't saved, your windows would be busted out in your Land Cruiser. We ain't takin' this." Sable jumped over the pew and headed straight up to the stage. The Armor Bearers tried to hold her back but she pulled out her mace and sprayed them in the eyes. Terrence burst past them, and made his way to Yolanda's side.

Total mayhem broke out. She saw Terrence grab Pastor Griffin by the collar. Sable poked her finger in Monica's smirking face. Candace ran up to push her husband in the chest, hurt by what he had done. But everything wasn't over.

On the jumbo screen, a presentation played. It started with Yolanda's past mug shot for stealing when she was nineteen. Followed by the news story of the drug bust Terrence had been involved in. Photos of Yolanda in the days of drinking and smoking with Michael came up next. She didn't even know where the film or pictures had come from. Lastly, pictures of Michael in the strip club getting lap dances scrolled across the screen. Yolanda was sick to her stomach.

"Church, we know all have sinned and fallen short of the glory of God," Monica's voice boomed. "She hasn't been clean with any of us. We knew she had a past but she never allowed us to see the entirety of it." She looked at Yolanda and smiled. "It's not that God can't use you, the question is how are you going to be a testimony when you haven't been transparent?"

"Her past, my past. It's under the blood." Terrence yelled, still holding Pastor Griffin by his necktie. "Why you digging all this up? You got your dirt, too."

"Simple. We need to know what and who we deal with." Monica said sharply. "Everyone knows my dirt, his dirt. But she wants to play like her past didn't happen. And she's still deceitful. Tried to set up people for a crime they didn't commit. Do we need to go there?"

"Oh, you don't want to because the truth is--" Terrence began.

Everything was interrupted by a shrill scream. "Is my mama dead?" Noel ran to the pulpit. Kennedy came up with Eddie. The congregation was in disarray. People moved into the aisles to get a better view of the service turned circus taking place before them.

"Call 911! Call 911!"

Yolanda had fallen unconscious. Pastor Griffin simply stepped back, like nothing was wrong. Candace couldn't believe her husband. She performed CPR on Yolanda as the thing Yolanda feared had come upon her. All her past secrets were revealed and she was judged for them. The pain of her past was too much to bear publicly. So much so, it finally took a toll on her.

Yolanda had a heart attack.

Pressing Past the Past

Chapter Thirty

Michael yawned, functioning on only half an hour of sleep. They'd rushed Chantal to the hospital when she went into labor. They gave her Demerol to take the edge off. At the moment, she was asleep. He looked at her in the hospital bed, her full face beautiful as ever.

At first, Michael was worried she was going into labor too soon. Come to find out, she was further along than they thought. He was excited yet nervous, anticipating the birth of his baby boy. He looked at Chantal not wanting to leave her alone. But he needed to clear his head.

A nurse popped in to check on her. Michael excused himself while she came in to check the monitor and determine when they would break her water. Chantal opened her eyes, groggy from the meds. "Hey baby," she whispered. "Where you going? Where Mama?"

"She went to Waffle House. I'm going to head to the vending machine. I'll be right back."

"Okay. Don't be gone too long. Text my sisters and them too, okay?" Michael gave her a tight-lipped grin and nodded. He had no intention of calling any of her family. They were a hood version of the "Beverly Hillbillies".

Michael closed the door behind him, pulled out his phone to let his boys know she was in labor. He didn't expect them to come but wanted to give them a heads up. He hadn't heard back from anyone, including Reggie.

As Michael headed into the elevator, he was shocked to see Kennedy, Eddie and his former first lady in there. He couldn't believe he was next to his ex-wife's best friend while his new girl was about to have his baby. *Really, Lord?*

Michael wondered if he should speak but noticed Kennedy's tear-stained cheeks. He knew she couldn't be in labor. At first, no one seemed to notice him. When they got to the next floor that changed.

The door opened and there was Sable and Noel.

"Nig- I mean – what you doing here?" Sable said. Noel slid in and hugged Michael. "Thanks for coming."

Michael was confused. "Coming? I had to. I'm...I mean she...we...the baby is coming." Noel's eyes widened. She moved away from him. Sable simply shook her head and muttered, "Humph."

"What's wrong? Why are you all here?" The door chimed and Eddie gave Michael a slight shove with his shoulder to move past him. Michael wanted to check him, but something told him now was not the time. "Kennedy, you good?"

Kennedy looked up. "No, I'm not," her voice cracked. "Not that you care, but my best friend– whom you cheated on with a wanna-be nurse stripper - is in danger of losing her life. You had her all messed up because you could never man up."

"Baby, he isn't worth it," Eddie said. He pulled Kennedy by the hand, with Candace rushing ahead of them. Sable gave Michael one more look of disgust, shook her head and walked away. She paused, looked over her shoulder and said, "Let her family worry about her. You run on back up to your whore. Congrats on the baby...better swab his cheek before

292

you sign." She sauntered off yelling without turning around, "Noel, let's go to your *mother and father.*"

"Noel, real quick," Michael whispered, motioning her to come close. "What's wrong?"

She burst into tears. "Daddy. Michael..." She sobbed and composed herself. "It was just too much. Me, the ministry, you, the pastor...Mama...had a heart attack at church."

Michael was floored. No matter what had happened, he would never wish this on Yolanda. After all, she had been the love of his life in his early years. His heart dropped into his stomach. He wanted to go see her, but knew that could make it worse.

"Did she make it?"

Noel nodded. "She's not out of the woods yet. They sedated her and are waiting for her to regain consciousness. Please pray she makes it."

"I will," Michael promised. He hugged Noel and whispered in her ear, "She'll be okay. God isn't through using her yet. I wish I could do something. Can I see her?"

Noel untangled herself from his embrace and firmly said, "No. I know you still care for Mama, but please don't. She is moving on and my...my...other dad..."

"No, it's okay. He is your real dad. I will always love you like a father, but it's okay Noel. You can forgive him. You can love him. If he's good to you," Michael stared into her eyes. "I can accept that. I'm so sorry we lied to you."

Noel took a deep breath. "My dad may not like you coming. Right now, he's there praying. He's been praying and fasting since we got here. Literally, the nurses have had to walk over him." Noel laughed softly and Michael joined in.

"Your mother would love to see him in action. She needs a man like that. But if you ever need me, I am still here."

Noel gave Michael a quick hug again before she ran off to catch up with her grandmother. Michael slowly headed back to the elevator in disbelief. When the door closed, Michael did something he hadn't done in a while.

He lowered himself to his knees and prayed. When he got up, the door immediately opened.

There was Reggie.

Although the check situation was in the back of his mind, Michael was glad to see him. He hoped Reggie could take his mind off Yolanda. But for some reason, Reggie looked startled.

"Hey man! I just texted you a little bit ago. You here already?"

"Aw...well..." Reggie's eyes shifted to the ground, with him faking a cough. Michael was puzzled but stepped into the elevator next to him. He wanted to bring up the check. He didn't really know how. For a minute, Michael thought about just letting it go. After all, he couldn't prove he forged a check yet the eerie similarity of the "I" and then the warning from Vera caused him to question for the first time ever if his number one boy was playing him. He decided to focus on making sure the baby got here before going there. He changed the subject.

"Man, how weird is it that I'm here having a baby..." Michael began.

"You not havin' nothin'. Let's get that right." He smiled broadly to cover his rough edge and playfully socked Michael in the arm. "I mean, if it were you having a baby literally, we got problems. There's something you ain't let me know, dawg."

Michael rolled his eyes at Reggie's dry humor. "I know, trust. And while my current lady about to have a baby, how about Yolanda is upstairs in intensive care after having a heart attack, man?"

"Man, fo' real?" Reggie looked sad. "I pray she makes it. Noel needs her. She got church business to take care of. Did you go see her?"

"I would have but Kennedy, Eddie, her mama, none of them are feeling me. I know I've moved on. She has, too. But, I can't help but wonder...did...did I..." his voice trailed off, afraid to admit he may have contributed to her current state.

"Did you make it happen?" Reggie finished his thought for him. "I mean, you did play her dirty."

Now Michael was getting heated. Reggie seemed to imply he was the reason his ex was lying at death's door. "Hey. I don't need all that. I know I did my dirt but who was with me encouraging it? You! So don't sit here and point at me like you a saint."

Reggie poked out his chest and walked up on Michael. He'd been smoking. Unlike some weed-heads, Reggie's "Kali Kush" mix made him bolder and quick to get angry. "I never said I was a saint." He was breathing hard, his nostrils flared in anger.

"You playing like the victim but you ain't been a victim ever since you hit it big. You set foot on the college campus, got your degrees, got your business off the ground, threw me some bones and now you want me to feel sorry for you?" Reggie looked Michael up and down. "I'm gon'

295

keep it one hundred. You played yourself. So, don't try to get no sympathy from me."

Michael was startled. The conversation he had with Vera was starting to be confirmed in his mind. "I didn't ask your opinion nor for you to be here. In fact, if you want to keep your job, I suggest you fall back. Let that weed wear off and then come holla at me. The rate you going, you about to get knocked out for real."

Reggie slowly backed up. "My bad, dawg. I just...just got a lot on my mind. I'll go sit in the waiting room. Do what you need to do." Before Michael could respond, he staggered down the hall, leaving Michael more confused than ever. He didn't know how Reggie knew Chantal was giving birth nor could he figure out what he was so mad about. Michael shrugged it off, heading back Chantal's room. Oddly enough, Reggie changed his mind about going to the waiting room and quietly followed. Although Michael was glad they weren't arguing, the quietness was uneasy.

"Michael! Your girl's door is wide open and your baby boy could be out any minute." Chantal's mother shrieked hysterically from the room. "You did this to her so get in here and help this girl." He shook his head as he hurried in. The biggest and best moment of his life was here and he wouldn't let her ghetto mama or his boy ruin it.

✟✟✟

Michael sat holding a little brown boy in his arms. He had a head full of curly black hair and a deep dimple in his chin, just like his mother. Michael's heart was filled with joy. Although from time to time, he did wonder how Yolanda was. Chantal was sleeping while her ghetto family had decided to go to Rib Shack for dinner. For some reason, Reggie had stuck around the entire time. Michael couldn't find the right time or

296

words to talk to Reggie about his suspicions about the check.

There was a soft knock at the door. "Excuse me," a friendly redhead nurse came in. "We need to take little Michael down for some routine tests. Do you all want to keep him in the room or the nursery for the night?"

Honestly, Michael didn't want to lay his son down but figured Chantal could use the rest. "We can give his mom a break." He bent to kiss his son on the nose. "Can I walk down with you?"

She smiled. "Sure. I know it's hard to let him go. He's adorable."

Michael smiled. He felt happier than he had felt in a long time. "He's big, too." Little Michael, or MJ, was nine pounds and twenty-two and a half inches.

When they arrived at the infant unit, Michael handed over his son to the nurse. "Bye, buddy. Daddy will see you later."

Michael reached Chantal's room. The door was ajar, though he'd left it closed. He got ready to burst inside but stopped when he heard familiar voices.

"I told you I would have got you the money. Why would you do that?" Chantal sounded frantic. Michael's ears perked up.

"You was getting too soft. I needed it then. But since you all in love now, you tryin' to play me."

Reggie.

It took all Michael's power not to bust into the room and see what was going on. But something told him to wait.

297

"I shouldn't have let you blackmail me. I should have just told him, but I was too embarrassed."

Michael heard a slap. "You take your clothes off for a living. Do you think that's not embarrassing enough?" Reggie laughed gruffly. "If it wasn't for me, you wouldn't have hit the jackpot anyway."

"Get out." Chantal screamed. "I will call the police. I don't work for you."

"Not anymore. You better make sure that baby ain't mine."

Michael's heart fell to his feet. His head was spinning. He was confused. Was Reggie messing with Chantal? And how did she 'work' for him? Michael burst open the door and immediately grabbed Reggie by his neck. Chantal hollered. Hospital security and two nurses rushed in.

Michael had almost choked Reggie unconscious. The security guard grabbed Michael's arms. Reggie fell to the ground. "Ma'am, do you want us to call the police?" The nurses looked scared.

"No, please don't," Chantal pleaded. "It's just a misunderstanding. We'll quiet down and handle it."

The security guards let Michael go. They gave him a stern look before backing out of the room. Michael knew he'd better keep his composure because they looked ready to send a brother to jail. He stood over Reggie, who was still on the ground, coughing while he clutched his throat.

"I heard y'alls little argument. Somebody tell me something." He looked at Reggie. "You been smashing my girl? Stealing from me, too?" Michael

298

was glad they were in public. He knew this was one time he could have shot somebody. The dude he thought was a brother to him was playing him – and it hurt.

Just like you hurt your wife.

Michael felt a pang of regret.

"Baby. This is the happiest day of my life. I am so grateful to you. What you heard...let me explain."

"Naw, baby. I got it," Reggie was on his feet, standing face-to-face with Michael. "So back in the day, when I was in my last foster home I met your girl. She needed a hustle so I hooked her up with dudes in the neighborhood. Every now and then, I'd hit it, but got the friend discount."

"Hold up," Michael said as pieces of the story were coming together in his mind. "You were his...'ho? I thought you went to school, got an associate's degree then decided to get an advanced degree in nursing."

Reggie laughed and sat on the bed. "How you think she paid for it? But when I got with Vera, you had your *business*." Though Reggie's lips were smiling, his eyes looked hard and mean. It actually made Michael pause and re-think their friendship. "So I stopped my mini pimping side-hustle, became your flunky and she started dancing." He paused thoughtfully. "I couldn't believe when you all met, once again you took what was mine."

Michael forgot about the threat of the police and punched Reggie in the mouth. Chantal flinched. She was too shocked to say anything. Reggie, bleeding from his face, laughed wickedly. "I'd punch me too if I got played like you did." Michael was fuming but regained his composure, shocked at Reggie's reaction. Reggie seemed intent on inflicting

299

emotional pain on him.

He took off his shirt and wiped his face. "I ain't mad at you."

"What do you mean I took what was yours again? It's not my fault you got infected by the system."

"You took the spotlight. When we were together, you always tried to outshine me. Got the grades. Did the sports. Anything to prove you was better than me." Reggie's pain showed on his face. "Had your parents, the girls...I was second fiddle."

"Man, my parents took you in. You were my brother. I never considered you second nothin'." Hot tears fell from his eyes, out of anger and the pain of betrayal.

"Don't cry now. You didn't cry when you went off to school. Sold a little dope. Got your degrees. Built a business. Gave me a hand-me-down job. You lived a perfect life. Then you took my girl." Reggie looked at Chantal. "She was supposed to be mine. She met you. You started paying her rent, buying her textbooks. She forgot we were a team."

Michael shook his head. He couldn't believe what he was hearing. "So you blackmailed her to keep it quiet?" Reggie said nothing. Michael looked at Chantal.

"I met Reggie and yes...I was...a prostitute." Chantal cried harder. Her body shook with sobs.

"I met you in a strip club. Why didn't you tell me?"

"Because I was ashamed. Stripping is not the best job but it's better than turning tricks with dirty old men, freaky women and being a sex

300

slave to married couples." She blew her nose on her hospital gown. "When I went back to school, it was my way to redeem myself. To this day, I can't believe some of the things I let *him* persuade me to do." She looked at Reggie, her eyes piercing him like daggers.

"So Reggie, you forged my signature on a check for a quarter of a million dollars? You know I could have you put away, right? How did you think you'd get away with it?"

"That's a good question! Actually, when you all *robbed your wife,* I told Chantal whatever you gave her, she needed to pay me to make me shut up forever. At first, I just wanted about fifty thousand. Then I decided I deserved more. Thought I'd get me a spot in Cali. Maybe send for Vera and the kids. I couldn't stay here and watch you win, man."

Michael always believed Reggie was his brother from another mother. But he had so much jealousy Michael couldn't believe he didn't pick up the signs any sooner.

"So you pimped my girl and stole my money, well tried. And now you think my son is yours?"

Chantal sat up. "No! MJ is yours. I promise you."

"I don't know because I still hit it every now and then. I blackmailed her for sex too, if you want to know." Reggie smiled, proud to cause Michael so much pain. "Let's not forget, she was a sidepiece for you until the baby came. Which is why you need to swab his cheek. We did it last – when, Boo? About Thanksgiving?"

Chantal sobbed. "Why are you doing this?" Reggie shrugged his shoulders – getting a kick out of the turmoil he was causing. For the first time, Michael knew what it felt like to hate someone.

301

Michael laughed gruffly. "Why you been doing *him*? I mean, was it to make a fool out of me?" Chantal continued to cry. "If you would have told me what was up, I could have fired him and had him out of our hair way before this." Michael shook his head. He turned to Reggie. "And you...you disgust me. Hatin' on me like you a girl. You are pitiful. Vera was right. You straight up jealous. I should press charges on you for this. But I feel so sorry for you, man. Stay away from me."

Michael had such a look of fury in his eyes Reggie shrunk back a tad. He knew when to back off.

"All right. I'm out. Sorry you had to find out like this, bro." Reggie looked down at his feet. "You were my partner but I was never your equal." For a minute, Michael thought he might apologize but he simply walked to the door and paused. "I'd still swab the baby's mouth to be safe. You can mail my last check." And with those words, he left.

Chapter
Thirty-One

Kennedy woke up. She was tired but too nervous to sleep in. She knew she wanted to go by the hospital and see Yolanda. She was concerned she hadn't gained consciousness yet. It had been three days since the heart attack. Kennedy was so distraught the only reason she ate was due to the life growing inside of her.

The life inside of *her*.

That was the next hurdle. Today was the day when they would confirm Marcus was the father of her baby.

It was a silent ride to Dr. Steward's office. When Eddie pulled into a parking space, he shut off the car and sighed before turning to Kennedy. "Baby, I am sorry I seem so distant. I'm trying to wrap my brain around what we are about to hear today."

Kennedy nodded. She knew he had been bothered by the situation. "I'd be lying if I didn't admit I been struggling with how I am going to accept an innocent child, yes – but one that isn't mine." Eddie's brow furrowed as it often did when he was upset. "He'll be a constant reminder of your transgression."

Kennedy gulped. "You said you'd be here." She was on the verge of tears. "You said God told you to forgive me and stay. Did you change your mind?"

He sighed again, this time harder than before. "If I tell God I'm going to do something, I am. The Word tells us to be careful not to make a vow before God. I can't say it will be easy or that I'm happy, but, all we can do is pray." Kennedy saw a tear in the corner of Eddie's eye and burst into full fledge sobs.

She paused to catch her breath. Eddie grabbed her hand and squeezed it. "Let's go." He exited the car and headed toward the office, leaving Kennedy behind. She was more scared than she'd ever been before – even more than the moment when she lost her purity early in life.

✞✞✞

Eddie read *Sports Illustrated,* mainly to keep from having to look at Kennedy. He was wrestling with his promise to God and being able to fully trust Kennedy and accept the baby inside her. He'd been praying and fasting for days unbeknownst to her. He asked God to change his heart and mind. That hadn't happened yet. He prayed for a miracle. He wasn't sure what kind God could do in this.

His thoughts were interrupted when a familiar voice said, "Today is the day the Lord has made. Let's rejoice and be glad in it." It was Mother Stone in a cotton candy pink suit with a green felt hat. Eddie was confused why she was there, dressed like she was an AKA.

"Mama, hold all that down. We're in a doctor's office." She balked at his aggressiveness.

"I'm going to let that slide. I'd be hot too if I had to deal with my spouse having a baby with somebody else's mate." She looked sideways at Kennedy.

"You do know how to handle it. Didn't your husband have kids not by you?" Kennedy responded dryly, not even looking up from her Bible.

"Look here, wench. Don't get smart with me. Yes, Eddie's daddy wronged me, but that's what men do. I ain't ever known a woman to be so loose she got pregnant not only by someone else's husband but another woman of God." She shook her head and fanned herself feverishly with a green peacock fan she pulled out of her purse. "The Bible says touch not God's anointed and do his prophet no harm. And you not only touched the anointed but slept with her husband."

"Mama, please be quiet." Eddie said forcefully. "Why are you here looking like you about to go to an AKA meeting?"

"I figured I needed to dress up for the occasion. Once we find out the results, which we already know, I wanted to be dressed appropriately to go straight to the midweek service and get us on an emergency prayer list. And you know I love me some pink and green, honey." She smiled broadly.

As if on cue, Monica and Marcus popped in the door, looking a bit disheveled. Monica wasn't her usual put together self. She had on a Royals t-shirt, baggy jeans, a baseball cap and some dirty Nikes. Her usually made up face was bare. Even her freckles showed, which she normally hid under concealer. Her eyes were bloodshot like she'd been crying or hadn't slept. Marcus had on a doo-rag and sweats.

"What the he..." Mother Stone caught herself. "Y'all look like you just left a pool hall and owe somebody money." She wrinkled up her nose, like they smelled.

Monica rolled her eyes. "It was a long night. Had a lot going on." Monica turned to Kennedy. "How's Yolanda?"

305

Kennedy slammed her Bible shut and stared Monica down for a good thirty seconds before she responded. Monica jerked her head back in response to Kennedy's stare down, appearing insulted.

"She's fighting for her life. You know — the life you tried to destroy because you're mad at me. So while we praying my best friend doesn't die and you trying to take her spot, don't ask me how she is. You put her there. If she dies, you killed her."

The room was completely silent. The couple of patients that were there looked uncomfortable, even Mother Stone didn't respond.

"Okay..." a cheery nurse came out. Perfect timing to interrupt a tense situation. "Need the Stones and Roberts. Dr. Steward is ready for you." The petite brunette smiled widely, easing some of the tension in the room.

"Let's go find out about this baby." Mother Stone grabbed her purse and got ready to head in, but the nurse stepped in her way.

"Heifer, you better get your little four-foot self out the doorway. We about to find out my son got a... what is it, daughter Monica? ...side baby, as you say?"

A rush of heat shot up Kennedy's neck. Since when did Monica become her mother-in-law's daughter and who was *she* to invite herself to their appointment?

Kennedy didn't have to worry long. The nurse, still smiling, said, "Dr. Steward made it clear only the *couples* need to come in and any detractors — specifically a Mrs. Myrtle Stone — is not to come in. So step aside before I call security." She smiled at Mother Stone making Kennedy laugh aloud. Mother Stone was livid.

"Eddie, you lettin' this girl run you? You better tell them you don't do anything without your momma. I will set it off in here! You don't want to see a church mother go gangster. It ain't good."

Eddie sighed. "Mama, please go. Think how the mother board would react to seeing you carried out by security. They may take away your parking spot."

Mother Stone straightened up. "I'll be here." She hurriedly walked away and plopped down in a seat, clasping her hands as if in prayer. *That woman*, Kennedy thought to herself. If you threatened her image, she'd get right. Suddenly, a thought came into her mind.

"Mother Stone, just come on in," Kennedy relented. Eddie looked at her like she was crazy. Kennedy would rather her be there than wait until they got in the lobby in front of people to act a fool.

Mother Stone took off her hat and smiled smugly at the nurse. She strolled past her switching her hips so much she hit her. Even Monica shook her head at her antics. They were all quiet while they followed the nurse into Dr. Steward's office. They sat down at the table in silence. When the nurse closed the door, Marcus turned to Eddie.

"Man to man, I'm sorry for my actions. I hope we can come to an agreement pleasing to all with no drama."

Eddie looked at him with his lips curled. "I can't talk to a brother man to man who has a scarf on his head." He shook his head. "Take that thing off and look like a father, boy." Much to Monica and Kennedy's surprise, Marcus removed his doo-rag and smoothed his hair down.

Monica cleared her throat. "This isn't easy for me either," she said pointedly looking at Kennedy. "I don't like being accused of killing someone – just like it's not easy to accept that I will have to care for a baby I didn't have."

Kennedy jerked her head to look at Monica. "Then let us have custody. Why you all up in the mix?"

"Because the baby is *my* husband's. It's not just yours."

"It's not your husband's baby, either."

Everyone turned around, surprised to see Dr. Steward standing in the door. Everyone was confused.

"Come again?" Eddie asked the doctor.

Dr. Steward walked to the table and sat down. She laid a manila folder in front of them. "According to the DNA test, Marcus Roberts cannot be the father. There was no genetic DNA connected to him."

Kennedy's heart raced. Monica appeared to be in shock.

"You mean you're such a slut you slept with someone else?" Monica laughed. "Go figure. Why you talking trash to me, your whorish ways done caught you."

Eddie's heart sunk. He had come to terms that Kennedy cheated with Marcus but there were others? *Sorry, God.* He silently prayed. *She needs to pack her bags today.* He was so angry he knew he had to be quiet or he may pop her like he did months ago. Marcus looked at Kennedy with disgust. He shook his head in disbelief.

"You played all of us? Acting like it was only us and we come –"

Julee Jonez

"Everybody stop!" Dr. Steward said sharply. She slammed her hand on the desk. "I know who the father is – and you do, too." She looked at Kennedy, who was speechless. She knew she hadn't slept with anyone else. Anyone except...

Her husband.

A slow smile crept across Dr. Steward's face. "It is 99.999% probability that the father is...your husband. Eddie Alfonso Stone."

"Say what?" Eddie exclaimed. "I had a vasectomy...decades ago."

"You did." Dr. Steward agreed. "My theory is, you were clipped – not clipped and burned and it seems your tubes grew back together." She laughed at the concerned look on Eddie's face. "Failure occurs when sperm finds a new way to enter the vas and make their way into the ejaculate, a process called recanalization. In our clinic, we may have 1 failure in 4,500 vasectomies." She paused as if she thought of something. "Did you ever have your sperm tested again after your vasectomy?"

"No," Eddie admitted. "But wouldn't she have gotten pregnant sooner?"

"It would seem likely but sometimes, women try to get pregnant for years and don't. It is possible, Mr. Stone, your vasectomy may not have even worked." She laughed as everyone else was still in shock at the news.

"Hold up." Marcus yelled angrily. He stood up. "So you mean, this is real? You're sure you not in cahoots with her?" Kennedy was amazed by his anger. Then it dawned on her.

He was angry he wasn't having a kid – even if it wasn't with his wife.

"Marcus, I can assure you as a woman of God," Dr. Steward began sternly, "I would never be in cahoots with anyone. I practice medical integrity and am insulted you would insinuate otherwise."

Kennedy's heart leaped. She looked at Eddie. He was sobbing with tears of joy. When he lifted his tear stained face, he kissed Kennedy passionately.

Kennedy was most grateful God wasn't a respecter of persons but could do anything.

He proved that today.

Chapter
Thirty-Two

"*T*ake my hand and follow me."

Yolanda felt she'd been hit by a truck. She couldn't move and didn't know where that voice was coming from.

"Take my hand and follow me."

Her eyes fluttered open and she glanced around seeing a bright white room. A shadowy figure was next to her but she couldn't identify who or what it was.

Though she was mentally foggy, it came to her that she was not at home. She slowly turned her head to the right and knew where the voice was coming from.

Terrence reached out and grabbed her hand, "Take my hand and follow me."

Though Yolanda was unsure of what had happened to her, those words struck a chord. Although at the time she couldn't fully recall where they had come from, she somehow knew she'd heard them before.

Her dream.

The dream of the dark cloud engulfing her came into her mind. She was in the church, everyone running and total chaos happening. Then, after panicking and being engulfed by the cloud she remembered the still small voice.

Take my hand and follow me.

Except this time, it was a reality. The voice was *real.* The nightmare had become real three days ago. Yolanda's mind recalled what happened. She had gone to church. Got fired from the church. Got embarrassed by the church. And now here she was. Yolanda realized she was in a hospital bed. Though she was fuzzy on how she got there, with the IV in her arm and strange gadgets taped to her, she knew the aftermath of what had happened must have taken a toll on her. A warm kiss was planted on her forehead.

Terrence. He smiled at her and sat on the bed, holding her hand. "Thank you, Jesus," he whispered.

"I guess I better let the nurses know you are waking up. You were out for a while then they had to do surgery." Her eyes seemed to ask a question. He nodded. "Sweetie, I thought we lost you. You have heart disease and after your...I can't call him pastor...a man who talks in your pulpit pulled that mess," his tone changed to one of subtle anger. "It was too much and you had a heart attack."

Yolanda looked away. To think she could have lost her life scared her. If she had one heart attack, wouldn't she be at risk for another? Yolanda didn't get it. She was in shape. She ate pretty well.

Terrence, seeming to read her mind, gently turned her head to see him and wiped the tears from her face. "You can't let stress get to you, baby." He kissed her softly on the head again. "You look like the picture of health but when you carry so many negative emotions, you can't take it. You really have to cast your cares on the Lord. You have walked around with fear of being found out, guilt from your past, anger from your recent present – it was too much."

She knew he was right. She recalled the physical pains she had suffered in the previous year. She wrote them off when they were actually, warning signs of a bigger problem. She realized her biggest fear of being publicly blasted for her past continually stressed her out.

"I know the nurses will be coming back soon and I need to go call Sable and Noel." Terrence stood up. "They decided to run to Chili's to break up the monotony. Anything you want me to get?"

"Was that you?" Yolanda managed to whisper.

"What?" Terrence looked confused at her comment.

"Take...my...hand." Yolanda was having a hard time putting her thoughts together. She was conscious but still not totally composed.

Terrence chuckled. "Yes," he looked embarrassed. "I didn't know you heard me. I was begging you."

"Begging me?"

"Yes. To forget your past and follow me."

Confirmation. The dream that plagued her for years now made sense.

Terrence continued to answer the questions lingering in her mind. "I prayed and fasted over these past three days and now, I know what God told me to do. And all I need for you to do is to take my hand and follow me as I follow Christ Jesus."

"First Corinthians 11 verse 1." Yolanda whispered.

"Yes...but when I said take my hand, I meant literally."

Terrence walked back over to her bed and took her by the hand. He got down on one knee and asked, "Will you take my hand...as my wife...the mother of my child...my ministry partner? Let me lead you and follow me as we follow God's will."

Yolanda couldn't believe it. Who would have thought the man she wrongly blamed for her mountains of deceit would become her Boaz? Yolanda knew in her heart that marrying Terrence was right. She nodded her head slowly, a smile spread across her face. She didn't have her church ministry. Didn't have a job. Didn't know what was next but was glad she had someone to share her load. And she trusted that Terrence would do right by her.

Terrence smiled broadly and got up. Bending over, he kissed her passionately on the lips. Electricity shoot through her body.

"She just had a heart attack. Don't send her into another one."

They turned around to see her doctor and two nurses smiling at Sable's outburst. "I guess she's awake. You nasty, seducing her in the hospital bed." Everyone burst into laughter. Sable moved quickly to her daughter's side and embraced her in a way she hadn't done in years. "Thank you, Jesus. I thought I lost you." She sniffled as she pulled away and dabbed at her eyes. For the first time in years, Yolanda could feel her mother's love.

"We're going to check your vitals, give you some meds and let you rest," the doctor said, his with a friendly twinkle. "You are loved, dear woman.

And you are a survivor. We will need to discuss the seriousness of your procedure, lifestyle changes and how we go forth."

"I will make sure my soon-to-be wife gets all she needs to live a long life, Doc."

"What I miss?" Noel pranced into the room. She burst into a huge smile seeing her mother's eyes open. She knew her dad had been praying and she begged God to let her mother live.

"Your parents are getting married, chile. Y'all about to be a real family. No baby daddy drama. No lies. Just a home with a real man of God." Sable stood back and grinned proudly. "Now if I can find me a man, I'll be all right."

Everyone in the room chuckled.

Pressing Past the Past

One Year Later Kennedy & Yolanda's Story

Eddie turned hot dogs on the grill, while Kennedy sat on the chaise lounge holding EJ in her arms. Her little brown bundle of joy was walking and trying to talk. It was unbelievable she was the mother of a one-year old, and recently she'd discovered she and Eddie were expecting *again*. When she broke the news, Yolanda was overjoyed joking that as soon as her six weeks were up, she was so ready to make love to Eddie she forgot it was *easier* to get pregnant. She and Eddie were surprised by the news and even more amazed that what they'd wanted for so long finally came to fruition. They never would have guessed he'd become a father twice over after turning 50, but God's ways were beyond understanding.

Eddie went back to his corporate job as a CPA, while Kennedy focused on making a happy home for her family. Although Eddie had trust issues and lurking resentment with Kennedy, once EJ arrived he was ecstatic. Kennedy was grateful that God gave her mercy, blessed her with forgiveness, and allowed her to keep her husband. It seemed like all their drama had been years ago. With God's blessing, they were moving onward and upward – even in ministry. She and Eddie left the church after the whole outing Yolanda situation and joined a small start-up church that had formed in the area.

They were at the church's weekly get together. While they were still small, they decided to take advantage of not having a lot of members by spending a lot of time together outside the church walls. The pastor made it clear the ministry would run on the realness of relationships with God, in His Word and with others. It was nice to be in a ministry, building it from the ground up. Besides, Kennedy adored her new first lady and pastor.

Terrence and Yolanda.

Yolanda was arranging snacks on the table when she looked up and saw Kennedy staring at her with a soft smile on her face. After Yolanda finished at the table, she hurried over to Kennedy, ready to kiss on her godson. She barely got to hold EJ when Yolanda or Noel were near. But she had to admit, she did appreciate the chance to relax while being baby free, even if it was momentarily.

"You know I love me some EJ!" Yolanda exclaimed covering his face in kisses, as he gave Yolanda a drooling grin. Yolanda and Kennedy cracked up.

"Are we officially ready to eat?" Kennedy asked. "You know this child out here and in *here* got me super hungry." Kennedy rubbed her protruding belly.

Yolanda laughed. "We will be. We're letting the kids finish one more round of kickball while Terrence gets the ribs done. He should be calling us any minute," Yolanda stated, looking around the park area.

On cue, Terrence waved Yolanda and Kennedy over to the grilling area to let them know it was time to bless the food. Yolanda, still holding EJ, reached out her other arm to help Kennedy up before they headed towards Terrence. Yolanda was relieved to have her friend back, have love in her life and even have this new ministry opportunity. It was like Joel 2:25: God gave her back the years the locusts had stolen.

Speaking of stealing, her ex Michael wanted to buy out her half of the construction business. She kept delaying it but wasn't sure why. She felt like God kept saying, "Not yet." Two days before Yolanda let him buy her out, his biggest deal for a commercial complex was finalized. Then it made sense. He'd wanted to buy her out *way before* the deal. Thanks to her patiently listening to that still small voice, she automatically got 51% of it. Selling her percentage afterwards was an easy decision, and it still left her a nice financial free fall.

One that landed her in the millions.

Before she left the hospital, she and Terrence married, right in her hospital room. After surviving a heart attack, she wanted to marry Terrence immediately. At the time, Michael had the audacity to be upset. He started with his whole spiel, "Of course he found Jesus. Most folks do who get locked up." when she called him to tell him the news.

"You just had a baby with your stripper mistress so tell me again why you're mad?" Yolanda had asked. He hung up in her face and called back later to apologize. He then revealed the Reggie-Chantal situation. When he told Yolanda Reggie suggested a DNA test, she weighed in.

"Maybe you should. You don't want to start another relationship based on lies," she warned. "You see what happened to us," she reminded him. The DNA proved he was the father. He was relieved, but unsure if he could trust Chantal. When he brought up the issue of infidelity and trust, Yolanda ended the conversation. "I will pray for you but remember, this is the bed you made so lie in it." Michael still kept in touch with Noel, but Yolanda had happily moved on.

"Before we bless our food, I just want to thank you all for being here today," Terrence stated. "Though we may be a family of thirty now, I know God is a god of increase. If we obey His voice and never forget from where He has brought us, the best is yet to come." The small crowd eagerly clapped, agreeing with him.

"On behalf of myself and my wife," Terrence continued, pulling Yolanda close to him. "Thank you for trusting this privilege of leading you in the call of God for Overcomers Through Christ Ministries, where we overcome by the blood of the lamb and the word of our testimony." After all they had been through, they finally pressed past their pasts and were going towards all that God had in store.

About the Author

Julee Jonez is a Radio Personality in Kansas City, Missouri. Born and raised in Kansas City, Julee always had a love for words even as a child. During childhood modeling, her mother recognized her penchant for writing while she created scripts for commercials as part as her modeling school assignments. Julee was always a talker, who often performed in school plays and was never afraid of speaking before an audience. In fact, assignments that involved public speaking were often the ones she thrived at the most during her high school years.

Although she initially wanted to study accounting in college, she changed her major to Broadcasting and Film after attending a student orientation. When she decided to finish her undergraduate studies at the University of Missouri- Kansas City, she did various internships but as destiny would have it, her last one was at KPRS Hot 103 Jamz. Unbeknownst to her at the time, KPRS would eventually be where Julee's radio career began and would continue for years to come.

Julee is married to Michael with whom she has one son. She is a passionate wife and mother, who believes in consistent prayer and faith in the Lord Jesus as the foundation for her family's success and strength.

In her spare time, Julee enjoys cooking, fellowship with her long-time friends, working out and partaking in women's Bible studies.

Julee is praying that God will continue to bless her with vision and imagination for future literary works and open doors for more public speaking opportunities. Julee loves talking to young women about bouncing back from a problem-some past, having healthy self-esteem, and how God uses all things for His glory when you give your life to Him.